**Praise for Chris D.'s DRAGON WHEEL SPLENDOR
and Other Love Stories of Violence and Dread**

*"Chris D. is someone who takes his dreams seriously, for, as Delmore
Schwartz said, In Dreams Begin Responsibilities. To that end, Chris
D.'s Los Angeles of the mind is awash with a heady mix of forlorn
delirium, nostalgia pangs, seductive ghosts, and dangerous desires."*

– Grace Krilanovich, author of
THE ORANGE EATS CREEPS

Praise for Chris D.'s novel, NO EVIL STAR

*"Chris D. has performed in his own bands, directed his own movie and
written books, from Japanese film studies to volumes of his own poetry.
Now he has written a crime novel, just another facet of the multi-
faceted inside of his head. Some people can do one thing – Chris can
do almost anything."*

– Mary Woronov, author of
SWIMMING UNDERGROUND,
NIAGARA, BLIND LOVE and SNAKE

*"A healthy authorial sense of curiosity and generosity lends weight
to No Evil Star's intersecting lives, where Chris D. ably traces out the
contours of human torment in a manner recalling American films of the
1970s."*

– Grace Krilanovich, author of
THE ORANGE EATS CREEPS

What Writers Had to Say About Chris D.'s Anthology
A MINUTE TO PRAY, A SECOND TO DIE

"Reading Chris D.'s blood-on-the-page prose is like running naked, screaming with terror and desire, through the fetid back alleys of American pulp culture. You're seduced, fucked over, doused with whiskey, set on fire, dragged by the getaway car, nailed by the hail from a 30.06 and still, still – you can't stop reading."

– Eddie Muller, author of
DARK CITY DAMES, THE ART OF NOIR and
the novels THE DISTANCE and SHADOW BOXER

"...he continues a tradition in writing that is all but lost; authors who use their powers of imagination and creativity rather than simply recounting or inventing a memoir. Like the outsider artists that Chris D. champions, he writes for the future, for art, to someday be truly discovered for the great talent he is."

– John Doe, singer/songwriter
of X and The Knitters

"Chris D. presents...such an immense encapsulation of his life's work that it reads as literary autopsy of a man not yet dead but of one who has died a thousand times and somehow miraculously between crucifixions used pen as shovel to prevent himself from being buried alive."

– Lydia Lunch, musician and author of
PARADOXIA and WILL WORK FOR DRUGS

"To my mind, the lyrics he wrote...are as blinding a display of raw, universe-gobbling intelligence as have ever been penned...The sources from which Chris drew his inspiration are a classic pop cultural blend – exploitation films of all stripes, pulp fiction, French decadent poets, hot rod gangs, mystical Catholicism, underground biker comix, beatnik booze into the hippie acid continuum, and on and on und on. This is a mix that has gained great subterranean currency over the past few decades, but when Chris was churning through these waters, they were

as yet uncharted. His written work (along with that of fellow travelers such as Exene Cervenka, Dave Alvin, John Doe and Claude 'Kickboy' Bessy) created a new, totally crazed hipster aesthetic that rejected punk orthodoxy in favor of something much more magnificent and inclusive."

– Byron Coley, writer for WIRE Magazine,
author of C'EST LA GUERRE:
EARLY WRITINGS 1978-1983
and co-author (with Thurston Moore)
of NO WAVE: POST-PUNK.
UNDERGROUND. NEW YORK. 1976-1980.

ALSO BY CHRIS D.

Double Snake Bourbon

A Minute to Pray, A Second to Die

No Evil Star

Mother's Worry

Shallow Water

Volcano Girls

Tightrope on Fire

NON-FICTION

Outlaw Masters of Japanese Film

Gun and Sword: An Encyclopedia of Japanese Gangster Films 1955-1980

DRAGON WHEEL SPLENDOR

and
Other Love Stories
of
Violence and Dread

If you enjoyed this book, tell someone about it.

A Poison Fang Book

© 2009, 2010, 2011 by Chris Desjardins, pka Chris D.

Front and back cover designs by C. D.

ISBN 978 0615869322

First published by New Texture, December 2011

First Poison Fang Books edition, October 2013

Printed in the United States

10 9 8 7 6 5 4 3 2 1

DRAGON WHEEL SPLENDOR

and
Other Love Stories
of
Violence and Dread
by
Chris D.

A POISON FANG BOOK

"It hurts to love. It's like giving yourself to be flayed and knowing that at any moment the other person may just walk off with your skin."

"To write you have to allow yourself to be the person you don't want to be (of all the people you are)."

Susan Sontag
REBORN
Journals & Notebooks 1947-1963

"Hell's gate is in your ear, a tiny atom of nothingness. Shove it over a quarter of a centimeter...and peer around it. You're kaput! That's all she wrote. Damned for eternity. Aren't you ready? You're not?...
A beautiful shroud stitched with stories–that's what the Lady desires. The last breath is all-consuming, the last movie and nothing to come afterwards. Most people can't know. You've got to knock yourself out. I'll work up to it soon...I'll hear my heart give its final sputtering click...and then pop! Arteries will tremble...like old broomsticks...it'll be finished. They'll slice them open to check on the autopsy table. They won't see my beautiful stories, nor my music either. The Lady will have taken eveything...Here I am, Miss, I'll whisper to her, you're the greatest connoisseur of all..."

Celine
DEATH ON THE
INSTALLMENT PLAN

FOR DONNA

Contents

INTRODUCTION

This collection came together rather quickly, and sprang into being for a couple of different reasons.

Roughly three years ago, in 2008, Brendan Mullen solicited a story from me for an anthology he was putting together of "punk horror" tales. The requirements were simple: a genre piece that could be of any length up to 10,000 words, and it could be based on incidents from real life – "true" horror stories – or from fictional elements, including the supernatural. The one other stipulation was that it should take place in – and be representative of – the late 1970s-early 1980s punk rock scene, preferably set in Los Angeles. I turned in "Nights in Venice," a fictionalized, autobiographical account of a traumatic period in my life. It was set against a backdrop of when I was just out of college and my first marriage was ending. Like me, the main character was teaching high school English, writing for a punk rock magazine and becoming enamored of the punk club scene in Hollywood, with all of its attendant exhilaration, implicit violence, substance abuse and promiscuous sex.

Brendan had collected most of the stories, as far as I know, by mid-2009, but was working on a couple of other much higher profile projects, books that, when finished, would have proved much more remunerative to him. The anthology was something he was doing for the love of it, but it was on the back burner while bills got paid.

Then, tragically, unexpectedly, Brendan had a stroke in October of 2009 and died. To my knowledge, the "punk horror" anthology he had been putting together was abandoned and, more than likely, will never see the light of day.

I am grateful to Brendan for asking me to write the piece. It stoked a fire under me. Although then sporadically working on a novel, *No Evil Star* (that I coincidentally – finally – just recently finished), I was not doing too much writing at the time. My high-pressure work as a film programmer was proving more and more stressful, in part because of the economic downturn, and I had just taken on an additional part-time job, teaching one day a week in San Francisco.

Having to write something to a specific word count in a specific genre inspired me. And 90% of the inspiration came from real situations I had experienced and real characters I had known. Even the supernatural events were partly based on fact: the apartment I lived in from June 1977 through January 1978, on Venice Boulevard not too far from the beach, was the only place I have ever lived that I am convinced was genuinely haunted. The first encounter with the invisible thing in bed happened – or so it seemed. Of course, I never saw or interacted with a visible manifestation of the ghost, as my alter ego Jack does in the story.

Throughout the year 2009, a number of harrowing events, as well as "artistically rewarding" things, occurred in my life. I also had a number of vivid dreams, something that does not necessarily happen that often but, when it does, the dreams and nightmares come in clotted bursts, usually concentrated into a period of a few days at a time. Two of the nightmares were so real and affecting, I decided to write them out as full-blown short narratives. The stories, "The Glider" and "Rail," were inspired by those dreams. I also got the idea to do three other stories with my alter ego, the Jack character from "Nights in Venice." More about these in a minute.

The novella, "Dragon Wheel Splendor," is based on a screen-play I wrote in 2005 as a follow-up to the only feature film I have, so far, written and directed, called *I Pass For Human*. Not a follow-up in terms of being a sequel, but a follow-up in terms of a similar kind of

downbeat tale about a similar kind of lonely, courageous character --
but without the supernatural trappings of the first film. Both screenplays
deal with strong-willed female personas who are spiraling out of
control from disillusionment, disappointment and personal tragedy,
characters who suddenly find themselves – partly through their own
fault – with no more viable options. I wrote the "Dragon Wheel
Splendor" screenplay for Eleanor Whitledge, who had starred as the
lead character, Jane, in *I Pass For Human*. Eleanor was committed to
doing it, but unfortunately, as is so often the case with trying to get film
productions off the ground, financing was never forthcoming.

"The Glider," as I've mentioned, was based on a dream,
specifically a nightmare fragment featuring a British female police
detective who becomes infatuated with a handsome young Belgian
man who picks her up on a country road when her car breaks down.
What she doesn't realize till a day or two later is that he is the serial
killer who has been terrorizing the rural villages on her beat. He is
also a hang-gliding enthusiast! Don't ask me where that comes from,
because I don't know. When I had the dream and subsequently began
writing the story, I had just finished reading four of Derek Raymond's
extremely downbeat and unorthodox police novels, as well as the first
installment of David Peace's *Red Riding Quartet*. So there was some
twisted, perverse British crime fiction permeating my subconscious at
the time.

"Rail" was from a realistic nightmare I had, a dream where
I was simultaneously watching and living inside of a film about the
self-destructive relationship between two tragically bereft characters
in a 1948 French mining town: a brothel madam (played in the dream
film by Simone Signoret) and a tormented drifter-turned-striking-miner
(played by Yves Montand). The last four or five pages of the story
represent the core of the dream.

The "Jack's Girlfriends" stories, "Cherie's Payback," "Nights
in Venice," "Assumpta" and "San Francisco Night" are all heavily
autobiographical, but with the characters' names, and about a third
of the locations, changed. The events in the stories are also time-
compressed and fictionalized to varying extent. No violent, fatal
vendetta served as a cathartic wrap-up for the gang-rape in real-life as
it does in "Cherie's Payback." Likewise, the character of May in that
story had no counterpart in reality. I've already talked about "Nights in
Venice." The tale, "Assumpta," probably comes closest to "real-life,"
but still, time-compression and disguising of identities puts this in the
realm of fiction. "San Francisco Night" is also fairly true to real events,

except the fight on the bus between the driver and a passenger did not end in violent death as it does in the story (though it seemed to me, at the time, it easily *could have*.)

These stories were the hardest for me to write; not in terms of creative flow, because they virtually gushed out. But I have mixed feelings about their confessional nature. Autobiographical details faintly morphed and molded into fiction can be extremely painful to write, and painful to read for anyone else who might recognize themselves in the stories. Ultimately, everything I've written, especially my vast catalogue of song lyrics and poetry, is personal. However, the confessional stripping of the soul in prose fiction is less abstract. Regardless, I felt I had to write them. This assertion may seem egocentric, annoyingly self-indulgent. But I felt as a if I had no choice.

As anyone familiar with my career as a musician and songwriter knows, I am obsessed with morbid romanticism and its consequences. *Amour fou* – crazy love or doomed love – is a staple of the song lyrics and fiction I have written. For some reason, from the time I reached puberty until now, I have fixated on those dark elements in cinema, music and literature. Why? I don't know. Trekking through my youth and middle age, have I carried out a self-fulfilling prophecy? I don't know, I don't think so. And, when you get down to it, who-the-fuck (besides me) really cares?

Although I am agnostic, all of this undoubtedly has something to do with what my long-time writer friend, Byron Coley, describes as, to paraphrase slightly, my "blood Catholicism." Perhaps, too, a lack of seratonin in the brain.

One of the things that has happened to me in the last several years, since I've been getting back into the daily habit of writing, is that I have attempted to search for some semblance of meaning in the poems, lyrics and fiction I have written. I admit this, once again, at the risk of sounding pretentious. To get too heavily into self-analysis is crippling for any artist and can help kill spontaneity. It can damage or subvert that tapping into the unconscious that makes the best fiction. Nevertheless, telling stories – for me, in any case – involves a character's search for meaning *where there seems to be no meaning*, even if this search is not consciously acknowledged.

The eternal quest for love, especially romantic love, is beset with all kinds of undermining forces, some self-created, some from external forces beyond one's control. Love of another, whether of a mate or of a family member, can give meaning where otherwise there may be none. And when that love is snatched away, either by design or by chance, all manner of horrific things can pop up in its wake. That is what these stories are about.

Chris D.
August 2010
Highland Park, CA

DRAGON WHEEL SPLENDOR

c. 2001, Los Angeles, CA

"Fuck you! Get off me!"

Anne's boyfriend's large, powerful hand held her down, pinned by the throat to the dirty hardwood floor. A slight trickle of blood issued from her lips, and she struggled to get a breath. She wasn't sure because it was night, but the room seemed to be getting darker.

"Get the fuck off me!"

Steve ignored her command, stuck in a different groove like a defective record. "Goddamn it, Anne. Why do you do that! You're always trying to make me feel small. Every other word that comes out of your mouth – "

Anne fought his choking grip to get out the words, "That's not true –"

"Shut up! You had your goddamn say! Now it's my fucking turn!" Steve's voice was ridiculously loud and, for a few seconds, he tightened his grasp. Suddenly he was near tears. He didn't let her up, but he loosened his hold so she wouldn't choke. For a seemingly eternal minute the only sound was their ragged breathing.

"I don't know what to do. I'm Mister Confidence all day long, nothing can get me down, then suddenly when I see you, it's...it's like

I'm a goddamn kid! I can't hold my head up. I feel like people are laughing at me behind my back. I feel like you're laughing at me."

"Don't put that on me, you fucking psycho. That's you."

Steve thrust the grimy index finger of his free hand into her face. "Shut up! I told you to shut your goddamn mouth!"

"No! You think talking this way, treating me this way is going to help? This isn't the way things used to be. I haven't been trying hard enough, I know. But you, Steve – you haven't been trying at all. Not for the last six months. Your trolley's off the goddamn tracks. You're in a goddamn shell and won't let anyone in. No one's laughing at you. It's all in your head. You need to work on yourself."

He didn't answer, then lashed out, slapping her hard across her face.

A wildcat expression rippled across her features, and she exploded, kneeing him in the groin. He gasped and reflexively drew his hand away from her throat. She elbowed him in the face, and he careened off her, crumpled, moaning on the floor. She picked herself up, tenderly touching her mouth, then gazed down at him.

"I'm not trying anymore, Steve. I don't take this kind of crap from any guy. Take your shit and get the fuck out. It's over."

Steve was crying softly. There was no other sound except the ambience of the deserted block of buildings through the open window. Startlingly, there came a shout from the street below.

"Hey, Steve! Steverino!"

Anne peeked out the window from the shadows and saw that Steve's two bedraggled friends, Manny and Terry, were looking up at her building.

"Oh, Steve! Stevie Dios! You didn't forget we were down here, did you? Take a break from beating the shit out of Anne for a while, why don't you, and come on down."

Anne stuck her head out into the corpse light illumination of the street lamp.

"Oh, hey, Anne. Could you tell Steven we've been waiting patiently for him to get his ass back down here. He said he was only going to be five minutes."

Anne didn't reply. She turned as she heard Steve stand up.

"Your homeboys need you. You better mosey along."

He stared at her bitterly, then swiveled on his heel, picked up a paper bag full of beer on the floor and split. The slamming of the door thundered in the room.

Anne grimaced and licked the blood from her lips. She caught sight of herself in the mirror through the open bathroom door. The one naked light bulb hanging over the sink gave her beautiful face a harsh, worn aspect. She had a striking presence at 5'10" with a mane of tangled chestnut hair falling to her shoulders. She looked good, but she didn't think so. Adding to her disgust, her jeans, T-shirt and denim jacket were filthy. Self-loathing surged through her soul. Forty-two years old, and she was still dicking around with guys like that in a hellhole like this.

Anne lived downtown, slightly east of Alameda near 3rd Street, in a falling-apart old building full of artist lofts. When she came out of the dilapidated ruin, she did what she usually did, which was to check her surroundings for homeless nutcases or desperate, needy drug addicts. There was a drunk passed out in a doorway a few buildings further south, but that was it. Stevie and his dipshit friends were nowhere in sight. She twirled her keys on her fingers as she walked to her late 1980s Buick that was parked across the street. It started after a couple of tries, and she rolled down the pavement, keeping an eye out for broken liquor bottles, something prevalent in the neighborhood. Four blocks further south, in the ancient and decaying rail warehouse district, she came to the club where the rave was happening. The music was so deafening you could hear it plainly from where she parked a half block away.

The club building was much taller than the deserted warehouses that surrounded it on every side. It stood like a beacon of depravity in a wasteland of crushed hopes. She sauntered lazily to the entrance, watching the shadowy figures of people who stood in silhouette against the bright yellow light of the entrance. She started to climb the steps but ran into Steve, who was coming out.

She muttered, "Shit!" under her breath.

"There you are. I thought you might show up here. Listen, I'm – "

"I don't want to hear it."

"I'm sorry, goddamn it. Can't I even apologize!"

They seemed to be circling each other warily, but Anne was trying to move around him without turning her back. She slowly ascended backwards up the four steps to the open door.

"Fuck, what is this? You think you're better than me now?" He took a deep breath, sighed, looked away, then up at the full moon. "Sorry, sorry. Really. I don't know what's wrong with me. I've got all this rage inside me, and I can't seem to control it."

At the top, she had stopped, turned her back and refused to look at him.

Steve began to weep. "Listen, Anne...I don't know how to say this. I don't feel like I can live without you."

"You're going to have to learn."

"Anne, please. Please listen to me. Give me another chance. I promise I'll – "

"I already gave you another chance. At least four times." She slowly turned to face him. "I can't stand it the way you are now. Ping-ponging back and forth between drunken caveman and big crybaby."

He stared at her, unable to speak, totally crestfallen and in despair. She cocked her head as she turned her back on him again. She raised her voice slightly to make sure he could hear her over the electronic din.

"Don't call me. Don't follow me. Just leave me the fuck alone."

Anne disappeared into the building, and Steve was left in the gutter, staring at the pavement.

Inside the music was blasting at an eardrum-piercing level, just the way she liked when she felt the need to obliterate consciousness. She moved through the crowd to a shadowy alcove where she leaned against the wall to watch the gyrating throng. Suddenly she pushed off and took up her station in a dark corner closer to the entry foyer. She sat down on the floor and watched people straggle in and out.

A well-dressed couple abruptly materialized out of the darkness outside, smiling, murmuring to each other. The woman was Japanese, in her late twenties and bewitchingly beautiful – ethereal, delicate. The man was ruggedly attractive, cruel-looking, in his late forties, with a full handlebar moustache and soul patch. He acted as if he had money. The pair moved to one side of the entranceway, whispering. The woman threw back her head, drunkenly laughing. A handsome Asian guy, probably Japanese, in his thirties with slicked, jet-black hair, appeared from inside the club, passed Anne and walked up to the couple with a big smile. He pointedly ignored the woman and pumped the man's hand, currying favor. The woman's expression sobered as she focused, realizing the younger guy was snubbing her.

A few more words were exchanged, then the older man leaned over, kissed the woman on the cheek – in what Anne thought was a patronizing manner – and quickly left. The woman and the younger man stared at each other with balefully ambivalent expressions. After a few seconds, the younger man took hold of the woman's forearm and dragged her with him back into the noisy, cavernous club. Just as they were passing, the woman glanced down at Anne and smiled a drunken smile. Anne's eyes followed them until they dissolved into the chaotic crowd.

Anne unlocked her car door. She slowly got in, wincing as if every bone in her body ached, switched on the ignition, then pulled away from the curb. The block ahead seemed deserted, though it was hard to tell since she hadn't washed her car in a while, and the windshield was caked with smeary dust. She took a shortcut down one of the disused old streets that held nothing but more decrepit, abandoned railroad warehouses. She was preoccupied, deep in thought, when she saw something ahead and braked with a screech. There was a huddled mass lying on the asphalt in the beams of her headlights. It looked like a woman's body. Unsure what to do, she studied the surrounding area, wary lest some predatory assailant be in the vicinity, then cautiously opened the door and climbed out. Glancing around, she made her way to the trunk, opened it and took out a tire iron. She approached the still form. A drunken howl echoed from somewhere a couple of blocks away, and she froze in her tracks.

She stood there, surveying the surroundings, then whirled as she noticed something out of the corner of her eye. A shadow scurried into the darkness on her right and disappeared. The palm of her hand was sweating, making the tire iron slippery. She waited almost a full minute before moving again, then finally stooped down beside the body and turned it over. It was the young woman from the club. She had been beaten, her face covered with bruises, and she was barely conscious.

"Jesus..." Anne gently shook her, patting her cheeks where they weren't black-and-blue. "Hey, hey, honey. Wake up. Are you okay?"

The woman moaned but seemed incapable of coming fully awake.

"Fuck..." she whispered, "Fuck, fuck, fuck." She hoisted the girl to a vertical position, half-carrying her, half-frog-jumping her to the car.

The door swung open, hitting the wall, as Anne burst in trying to steer the barely conscious girl toward the bed. She let her fall diagonally across the unmade mattress. She exhaled and propped her hands on her knees as she bent over, trying to catch her breath. It had only been two floors she had had to climb with her, but she was out of shape and

winded. She scanned the room, spotted the three quarters-full fifth
of vodka on the table amidst her acrylic paint tubes and brushes and
grabbed hold of it. She took a swig, then wiped her mouth.

She noticed the washrag on the floor next to the open bathroom
door, reached for it, held it under hot, then cold, running water in the
sink and wrung it out several times. She sat down beside the young
woman, wiping the girl's face and cleaning her up.

A few minutes later, Anne was sitting by the open window,
smoking a cigarette and looking out over the quiet street. A sound from
the bed made her turn. The girl was stumbling into the bathroom. Anne
got up and went to see what was going on. The girl was clutching either
side of the toilet, staring down into the bowl. Anne held the girl's head
as she began to retch.

It was near dawn, and Anne still did not felt sleepy. She was unusually
depressed. She swiveled her head, examining her single apartment.
The torn-up couch looked like hell, but she liked it like that -- it was
comfortable and felt good under her. Her few paintings were stacked
against the opposite wall, directly across from her. She thought of her
late, lamented first show that had recently, literally, gone up in flames
just five weeks earlier. Hadj Pizzaro, an influential gallery owner, had
scheduled a whole month devoted to what he believed to be her best
work. Then two days before the opening, he had had a fatal heart attack
when the gallery had caught fire in the wee hours of the morning. By
the time the fire engines had arrived, not only was Hadj dead, but the
inferno had incinerated thirty paintings, at least two thirds of her output
over those past three years. The one she was working on now – it had
actually been almost a week since she had touched it – sat on its easel
on the other side of the far second window, an oilcloth draped over it.
Cigarette butts overflowed from the ashtray, centered amidst scattered
brushes and nearly squeezed-dry paint tubes, on the rickety coffee
table. She sipped some more vodka and watched the sleeping girl on
the bed.

Unbeknownst to Anne, the young Japanese man with slick, jet-black
hair was leaning against his black Lexus on the other side of the street
from her building. He was parked directly behind Anne's Buick. He
sat there, motionless, staring up at her windows with a lit cigarette
dangling from his thin lips.

The sun had been up for almost an hour. Anne dozed fitfully on the couch. The girl, now sober and comparatively recovered, stood gazing down at her benefactor. She opened a piece of paper she had folded in her hands, guiltily glanced at it, then quickly refolded it and set the note down beside the sleeping woman. As she straightened, she spotted the vodka on the floor. It was now about a quarter full. She belted a good swallow and placed it on the coffee table. Wringing her hands and anxiously glancing about, she hesitantly walked to the door, then quietly opened it and left.

When Anne opened her eyes, she almost immediately saw the note.

"I don't know your name. But whoever you are, thanks for being kind to me. It means more than you'll ever know... LISA"

She stared off into space as she refolded the note and gently set it back on the couch.

The rave club was comparatively dead; then again, it was a Tuesday night.

Anne and another younger, slightly shorter woman with black hair, named Eve, stood against the wall in one corner. Eve laughed, conspiratorially leaned onto Anne's shoulder and whispered in her ear. Anne tried not to smile.

Lisa, the young Japanese man and the older, rich-looking guy appeared out of the depths of the club, on their way out. They paused as the older man said something to the doorman. The younger one drifted outside, lighting a cigarette and scanning the street for the valet attendant and their car. Lisa saw Anne and stopped. The two women stared uncomfortably at each other.

Eve picked up on the vibes right away and looked at Anne, puzzled.

Lisa timidly smiled and gave a shy wave of her hand.

Anne was stone-faced.

Suddenly, the young Japanese man was at Lisa's shoulder, whispering in her ear. He gave Anne a poisonous look as he yanked the girl to the entrance. The older man stood behind them, off to the side, watching the scene with a stoic expression. Lisa let herself be led, but she shot one more surreptitious glance over her shoulder as she was hustled out of the club.

Anne sat behind the wheel, gazing distractedly out the windshield as she drove, while Eve sat sideways on the opposite end, staring at her.

"That's the girl you found in the street?"

Anne just nodded, not looking at her.

"Lisa Masuda? Jesus, you're crazy! You know who those two guys are?"

Anne had a can of beer tucked between her legs and took a swig, then finally turned her head to look at Eve.

"Tell me."

"The younger one, the Japanese guy, Shingo, is yakuza. Speaks English like he was born here. Fucking mean son-of-a-bitch. He's like her handler, her pimp, I guess. He's got at least three other girls on a string in Little Tokyo and a couple more further downtown at the Biltmore. He probably has more. He tried to pull me once. I told him to fuck off, and I got a black eye for 'disrespecting' him. If there hadn't been a couple of other people a half a block away, he probably would have really kicked the shit out of me."

"Disrespecting him, hunh?"

Eve laughed bitterly. "Yeah, it was worse because I did it in front of Del Lynch, the older one, the other guy that rounded out their adorable little threesome tonight."

"What makes him so special?"

"He's a high roller, a lawyer. Rich as fuck from all kinds of illegal crap. Pulls strings downtown. He's got a real sick scene going on up in the hills in Silver Lake at his house."

"What kind of scene?"

"You name it. Sex and drug parties for various rich fucks; you know, politicians, CEOs, movie stars. S&M dungeon with religious motifs in the cellar."

"How does Lisa fit in?"

"Del more or less adopted her after her folks died. She'd just turned thirteen. Adopted...that's a joke."

"Why?"

"Del was her dad's business partner. I hear he was like a part of the family. Like an uncle to Lisa. But he was doing all kinds of shit behind their backs. Jack Bennett, you know the artist who lives down the block from you? He got close to Lisa for about a minute. Before Shingo tightened the screws. Jack thinks Del drove her dad out of the business, although it was so smooth you could never prove it. When Lisa's dad came home early one day and found Del in bed with Lisa, that was the final straw."

"Christ." Anne looked out at the dead buildings lining the street. "Then what? How did her parents die?"

"Murder/suicide. Her dad killed the mom, then turned the

shotgun on himself. At least that's what the cops said. I've always wondered..." She paused. "Lisa was the one who found them. I wouldn't put it past Lynch to have rigged up the whole thing."

They were quiet for a few seconds.

"Why are you so interested?"

Anne nonchalantly glanced over, then back out the windshield.

Eve's smile grew wider. "Oh, no. That's too much! I didn't know you swung both ways."

"Fuck you. That's not it."

"It's not? Then why?"

"I don't know why. It's not sexual. She made me feel a certain way I've never felt before. But it's not sexual."

"Yeah? My lady doth protest -- "

"Shut up." Anne shook her head, frustrated.

Eve reached out to sympathetically touch Anne's shoulder. "Anyway, Lisa's on the same wavelength. She likes the girls, only goes with men for money."

"You really are getting on my nerves, Eve."

"So, what's going on with you? I know it's been slim pickin's in the guy department."

Anne shot her a dirty look. "Nothing. Nothing's going on with me."

"You given up on guys since the Stevie Dios nightmare?"

"Stop."

Eve was suddenly curious. "Hey, whatever happened to Adrian? Now there was a hot guy!"

Anne's face colored. "I said drop it."

"Jeez, don't take my head off."

Anne remembered the first time she had met Adrian. She had been lying on her back on a blanket in the grass of the park, reading a book by Colette. Suddenly a good-looking guy about her age had walked over. He'd been clad in a business suit, but his tie was loosened and his jacket slung over his shoulder, like he'd been headed down to the local bar to meet Frank, Dean and Sammy. She had squinted up at him as he'd loomed over her.

"You're Anne, right?"

No matter how good-looking he was, she had not been happy that he had known her name.

"Yeah... what's it to you?"

"I'm Adrian Greer. Eve Sandrelli introduced us at that party a couple of weeks ago."

"Hunh...I kind of remember."

"You got away before I could get your number."

"I was drunk and smoked too much pot. It made me nauseous and paranoid, and I cut out."

Adrian had crouched down beside her. "Well, I've been thinking about you."

She had looked at him strangely.

He'd laughed. "No, really, no big deal. I was just thinking it might be fun for us to go out together sometime. For a drink or bite to eat."

Anne had thought for a few seconds about what to do, then had taken a slip of paper she'd been using as a bookmark and had written her number down. She handed it to him.

"Call me." She had finally smiled.

"Whoa!" Eve pointed up ahead, laughing incredulously. "What's that fuckhead doing up there?"

Anne slowed the car to a crawl. Both the front windows were open, and they could hear the bald-headed, burly bear of a guy in sport shirt and shorts yelling his head off. He was still almost a block away.

"Goddamn it! Goddamn you, you fucking little son-of-a-bitch! I can't believe you!"

There was a tiny terrier on a leash looking up at the wildly gesticulating man. Torrents of verbal abuse were being hurled the dog's way.

"I gotta retard dog! Stupid mutt!"

Anne and Eve were hypnotized by the scene.

Suddenly the man grabbed the dog and dropkicked it like a football so it yelped and went flying down the street.

"Jesus! The bastard!"

"Fuck! The guy's nuts!"

Anne honked the horn. Eve tried to reach across her.

"Flash your lights at the prick!"

Anne flashed the headlights off and on.

The squat little man turned and started their way. "What-the-fuck's your problem!"

He reached them, kicked the fender and came around Anne's side. He bent down. "Can't mind your own goddamn business?"

"Fuck you, prick!"

"Yeah, fuck you, ya yellow coward!"

The man could not believe his ears and reached through the
open window. "Cunts!"

Anne pulled away from him as he clutched at her hair,
pushing the button so the window rolled up, trapping his arm. He tried
to grab at her, but she easily deflected his limited reach. Eve slapped the
dashboard, laughing. Anne leaned over onto Eve to avoid the clutching
hand.

He was beside himself. "Lemme go, goddamn it! You bitches!
Lemme go!"

Eve flipped him off. The man began to panic. He kicked the car
door. Anne slowly began to drive away, dragging the man with them.

Now he was scared. "Hey, quit it! You're hurting me!"

Anne gradually sped up. Suddenly she rolled the window
down, the man tumbled and fell, and the car peeled away. He landed on
his ass in the gutter, holding a scraped arm and staring after the car that
was already halfway down the block.

Anne stopped the car. The man awkwardly regained his feet
and stumbled towards them.

"I'm gonna kill you, you bitches! Kill you!"

Anne ignored him, scanning the street.

"What-the-fuck you doing!"

"Looking for the dog."

Eve shook her head. "Girl, he's long gone."

The man was nearly on them again, roaring his lungs out. "You
goddamn bitches!"

Eve glanced back. "Forget the damn dog!"

Anne stepped on the gas. The man tripped and fell in a heap as
the girls careened around the next corner.

Anne was starting to have trouble with the Buick's timing, the motor
occasionally stalling, so she kept the engine revved while she idled in
place in front of Eve's building. Eve shut the passenger door and leaned
back in through the open window.

"Thanks."

Anne faintly smiled but didn't say anything.

"I think you're nuts, but if you're interested, there's a little bar
downtown where Lisa hangs. It's called Komaka now, but last time
I was by there, they still had the old sign out front. I can't remember
the old name. It's on the edge of Little Tokyo on 3rd Street. Almost all
Japanese clientele. You'll stick out like a sore thumb."

Anne turned her head, once more staring straight ahead.

"Good night, honey." Eve disappeared up the walk.

Anne was parked at the curb a couple of doors down from the bar. There was no sign outside at all now. She had asked a homeless man if he knew where Komaka was, and he had pointed it out to her. You never would have guessed it was open, except Anne had seen a couple of customers leave. It was after 1:00 AM, and everything was quiet. She glanced in the rearview mirror, then sank down in the seat. She tried to keep awake, but she was seriously underslept and soon dozed off.

Shingo, the Japanese man with slick black hair, strutted out of the entrance, stretching and yawning melodramatically, then looked up and down the deserted block. He paused on the sidewalk to light a cigarette. As he pocketed his lighter, he spotted her. He casually walked over and banged on the hood with the flat of his hand.

She awoke, startled, and recognized Shingo. He laughed drunkenly, contemptuously flicked his cigarette at the windshield, then pivoted and walked off into the shadows in the opposite direction. She vigorously rubbed her face with both hands and started the car.

The next day, Anne had to get up comparatively early. She had a 10:00 AM appointment at the employment agency.

She was in a dress for once, and she stood fidgeting at the counter. A woman recognized her and came up.

"I'm sorry, Anne. When I checked earlier, the position hadn't been filled. But apparently Jerry at the next desk didn't realize I'd called you to come in. He gave it to another woman who showed up with the same qualifications."

She couldn't motivate herself to feel disappointed that she'd been screwed out of work.

"You okay?"

Anne nodded.

"You still getting unemployment?"

"For another few weeks. I've got a little in savings. But I wanted to quit dipping into that."

"Sorry, honey. I should have something soon."

"I'll call you."

The woman smiled, and Anne pushed herself away from the counter and left.

It was dusk. Anne lay on her stomach on her unmade bed, paging through an arts magazine. Suddenly disgusted, she heaved it across the room and flipped over on her back to stare at the ceiling.

The Komaka bar was dark inside, much darker than most bars, something Anne liked. She sat at the counter on a ripped, red leather-upholstered stool, nursing a beer. There was virtually no one there. The old bartender eyed her suspiciously from where he conversed in Japanese with the one other patron, a tired-looking businessman, at the opposite end of the bar.

Shingo burst through the door behind Anne, started to pass by, then did a double-take. He lit his customary cigarette as he stared hard at her. She swiveled slightly on the stool to look at him.

He beckoned to her. "You got a minute?"

She didn't reply.

He laughed, and the guttural tones came out juvenile and immature. "Come on, I want to show you something."

"What?"

He reached out and clutched her upper arm.

She jerked away. "I don't fucking know you, so don't fucking touch me!"

He took a deceptively casual puff on his smoke and dropped it to the floor, grinding it out with exaggerated emphasis. Abruptly, he lashed out, slapping Anne on the back of the head and grabbing her by the neck in a viselike grip.

"Fucking let go, you prick!" Anne was shocked and frightened. The adrenaline pumping through her sobered her, and she squirmed to get free, but it was no use. Shingo bent down close to her ear, his grip, now switched to her arm, cutting off the circulation.

"You're going to hurt yourself, bitch. I'm going to show you something. For your own good."

He steered her along the bar towards the rear. The bartender and the businessman watched in silence. Shingo freed up one hand to open the door to the back room, and she immediately tried to shake herself free. Shingo tripped her, then pulled her up again to a standing position.

"You *really* are going to hurt yourself," he hissed, "I am not fucking around, *cunt*."

Once they were through the door, two men with their backs turned, standing under a naked low wattage bulb, blocked most of the view of a billiards table. One of them glanced over his shoulder, then, when he saw it was only Shingo, shrugged and turned back.

Anne was shuddering, partly from anger and partly from fear. Shingo seized a straight back wooden chair and dragged it over, positioning it between the two men.

Then she realized what was going on. She saw now, and the sight of what they were doing paralyzed her. Shingo forced her to sit, using one of his hands to hold her in place by her right shoulder and the other hand so she couldn't turn her head to look away.

"This is something you need to see."

The two men, who were now on either side of her, laughed.

She tried to move her head, but Shingo forced it back into place. Right in front of her, a third gangster had Lisa spread-eagled on the billiards table. His pants were down around his ankles, and his fat, hairless ass heaved to and fro as he fucked her. Lisa was making squeaking and grunting sounds of pain, though there was a glazed, blank expression on her face. Tears periodically dripped down her cheeks. She hadn't realized yet that Anne was there, watching.

Anne wept soundlessly, her rage boiling over and erasing her fear.

Lisa sensed something and slowly turned her head to stare at Anne. Her silky flesh bloomed with a hot flush of sweaty pink color. There was a resigned humiliation in her eyes. Her spirit was broken and shamed beyond words, and she meekly tried to smile.

Anne didn't think she could take it much longer. She wanted to kill Shingo and his pals with every fiber of her being.

She knew she should consider herself lucky. Even though Shingo had made her watch as the other two men had taken their turns with Lisa, they had not raped her. After they were done with Lisa, Shingo had quickly hauled Anne out the back door of the place as if she was a load of garbage and had unceremoniously dumped her without another a word.

She crouched over the trash can in the alley, vomiting. She finally straightened, wiped her eyes with the sleeve of her denim jacket, then her mouth. She sank back, leaning against the grimy wall and looked up at the brightly blinking stars in the night sky.

Inside the club, the industrial music was deafening, soul-destroying. Anne was ferociously drunk. She stumbled through the oblivious crowd and into the shadows in the back of the huge auditorium. She fell, sprawling on the floor next to the wall amidst discarded bottles and cans and promptly passed out.

A vase full of yellow flowers – flowers she didn't know the name of – sat in front of a wall on a waist-high table. Two very tall windows with sheer lace curtains let in sunlight on either side. Somehow Anne knew that the water in the flowers' vase had been collected from Lisa's tears.

The strange thing is they were playing such loud music in this tranquil setting.

She came to with a start in the crushing din of the club, shaken into consciousness by some huge guy in silhouette. Then she saw it was Steve, and she instinctively jerked away as he tried to help her to her feet.

"You all right? You look tore up."

She dumbly stared at him as she arose on wobbly legs. He reached out his hand again to steady her, but she slapped it away.

"I don't need your fucking help."

"C'mon, don't be that way. You shouldn't be here fucked up like this. One of the security guards'll come by and throw you out. Or worse, call the cops."

She swayed uncertainly.

The next thing Anne knew, they were sitting on a bench about a block from Alameda. She hunched herself over, laid her elbows on her knees and her head in her hands as she stared at the ground. Steve bent to look at her, then leaned back.

"What's going on?"

"Nothing." She paused, and bitter poison crept into her voice. "Just reveling in the wonderfulness of the male sex."

"I saw Eve."

"So?"

"So she's worried about you."

"Did she say why?"

"Wouldn't tell me."

"That's a nice change of pace." Anne moaned, then leaned back, making a face.

"I feel sick."

"I'm not surprised."

"I haven't eaten all day, and I drank a whole pint of vodka in about half an hour."

"Ouch."

"I don't think I can make it home."
Steve glanced at her, put out his cigarette and stood up.
"Come on."

Anne and Steve stood at the open, broken door of her
apartment building. An awkward silence between them amplified the
whole block's strange ambient noises.
"I can make it the rest of the way."
"You sure? You got a mean staircase."
She smiled, started to nod, then stopped herself, confused. "Go
on home, Steve. I'm all right."
He hesitated, something battling inside of him, disappointed he
couldn't play nursemaid. "I hope so."
She frowned as he walked off. She propped herself against
the door, watching him go, praying that she could make it upstairs and
inside before puking. Somehow she did it. She had difficulty with the
lock at first, something that happened even when she was sober. But her
blurry vision made it worse. Finally, she shambled in and shut the door.
She haphazardly navigated across the clutter to the bathroom, switched
on the light and sank to her knees. For almost a full minute, she just
knelt there, staring into the bowl, her head pounding and her gorge rising.
Oh, yes! Drinking made her memory of what happened to Lisa
so, so much better. Why did she keep on? It wasn't working anymore.
If anything, the vodka had made her more upset about Lisa,
emblazoning nightmare images onto her spiritual retina, fermenting
her blood into vitriol. Then it came up, and she puked her guts out for
what seemed like forever. At last, the convulsions of her stomach and
esophagus subsided, and she lay down on the cold tile floor. With
Herculean effort, she turned over and crawled to the bed, hoisting
herself up. She plopped face down with her head at the foot of the
mattress. She tried to keep her eyes open but couldn't.

There was that vase of yellow flowers again, this time in the middle
of her floor. Light was streaming out of the open bathroom. It hurt her
eyes. A bishop in full vestments, complete with the split dome hat and a
chalice of communion hosts, stood in profile with the toilet behind him.
His face was in shadow. Anne crawled towards him on her hands and
knees. She stopped at his feet, raising herself up to a kneeling position.
As the cleric removed a host from the chalice, Anne distinctly heard
the sound of a trouser fly unzipping and a man's heavy breathing. She

opened her mouth, closed her eyes, and the priest's hand placed a host on her tongue. There was the sound of a man sighing with ecstasy, and now she was breathing heavily herself. She smiled with sexual delight. The host tasted like cum, and a thin stream of white viscous liquid trickled from between her lips down one side of her chin. She brought up one hand, licked her fingers, then her lips, smearing the stuff. Some portent of doom made her open her eyes, and they went wide with shock. She stared up into the face of Del Lynch who was looking down at her with a demonic smile. She heard the very loud zipping back up of his fly.

She raised her sweaty head from the mattress, rapt with horror at the unfolding vision. She was outside of herself looking on – she saw herself plain as day, kneeling on the bathroom floor in front of Lynch who was gazing lewdly down at her. There was a loud crash as she fell off the bed, and she looked up, startled, propping herself so she was leaning on her elbows.

Lisa stood in the open doorway of her apartment.

"It wasn't locked...you okay?" Lisa smiled. She came in and shut the door. "I wanted to see you..." Suddenly her smile was gone. "I couldn't take it anymore...I didn't know where else to go."

Anne dumbly looked at her, as if she was from another planet and, suddenly remembering her vision, whipped her head around to stare into the bathroom.

She groaned. "Oh, God..." She crawled back to the toilet and was sick again. Lisa came in and gently held Anne's head.

Much later, Lisa was sitting on the bed, her back against the wall, and Anne was resting her head on a pillow in her lap. Lisa smoothed Anne's tangled, dirty hair. They'd been like that for almost an hour.

Lisa carefully eased herself off the bedspread, walked to the bathroom and shut the door. When she came back out a few minutes later, she slowly started to peel off her clothes, staring tenderly at Anne. Anne watched, mesmerized, and the sight made her unexpectedly emotional. She wiped away a tear. At last, Lisa was naked. She settled down on the edge of the mattress, leaning on one elbow, never breaking eye contact with Anne. She scooted over and lay down very close to her. She cupped one side of Anne's face in her left hand, then bent over to kiss her, but Anne drew back and put up her hand.

"I'm sorry. I've never been with a woman before. You're going to have to give me some time."

Lisa took Anne's hand in both of hers, kissed it, then let it go.

Anne felt foolish, like she needed to explain. "I have to get used to the idea. If I can."

Lisa relaxed and nodded almost imperceptibly.

Anne turned over on her side, away from Lisa. Lisa rolled slowly onto her back and gazed up at the ceiling.

A few short hours later the dawn light threw shadows on the ceiling. Lisa was fast asleep. Anne, bleary-eyed, painfully pushed herself up to a sitting position. She glanced down at Lisa, then swung her feet off the bed. She stood with difficulty, and swayed over to the bathroom. She turned on the water and cupped both hands under it, splashing the liquid all over her face. She repeated the action several more times, finally had had enough and grabbed a towel to dry herself. Lisa appeared beside her, fully clothed.

"Wow, dressed already? You were asleep only a minute ago."

Lisa blushed. "My cherished 'business associates' have taught me well. I am an expert on how to dress quickly." Her sarcastic tone disappeared. "What are you doing today?"

"Hoping to overcome my hangover and go try to find a job. But I don't absolutely have to."

"Can we take your car and go somewhere?"

"Where?"

"Just someplace I want to show you. I used to go there a lot when my dad was still alive. When I was a lot younger."

Anne hung up the towel. "Okay."

Downtown the temperature had been muggy and in the low 90s. But along the coast the weather was beautiful, in the low 70s with puffy clouds creeping across the blue sky.

They had to drive up Pacific Coast Highway for almost an hour before hitting the area Lisa was looking for.

"Is this it?"

Lisa nodded excitedly. "Take that next exit on the left."

It was a semi-wooded area, no more than fifty or sixty yards from the water. Anne made the turn and followed the narrow winding road down a gradual slope. They entered a deserted dirt parking lot, but Lisa instructed Anne to keep going. There was a solid dirt road running between the trees, lightly dusted with sand. Anne continued, at last braking the car to a halt at the edge of a small clearing. They could plainly see the breaking surf, framed by the overhanging branches on either side.

Lisa suddenly became emotional. Tears flowed freely down both cheeks. Embarrassed, she swatted at them with her delicate, perfectly manicured hands. An impulse overcame Anne's timidity about physical contact, and she spontaneously threw her arms around Lisa's shoulders, hugging her. Lisa nervously laughed and gently threw off her embrace, trying to smile.

"Let's get out."

They walked only a few yards from the car, and the sound of the waves became dramatically louder.

"This is amazing."

"I wish I could build a house here and just live. I'd never have to go back to the city."

Anne smiled sympathetically.

That night, Anne sat on the bed with her back against the wall, barefoot, clad in jeans and a tanktop. Lisa lay beside her.

"You don't like TV, hunh?"

Anne slipped out of her reverie. "What?"

"You don't have one."

"It's in the pawn shop at the moment. It's just as well. It used to keep me from working on my paintings. Not like I've done too much of that in the last couple of weeks."

Lisa pointed at the long, tall bookcase next to the couch.

"You have a lot of books."

"I used to have more. I used to have a lot more of everything. CDs, records, DVDs. I've sold a lot. Besides needing the money, it was weighing me down."

"I know the feeling. I've only got a suitcase full of clothes. And sometimes it feels like a ton of bricks." She softly laughed.

Anne awoke from a nightmare that she immediately forgot. She sat up, confused, glanced at sleeping Lisa, and swung her feet off the mattress to a sitting position. She quickly pulled her jeans on over her panties, then went into the bathroom to begin her morning ritual. She'd had only a couple of drinks the previous night and felt far superior to the day before. Thankfully I've got some energy today, she thought. She returned to the big, combination living room/bedroom and continued to towel her face. She stopped at the window, glancing outside from habit, and froze. Ducking behind the curtain, she peered through a tear in the dirty, purple velvet fabric.

Shingo was casually standing on the sidewalk, leaning against a wall on the other side of the street. His shiny black monster of a Lexus was parked only a few feet behind Anne's Buick. He was smoking, as usual, and didn't seem to have seen her.

Lisa sat up in bed, yawned and ran her fingers through her long black tresses. "What's wrong?"

Anne turned to look at Lisa but didn't answer. Lisa could tell something was not right from Anne's expression. She rose, clad only in her panties, slipped on her sheer blouse and slowly walked over. When she was a few feet away, Anne quickly peeked out the window, then held out a hand to stop her.

"Stay there."

"What?"

Anne backed towards her in a hunched-over crouch, skirted the coffee table and sat down on the sofa.

"Your – 'friend' – what's his name? Shingo?"

"No...no..." Lisa dropped down beside Anne, her already pale face going white.

"Yeah...the prick."

"He must've followed me."

They both instinctively looked over at the window. Lisa touched Anne, and Anne jumped.

"Shit."

"I'm sorry." She swallowed. "How did you know his name?"

"Eve."

"Eve?"

"A mutual friend of ours. Eve Sandrelli. She's a couple inches shorter than me. Black hair. Wears tie-tops and bell bottoms a lot."

Lisa gradually put the name and face together. "Yeah...I know her. Kind of. She's a friend of Jack Bennett. She must have told you my name, too."

"Lisa Masuda," Jane offered.

Lisa meekly nodded.

"I haven't told you mine."

Lisa composed herself. "Of course I know your name. Anne." She paused, embarrassed again. "I don't know what I was thinking just showing up here unannounced. Now I've dragged you into all this."

Anne leaned back, sinking into the couch, overwhelmed.

Lisa frowned. "I was a little drunk the other night. Otherwise

--"

"Stop. It's okay."

"No, I should go." Lisa got up and walked to the bed. She hurriedly pulled on her skirt and her sleeveless jacket top.

Anne watched her, then swiveled her head to peer surreptitiously out the window.

Shingo was getting something out of his car.

Anne bent over, crouching, then straightened when she knew she was far enough away from the window that he couldn't see her.

"You can't. I could never live with myself knowing I'd let you go back to that."

Lisa smiled, sadly and strangely resigned. "It's okay…it's my fate."

The words made Anne angry. "It's nobody's fate!"

Lisa stared into space, then silently laughed at a private joke and collected her purse off the nightstand. She stood for almost an entire minute, staring at the floor, seemingly afraid to look at Anne.

"Goodbye, Anne. Thanks for everything."

At last, she moved towards the door. Anne reached out, grabbed her around the wrist and yanked with all her strength. Lisa lost her balance and was catapulted onto the bed.

"I said no."

Lisa propped herself on her elbows, shocked.

There was an abrupt, loud knocking on the door. Both women froze, petrified.

Anne screwed up her courage. "Yeah? Who is it?"

"It's Steve. You all right?"

Anne let out a deep sigh of relief.

"Hey, Anne, what's going on? Can you hear me?"

Anne whispered to Lisa. "I never thought I'd be glad to hear that voice…"

She spoke louder as she moved to the door. "Yeah, coming." She unclicked the deadbolt, but left on the chain, opening it only part way, trying to obstruct Steve's line of vision.

"What gives, baby?"

"Don't call me baby."

"Sorry." He fidgeted. "I was worried. I tried to call, but your phone is still disconnected, and your cell went straight to message. "

"Thanks for reminding me. I need to put it on the charger."

"I just had a bad feel – " He stopped short as he caught sight of Lisa over Anne's shoulder. "– sorry, I didn't realize you had company."

"It's okay." She undid the chain, pushed him out onto the landing and followed, almost completely closing the door behind her. She conspiratorially lowered her voice. "Look, Steve, could you do me a big favor?"

Steve grimaced. "I should've seen this coming."

"Okay. Forget it." She cracked the door and backed into the apartment, but Steve reached out and softly touched her arm.

"Shit, I didn't mean it that way. What do you need?"

Anne sighed. "I don't have any food in the house. She's not well...I don't want to leave her by herself." She whispered, "Drugs."

Steve looked over Anne's shoulder, trying to get a glimpse of Lisa, then stared down at Anne.

"Yeah, I get you. Okay."

Anne smiled. "Wait here a minute. I'll make you a list and get some dough."

As Steve came out of the building, he noticed Shingo and paused, giving him the once-over. Shingo barely turned his head, warily watching Steve.

Anne was stationed at the window behind the curtains. She watched as Steve turned on his heel and walked the other way down the block.

"Who was that guy?"

Anne rejoined Lisa on the bed.

"My latest ex. He can be a real prick. But he seems to be behaving himself at the moment."

"What did you say to him? Did you tell him I was on drugs?"

Anne laughed. "Yeah, sorry. I had to come up with a reason I couldn't leave you alone." She became more serious when she saw Lisa's expression. "Why? Are you?"

Lisa lay back on the unmade mattress. "Not me. My mother was strung out the whole last year before she died. One of the perks of hanging out with Del Lynch."

"Your...guardian?"

Lisa laughed derisively. "Eve sure gave you a full briefing."

Anne blushed.

Lisa was dismissive. "It's cool."

"I wanted to know more about you."

"'Guardian'. That is so pathetically funny."

Anne lay down next to her.

"What are we going to do?" Lisa averted her eyes towards the window. "About him?"

"I don't know."

"Is there a back way out?"

"It's blocked off. The landlord's remodeling. The fire department would pitch a fit if they knew."

"He's probably got one of his goons watching the back anyway."

Anne sat up again. "How come he hasn't come up here and made a scene?"

"He works for Del. And Del likes him to keep a very low profile."

"I thought Lynch was some kind of big shot."

"He is. But the reason he is, he's never had anything blow up in his face. I've seen him get crazy, but only in private, only in front of the flunkies on his payroll. He's a fanatical control freak. He likes his hired hands to be extra-cautious, especially in broad daylight. No little scrapes with the law."

Anne volunteered, "I don't really want to, but I suppose we could call the police."

"No."

"Why?"

"I'd just...rather you didn't." Lisa paused, staring at the ceiling. "Probably what Shingo will do is suddenly disappear. But he'll be watching from some place close by. We walk out, thinking he's gone, then suddenly the son-of-a-bitch materializes with a nasty grin on his face."

"The night you got the shit kicked out of you? Was that Del or Shingo?"

Lisa wagged her head at the window. "Him."

"Fuck."

Anne lay down again on the mattress. Lisa watched her, slowly propped herself on one elbow, then lowered her face as if to kiss her. Just before her lips reached Anne's, Anne jerked her head away, raised herself and moved to the edge of the bed, staring fixedly at the window.

"I'm sorry," Lisa whispered.

Anne whirled to look at her. "Goddamn it, stop apologizing every five minutes. It's okay. I'm just not ready. It's all the programming that's been burned into me since I was a kid."

"You've never been attracted to a girl?"

Anne calmed down and looked back at the window. "Yeah, a couple of times. I came pretty close once when I was drunk. But the attraction's just never been strong enough."

There was a loud knock at the door, and they both jumped. Anne got up, walked a few steps closer to peek through the window to make sure Shingo was still outside. When she saw him smoking his perpetual cigarette, she backed away and moved to the door.

"Yeah?"

"It's me. Open the fuck up."

Anne unbolted the lock and let Steve in. He handed her the bag of groceries but stared down at Lisa, distracted. Anne could tell he had a wild hair up his ass.

"You must think I'm pretty stupid."

Lisa perched herself on the edge of the bed, alarmed. Anne was fed up with him and put her hands on her hips in a defiant pose.

"Now what?"

Steve pointed at Lisa. "Her! That's what. I know who she is now. I thought she looked familiar. Then I saw that ass-wipe pimp across the street, and I remembered. She's one of his stable he works out of the Alexandria Hotel."

Anne sat down next to Lisa and took hold of one of her hands.

"I never worked out of the Alexandria Hotel..."

Steve ignored Lisa and petulantly stared at Anne. "Well! Don't you have anything to say?"

Anne leapt to a standing position, getting right in his face. "Who in the flying fuck do you think you are! What the fuck, Steve!"

"What's she doing here? Are you nuts?"

"I don't owe you a goddamn explanation. Just because we had sex a few times -- "

Steve was stung to his core. He looked at Lisa, then towards the window.

"Yeah, I forgot. I'm supposed to stop caring about you now that we aren't crackin' sheetrock anymore."

Anne disgustedly shook her head, sick of his cornball histrionics. "Stop it."

"You really *have* lost it, Anne. I know about that guy and the sons-of-bitches he runs with. They don't screw around. *They play for fucking keeps.*"

Anne stared at the floor and refused to make eye contact with him. After a few seconds of uncomfortable silence, he quietly opened the door and left. Anne glanced at Lisa.

"He's right," Lisa whispered.

"Stop, goddamn it."

Suddenly they heard shouting in the street.

"Hey, motherfucker!"

They darted to the window.

Steve was shouting, inches from Shingo's face. "What-the-fuck you lookin' at, pimp!"

Shingo turned away from him, smoking, trying to pretend he didn't care.

"What's the matter, dickwad? You think you're a fucking gangster? You look more like a fag to me."

It was obvious, even from their window vantage point, that Shingo was on fire with rage, but he displayed no overt reaction. Steve shoved him, and Shingo hit the boarded window of the building behind, his cigarette comically flying from his mouth. Without warning, his fist flashed up, popping Steve in the mouth. Steve backed off, spitting blood, some of which hit Shingo's trousers. Steve held his hand under his chin to catch the dripping redness.

"Oooh, now you've done it – " Steve gave a mirthless laugh as he licked his bloody lips.

Anne and Lisa could barely hear Shingo as he lowered his voice, controlling his temper. "Get the fuck out of here, before you really get hurt." He slipped his right hand inside his suit jacket, implying he had a gun. But when his hand partially emerged, it was holding what looked like the handle of a knife.

Steve hesitated. "Don't worry, I'm leaving. But you're going to pay for that. Just wait."

They stared at each other for several tense seconds. Finally, Steve stalked off, glancing over his shoulder at Shingo as he made his way down the block. Once he was out of sight, Shingo slowly turned to stare up at Anne's window.

Anne and Lisa backed away, out of his line of vision.

Shingo's cell phone rang. He took it out of his jacket pocket and checked the number. It was Dell Lynch.

"Well?"

"She still hasn't budged. But some guy, a friend of the girl she's staying with, came by. I've seen him at the club. I know a couple of his friends. They've been down to the Alexandria and the Biltmore. To see the girls. He went off on me, tried to pick a fight."

There was silence at the other end.

"You still there?"

"Yes."

"What should – "

"You didn't respond, I hope?"

"To the asshole? No."

"You didn't hit him or make a scene?"

Shingo hesitated because he was going to lie. "No…of course not."

"You're sure? You know how I feel about that kind of thing before the sun goes down."

Shingo rolled his eyes. "I understand. What should I do?"

"Stay put. She'll have to come out eventually. You've got the rear exit watched?

"They can't get out that way. It's blocked off. And there's no fire escape on their building."

"I know that neighborhood. All those buildings are fire traps. It'd be a shame if any unforeseen accidents happened. Any acts of God."

"It can be arranged."

"Not yet. Let's wait to see what happens. There's no hurry. I'll call you again. Be sure to let me know of any developments.

"Sure thing."

There was an audible click from the other end. Shingo absent-mindedly pocketed his phone and fixed his gaze on Anne's window.

Del Lynch gave his cell phone a dirty look and exhaled with a sigh. He was sitting in an antique French chair, probably dating from 1850 or so, enjoying the pleasant breeze from the French windows that opened onto his huge, gently sloping garden. He contemplated the figure of his only living relative, his brain-damaged cousin, Bennie, who was seated, back turned, on a long, ornamental concrete bench about twenty feet away. Bennie had been a professional wrestler living in Georgia until a horrific car accident had cut short his booming career five years earlier. He had had the misfortune of being in the passenger seat of a Dodge Charger going a 100 miles an hour when it had plowed into a very sturdy, very solid brick wall. It had rocketed him headfirst through the windshield, slamming his unusually hard noggin into the immovable mass. It was a miracle he had survived, even as a retarded near-vegetable. The driver, a hellraising biker mama from Baton Rouge, had perished.

Large, simian-looking, one-eyed Bennie stood 6'5" when fully erect and was presently dressed in tanktop and hillbilly bib overalls. His bad right eye was sewn shut and a sizeable railroad track of a scar

ran down the side of his left cheek. He lustily chomped on a nearly
devoured turkey drumstick. His mouth was an unsightly mess. Three
large front teeth protruded in an underbite, gouging his greasy top lip.
He smiled as he watched the butterflies flitting to and fro amongst the
profusion of multi-colored flowers in front of him.

Del realized his elderly, cadaverous butler, Elias, was standing
to one side. He looked up at him appraisingly.

"I was just wondering, sir, if you required anything more before I took my afternoon nap?"

"No," Del dismissed him with a wave of the hand, then
immediately thought better of it. "On second thought, Elias, go out in
the garden – " Del smirked, "– and see if Master Bennie is still
hungry."

"Very well, sir."

It had been an unusual sunset. Unlike most summer nights, darkness
had fallen like a black curtain around 8:00 PM.

They hadn't spoken more than a few words. Both of them had
no appetite, so they ate little. They sat in the shadows and didn't turn on
any lights once the sunlight disappeared.

Now it was nearly 11. Lisa was asleep. Anne stood in the
middle of the floor in a blind spot, staring down out of the window.

Shingo was taking a ridiculously long drag off his perpetual
smoke.

Anne spotted her cell phone on the table and plugged it into the
charger. As she grabbed her keys, she knocked over Lisa's purse, and
her phone and something else fell out. When she picked up the items to
replace them, she noticed the straight razor. Fascinated, she carefully
unfolded it and studied the blade. She glanced over at slumbering Lisa,
marveling at the incongruity, then quickly flipped the razor closed and
put it back.

She quietly let herself out. She locked all the locks with the
keys and pocketed them, then headed slowly down to the first floor,
peering cautiously round every bend in the stairwell. When she reached
the ground floor, she glided softly down the hall leading to the back
of the building. It was just as she had feared. The rear exit was all but
obscured by a mountain of obstacles – stacked paint cans, sawhorses,
pieces of scaffolding. To make matters worse, the bar release
opening mechanisms on the double doors were chained together, held
by an industrial-strength padlock. Even if the miscellaneous crap that
was blocking the exit hadn't been there, they were fucked.

Anne knew she needed to be getting back to her apartment. She padded at a loping run up the two flights of stairs, silently re-entered, locked the door and set the keys on the night table. Lisa was still asleep. Anne stood there staring at her for nearly five minutes, paralyzed by indecision. Finally she broke the spell and edged toward the window to peer outside.

Shingo's Lexus was there, but she didn't see him.

Still fully clothed, Anne tossed fitfully where she'd fallen asleep on the couch. It was nearly 10:00 AM before the sun shone directly onto her closed lids. She squinted and peered out at the blinding morning. She stretched, yawned and looked over at the bed, then walked over to the small refrigerator sitting on the floor next to her paintings. She took a swig from an orange juice carton, then replaced it. At last, she furtively moved to the window to check on Shingo.

Both Shingo and his car were gone. Anne's Buick was still parked in the same spot. She was surprised – happy but wary. She stuck her head out of the window, surveying the scene in both directions. The gangster was nowhere in sight.

Anne darted across the room, sat down on the mattress and shook Lisa's shoulder. Lisa groggily came to and struggled to a sitting position.

"It's too good to be true."

"What?"

Anne hooked her thumb over her shoulder. "Go look."

Lisa jumped up and ran to the window, peeking out from behind the curtains.

"I don't see him. Or the car."

"I don't know if he's still around or not, but he's nowhere in sight." Anne walked over to stand beside her.

Lisa was incredulous. "I can't believe it. It is too good to be true. He's trying to draw us out into the open."

They turned to face each other.

"I'm going down, but I'm going to leave my keys up here. Just in case he's still in the vicinity and catches me. That way he won't be able to just waltz in and get you. At least we won't make it easy for him."

Lisa started to panic. "No...please...please don't."

"Don't be silly. We can't stay locked in here forever. Look, don't freak out. I'll be right back." Anne hugged her, managing to coax a reluctant smile from the scared girl. "Don't be frightened."

Anne tentatively stuck her head outside of the building, looked up and down the street, then crossed to her car. She slowly circled the vehicle, surveying the block in all directions, hoping against hope that Shingo was really gone. When she came back full circle to the rear of the car, she noticed something odd.

The trunk was ajar.

Alarmed, she pivoted her head like a nervous bird, studying the street. As usual it was pretty dead. A mailman was slowly making his way down the next block. In the opposite direction, two junkies were perched on a doorstep, deep in conversation. Two blocks over, on the southeast corner, three winos were drunkenly singing an obscene, improvised rap.

She took hold and hoisted the trunk lid. Her eyes went wide, she gasped, but she tried to suppress her reaction. Shingo's battered dead body was curled up, jammed in a fetal position around the spare tire.

"Is that your car, miss?"

Anne slowly closed the trunk and made sure that it was locked. She turned around to face a plainclothes cop getting out of the unmarked police car that had just parked behind her. She hadn't heard him pull to the curb. He looked to be around fifty, with thinning grey hair. His hard face was borderline good-looking, but his features were neutral and held no emotion. He casually strolled up.

"Yes, it's mine."

Lisa was beside herself with anxiety as she watched from the window.

"You've had it parked in the same place and haven't moved it for several days."

"Oh, no, officer, I've driven it a couple of times, just yesterday in fact. I've just been lucky and always gotten this same spot. I live across the street."

"Uh, hunh..." He stared at the license plate and frowned. "I didn't notice it before, but your registration's expired, too."

Anne followed his stare, beads of sweat breaking out on her forehead. "Oh, wow."

"A couple months out of date. That's not good. Let's see your driver's license."

Anne was getting flustered. She dug in her jeans, came out with her license and gingerly handed it to him.

"Yeah, you know I have the registration upstairs. I just completely forgot to put the sticker on."

"Unh, hunh." He gestured at her building. "So, you say you live there?"

She nervously nodded.

"Go up and get it. I'll wait."

She hesitated for a second, then walked across the street.

Lisa watched as the cop casually circled the car. The sound of the apartment door opening made her turn. Anne had left it wide open and was frantically searching through a pile of envelopes on the nightstand, oblivious to Lisa. Not finding what she wanted, she moved to the coffee table and rifled through a pile of envelopes haphazardly stacked next to the ashtray and beer cans.

"What's wrong?"

Anne didn't look up. "He wants the registration."

"Is that it?"

Anne was losing her patience. "So far..." She threw the pile of envelopes back down, scattering them. "Shit!" She stealthily peeked out the window. The cop was kneeling behind the car, apparently examining the license plate.

Anne ran to the closet, opened it and rummaged through more papers and envelopes that were strewn on the floor amidst art supplies.

"Here it is. Thank fucking God!"

Lisa watched her as she quickly bent down to pick her keys off the floor, then disappeared.

Outside in the blistering sun, she raced up to the cop.

She smiled. "Here you go."

He lackadaisically straightened and took the papers from her. He took a good couple of minutes studying them.

Abruptly, he smiled. "Anne Bowen. I knew you looked familiar. Didn't we meet at a party about six or seven months ago? I think it was over at Adrian Greer's."

This was too fucking weird. Adrian would be the kind of guy to be friends with a cop. She nervously smiled.

"Oh, yeah, I know Adrian."

"Yeah, yeah, sure. I know him, too, from the DA's office. Weren't you two going out?

Anne nodded uncomfortably. "We went out a few times."

"Oh, you two aren't an item anymore?"

Anne remembered the party, but not the cop. She had been clad in a black, low cut sheath dress and extremely drunk. She had been jumpy because no one from her own small circle of friends, not even Eve, had been there. In the wee hours, as people had been leaving, she had slipped, falling on her ass, and had been unable to stop laughing. Most of Adrian's friends had muttered disparaging remarks and given her withering looks.

"I…I don't know if you could say we were really ever an item…"

The cop nodded thoughtfully as he handed back her registration and license.

"This stuff's all okay. You better put the sticker on, though. You're lucky it was me and not somebody in the traffic division. Some of those guys are cocksuckers. I wouldn't have even stopped, it's just I'm down here a lot on vice, and I notice things. This is a bad neighborhood. Two blocks further down, I guess you know, there's tons of drugs and prostitution."

"Yeah…but there are a lot of artists and writers who live here, too." She unlocked the front passenger door, opened it, pulled off the registration sticker, then placed the rest of the registration papers in the glove compartment.

The cop suddenly kneeled down behind the car again. He stuck his head up over the trunk. "Hey, did you see this? This is exactly what I mean."

Anne circled around. He fingered an area on the trunk lid's edge, right below the lock. He looked up at her meaningfully. "Pry marks. Like someone was trying to break into your trunk."

She nervously laughed. "That's from me. I lost my keys for a few hours last week, and I thought I might have locked them in there. I tried to pry it open. It didn't work, though."

The officer stood up. "You should be careful. You'll ruin the resale value."

Resale value? Was he kidding? The car was a piece of shit.

"I hadn't thought of that. Thanks." She was watching his every move, trying to contain her anxiety.

He slowly headed to his car, but he was reluctant to part company and turned again.

"Hey, I just thought of something…"

"Yeah?"

"You and Adrian aren't going out anymore, right?"

Anne shook her head, blushing and leery of what was coming.

"Maybe the two of us could go out for a hamburger and a movie sometime – "

"You know, I'd love to, but – "

"Yeah?"

"– I just started seeing someone else."

He nodded, disappointed. He smiled as he climbed into the car. "Oh, well, my loss. Didn't hurt to ask."

She grinned. "Yeah..."

She bent down, putting the sticker on the license plate as the unmarked car pulled away. She watched it until it disappeared around the corner two blocks further down, then straightened and stared up at the window.

Lisa was drained and drifted listlessly from the curtains to sit on the couch. Anne walked in, supercharged with adrenaline, and went directly to the window, gazing down at her car.

"So everything's okay?"

"Not really. I don't want to freak you out, but I know the reason why Shingo isn't standing there anymore."

Lisa sat forward, dreading some new traumatic revelation. "What?"

"He's dead."

Lisa put her hand to her mouth.

"– and he's in the goddamn trunk of my goddamn car."

"But... who killed him?"

Anne sat down next to her. "I don't know. The logical choice would be Steve after what happened between the two of them. But I can't imagine Steve actually killing anyone. Beating the shit out of someone with hardly any provocation, yeah. But not killing them."

"It's got to be him."

She creased her forehead, concentrating, then realized she was wasting time. "We can't worry about who did it at the moment. We've got to get rid of him."

"Where?"

"I don't know. Not around here. I've been trying to think. Maybe up along Angeles Crest."

They paused in the building doorway and anxiously scanned the street for signs of other Lynch henchmen. When they felt relatively certain they were safe, they crossed and quickly got into Anne's car.

A few minutes later they were headed into Pasadena on the 110 Freeway. Once the freeway ended, they continued north, jogging over to the 210 towards La Cañada. They got off at the Angeles Crest Highway connector and drove northeast for nearly forty minutes before Anne was satisfied that the traffic was sparse enough to risk dumping Shingo. There was little conversation between the women; both of them were caught in their own nightmare mazes of introspection.

Anne pulled over a little beyond the Devil's Canyon trailhead, maneuvering the car close to the edge of a brush-covered slope at the mouth of a disused fire road.

"We better do it now while there's no one coming."

Lisa nodded, terrified.

Anne swiftly sprung open the trunk, looked around one last time, then reached under Shingo's arms. Petulant anxiety welled up in her voice. "C'mon, Lisa. I need your help. Take his legs."

Lisa reluctantly pitched in. They carried him about ten feet, setting him down behind some bushes right on the edge of the gradual slope.

"Christ, it looks like someone killed him with their bare hands."

Large fingermark bruises were clearly visible on Shingo's throat. His windpipe looked crushed.

"C'mon, let's get him a little ways down the hill."

Lisa tried to avoid eye contact with Anne. "I can't. I can't touch him again. He's so cold." Lisa raised her eyes, then suddenly clasped her hands over her mouth as she threw up. She hovered above a dried-out husk of a tree trunk, spewing. Anne put her arm around the girl's back, supporting her. Once Lisa's convulsive anxiety dissipated a bit, and she seemed to be done, Anne took a handkerchief from her denim jacket and wiped Lisa's mouth. A car going way too fast whooshed past them. Anne looked after it and sighed, frustrated.

"Okay, stay here." She bent over and hooked her hands underneath Shingo's armpits. "I'll be right back." Anne dragged the body down onto the brushy slope.

Lisa dejectedly shuffled to the car, sitting down in the passenger seat with the door open. She dug in her jacket pocket and withdrew a very small, furry dragon doll. It fit comfortably in the palm of her hand. Anne's words echoed in Lisa's head: "Christ, it looks like someone killed him with their bare hands."

She remembered Del in his garden, reading the Wall Street Journal. She knew he had thought she hadn't noticed, but she'd been able to tell he was watching her over the top of the paper. Lisa had gotten up from Del's side and walked to where Bennie was sitting on his favorite bench, observing the bees and butterflies. Lisa had bent down and given him a present.

"I know you always wanted a little doll like mine, Bennie. So this is for you."

Lisa always winced when she saw the scars crisscrossing the backs of Bennie's large, powerful hands, and that time had been no exception. She had had to use every ounce of fortitude to take his right hand in hers and place an exact replica of the tiny dragon doll in his grasp.

"Now we both have one..."

Bennie had laughed with joy in his own pathetic, brain-damaged way.

Before she returned to the top, an idea occurred to Anne, and she went through Shingo's pockets. Astonishingly enough, they were empty. She was hoping to find a weapon of some kind – a gun, even a knife, something. But she came up empty-handed. Anne was already tired, but she knew she couldn't waste time and began her ascent. At the very top, she climbed over the ridge on all fours with difficulty, straightened erect and dusted herself off. She raised her head.

"Thank God that's over with."

Alarm bells went off inside of her.

Lisa wasn't in the car, and she was nowhere in sight. Anne rapidly circled the vehicle, looking for her, trying to fight her rising panic. She hurriedly trekked twenty yards down the road, searching, then raced up ahead of the car in the other direction. The aroma of pine needles, a smell she usually loved, was having an unpleasant effect on her, making her throat feel raw and scratchy, and the cooler temperature at this higher elevation, compared to the heat of the city, chilled her to the bone.

"Lisa! Lisa! Where are you!" Anne's voice echoed in the canyon, and she shivered at the spooky loneliness of the sound. She called several more times over the next ten minutes. But it was no use.

She was gone.

They had been watched and followed.

Resigned, Anne sank down into the driver's seat. She was about to start the car when she noticed that the passenger door was not completely shut. As she reached over to pull it closed, she caught sight of something on the floor. She picked up Lisa's dragon doll.

Anne parked across the street from Steve's house in Highland Park. She hesitated before getting out when she spotted a black-and-white as well as an unmarked police car in the driveway. A uniformed cop stood against the low retaining wall in front. She climbed out and crossed the street. He slowly looked over at her.

She tried to smile. "What's going on?"

"Police business."

"I kind of figured that out."

"Then you also should've figured it's none of *your* business. It's a crime scene."

"I'm friends with one of the guys who lives here. Is everything okay?"

His expression changed, and he gestured toward the backyard. "You better go talk to Detective Mason. He's behind the house."

Anne had a horrible presentiment as she moved up the uneven walk alongside the building. When she rounded the rear into the tiny yard, she spotted two men in suits with their backs turned, both staring down at something. She paused for a couple of seconds until it registered what they were looking at.

"What do you think? The way he's cut up –?"

"I dunno. The cuts are strange. Pretty fucking deep."

Anne walked forward. Suddenly an old-fashioned metal garbage can with two bloody legs protruding, knees bent and hanging over the edge, became clearly visible between the two men. Mason, a 50-ish, tall, heavyset man with jowls and a shock of grey hair, sensed Anne's presence and turned.

"Ma'am, you're not supposed to be back here. You don't live here, do you?"

"No. What's going on?"

"Who are you?"

"My name's Anne Bowen."

"Yeah? And – ?"

"I know one of the guys who lives here, Steve Dios." She was scared. "Where is he?"

"Were not 100% sure yet."

Mason's colleague, Velkovsky, a skinnier, shorter, younger man with a purple shirt and black silk tie, chimed in, gesturing at the body in the garbage can. "This might be him right here."

Mason frowned at his partner, then smiled at Anne. "You think you're up to taking a look?"

Anne felt paralyzed, but she nodded. She leaned over and gazed down into the can. She slowly raised her head, looked from one man to the other and nodded again.

"*That's* Steven Dios?"

Anne was shaken. "Yeah."

Mason softened his tone, trying to be gentle. "When was the last time you saw him, Anne?"

"Y-Y-Yesterday afternoon...d-d-downtown in the warehouse loft district where I live." Oh, God, she thought, now I'm fucking stuttering.

The next thing she knew, she was sitting on the curb in front of the house, holding a warm can of Coke. Mason was sitting beside her. She thought she must have blacked out.

"So, Anne, you feel a little better? Can you maybe answer a few questions? You might be able to help us."

"Go ahead. I doubt I know anything that can help."

Mason smiled a patronizing smile as he got out a small notepad and pen. "That's okay, let me be the judge of that. You never know."

She nodded.

"What was your relationship to the deceased?"

"We went out for a couple of months."

"When did that end?"

"Earlier this week."

"You mind if I ask why?"

She hesitated for only a second. "We both decided to start seeing other people."

"Unh, hunh." Mason looked at her thoughtfully for a few seconds, then flipped a page back on his small notepad. "I understand two other white Caucasian males live at this address? A Manfred Silverberg aka Manny and a Terrence Connelly?"

She nodded.

"Know where they are?"

"Uh, if they're not here, they're probably at work. They paint houses most days."

"Do you know anyone who would have wanted to do harm to Steve?"

She shook her head. "Not that I know of."

Mason frowned. "Can I get your phone number? We may want to contact you again."

She recited her number for him, then, thinking maybe she had better tell him, she added, "I do know that there was a guy who recently threatened Steve."

"Oh?"

"Yeah. A Japanese guy down in Little Tokyo. A gangster-type named Shingo. I don't know his last name. I heard he worked for a lawyer named Lynch."

"Lynch? Del Lynch?"

"Maybe. I'm not sure."

He frowned again, distracted and looked down the street. The neighborhood was suddenly filled with kids getting home from school. Suddenly he turned back to her and put on his best public relations smile.

"Very good, Anne." He put his pad back in his jacket. He slapped his knees as he got up. "Well, thank you. You're not leaving town anytime soon, are you?"

"No."

"Fine. No big deal. Just call me and let me know if you do. Here's my contact info." He handed her his business card.

She took it from him as she stood up. "Thanks."

Anne parked across the street from her building. She was a nervous wreck. Before getting out, she picked up her cell phone and dialed Eve.

"Hello?"

"Eve? Can you come over? Right away?"

"What's wrong? You sound awful."

"Something horrible's happened."

"What is it?"

"I don't want to tell you on the phone. Please, come over. I feel like I'm going off my rocker."

"Okay. I'm already in the car, and I'm not too far from your place. See you in a few minutes."

"Thanks."

Anne clicked off the phone and leaned against the headrest. The day's events had completely drained her.

She had dozed off on the couch, her head slumped back at an awkward angle. There was an insistent rapping on the door. She finally roused herself and jumped to her feet.

"It's me. Eve."

She rushed to open up, rubbing her stiff neck. Eve came in, and Anne hurriedly shut the door behind her, locking both locks.

"Sorry it took me so long to get over here. Rush hour traffic was a bitch. You okay?"

Anne shook her head, tightly holding her arms in a defensive posture.

"Yeah, you don't look okay. What's happened?" Eve pulled her to the bed.

"C'mon, let's sit down." They perched on the edge of the mattress, facing each other.

"Lisa came back the other night. But Shingo followed her. He was waiting outside across the street all yesterday and all last night.

"Fuck."

"That's not the worst of it. Steve comes by during the day, puts two-and-two together and flips out on Shingo. He picked a fight. Shingo bloodied his nose. Then Steve threatened Shingo and split..." She paused for a second, took a deep breath and let it out. "This morning, I think Shingo is gone. But he isn't."

"Where was he?"

"In the trunk of my car..."

"Jesus..."

"Needless to say, he was dead."

"Do you think it was Steve?"

"I thought maybe it was, at first. But now..."

"What happened to the body?"

"Lisa and I dumped it along Angeles Crest. I dragged it down a slope. But when I got back to the car, Lisa was gone."

"I don't believe this. It's her, Anne. That girl's bad luck. She -- "

"Hold on. I'm not finished. It keeps getting worse. Not only can I not find Lisa, I go over to Steve's to confront him about Shingo, and I find the cops there. And Steve's dead, too. Murdered."

Eve was shaken and didn't know what to say. She was too dumbfounded to speak.

"I'm scared for myself. I'm scared for Lisa. God knows what's happening to her. Those guys use her like she's some premium-grade blow-up doll. I've been around twisted fucks before, but never anybody like them."

Eve muttered. "I warned you it was a bad scene."

"She doesn't stand a chance. There's no contest. It's like pulling wings off a butterfly." Anne stared into space.

"You got a drink?"

Anne pointed to a bag on the coffee table. "I bought a bottle on the way home."

Eve shot over, grabbed it, dredged the fifth of whiskey out, anxiously tore off the wrapper, unscrewed the cap and offered it to Anne.

"Go ahead. I don't want any right now."

Eve downed a healthy swig.

"I wasn't sure how much to tell the cops."

Eve wiped her mouth. "Did you mention sweet, darling Shingo in your trunk, then rolling him down the mountainside?"

Anne gave her a dirty look. "What do you think?"

"I don't know. I wouldn't have told them jackshit to begin with."

Anne frowned. "I wasn't going to, then I thought I couldn't get much more fucked than I was already, so...I told them I thought Shingo had threatened Steve. And that he worked for Lynch."

"That was smart. Real smart."

"Shut up."

"*Don't* you *think* that'll get back to Lynch?"

"I didn't think about it...at the time. But the detective did act weird when I mentioned Lynch."

"I'll bet."

"Maybe it's just as well if it does get back to the prick. I'm fucked whatever happens. Maybe this way it'll bring things to a head a lot faster. I don't want to sit around here waiting for days, not knowing if I'm next."

"Is that all?"

"Yeah. Isn't it enough?"

"Well...in a way, you're lucky. So far."

Anne grabbed the bottle from Eve, pissed. "Christ, Lynch isn't some kind of invincible force. You're making him into a fucking god who sees all, knows all!"

"He thinks he is. And he acts like it. Two people wouldn't be dead otherwise."

"You think he might have had something to do with Shingo's death? The guy worked for him."

"Who fucking knows. Lynch isn't sane."

Anne took a gulp from the bottle and coughed.

Eve patted her on the back and made a suggestion. "Maybe we should try to get Steve's pal Manny and his buddies involved. They've got connections with Tony Rubio and some bikers. We could all go to Del's place, rescue Lisa and fuck him up."

Anne was incredulous. "You're crazy. You think you're in a fucking movie?"

Eve was embarrassed and reached for the bottle. Anne slumped flat on the bed for almost a full minute, then sat back up.

"Do you know where Lynch lives?"

"Pretty much. It's up in the Silver Lake hills. Right off the corner of Esplanade and Gentry...why?"

Anne shook her head. "Nothing..." She plopped down again on the mattress. After a few swigs, Eve set the bottle on the floor and stretched out horizontal. Both of them lay there, staring at the ceiling.

Later, both of them were still lying across the width of the mattress in their underwear, sleeping, turned on their sides and with their backs to each other. Anne's pupils convulsed beneath her eyelids in REM.

She was in the foyer of the big, old white house. There were the two tall windows with the sunlight streaming in and that table again, with that vase of yellow flowers, standing between them. This time there was a very old-fashioned sewing machine sitting on the same table. It reminded Anne of her mother's. Otherwise, the room was virtually empty. She withdrew one of the flowers from the vase and began pinching off the petals just as the sewing machine vanished into thin air. Anne put the yellow petals into an empty matchbox on the table.

She abruptly realized what she was wearing and was shocked to see she had gone out in only bra and panties. A closet door on the left, located under the staircase, soundlessly opened, and Lisa popped out her head, smiling. Anne pivoted completely around to look at her. Lisa's slurred, distorted voice, her words belied her happy expression.

"Help me stop them."

"Who?"

Lisa withdrew her head into the closet, and Anne just made out her answer as she quietly closed the door. "Them..."

Anne suddenly realized her bra and panties were gone, and she tried to use her hands to cover her breasts and shaved pussy. Why was she naked? It felt good, not wearing clothes, but she also felt ashamed and vulnerable.

Anne drifted to the closet door and opened it. Lisa was no-where to be seen. She grabbed a black leather raincoat, the one lone piece of clothing hanging there, and put it on. She then spotted a sawed-off, double-barreled shotgun that was leaning against the wall. She picked it up and cracked it open. Both barrels were empty. She was disappointed, and she began looking for shells. Suddenly, she had what she thought was a brilliant idea and carried the gun out to the table. She plucked the yellow flower petals from their stems and poked and squeezed and jammed them into the barrels of the still-cracked-open weapon. When she thought she'd loaded in enough, she slammed it shut.

A big wild rabbit scampered into the room through two big French windows that she hadn't noticed before. Anne watched the animal with trepidation, and slowly, almost imperceptibly, it changed and grew. Before long, it was just a huge blob of undulating fur, gradually spreading across the floor toward her. Anne raised the shotgun, aimed it where she believed its heart would be and pulled the trigger.

A loud clanking noise just outside her apartment made Anne wake with a start, and she sat bolt upright. Oblivious Eve was still asleep.

Anne pulled on her jeans and went to the door, carefully opening it and peering through the crack left by the chain. Seeing nothing, she closed it, undid the chain, then cracked it open again. She quietly moved out into the hall. There was no one about.

Prowling toward the staircase, then down the steps, her bare feet were soundless on the worn hard wood. She came to a tentative stop on the bottom floor. No one. Once she had been standing there for a moment, she began to discern the old building's familiar noises -- weird creaks of wood and the thuds and clankings of hot water pipes. Anne tilted her head, peering up between the stairs.

Nothing was stirring.

Then the Santa Ana winds, which had been mild earlier, must have picked up, because they became clearly audible. The glass panes in the building's entranceway rattled. Restless air currents sighed and whined, whooshing to a soft roar as they whipped around the building.

Anne climbed back up the steps, but she didn't stop at her floor, and she only hesitateed for a moment as she passed her slightly cracked door. When she got to the next landing, there was an abrupt, soft cry and a ferociously loud crash from what seemed to be her apartment. She froze, scared stiff, but paused for only a few seconds before bravely heading down again. Once she was only a few steps away, she saw that her place was now wide open. She leaned over the railing, trying to peer into the dimly-lit room. The lamp on the other side of the bed, which had been off, was switched on, and it lay overturned on the floor, flickering, throwing strobing shadows around the walls.

Eve was no longer on the disheveled bed. She had vanished. The blanket and sheets lay in a pile beyond the far end of the mattress, closest to the darkened bathroom. Anne felt she was being foolish, but she had to find out what had happened, and she stealthily walked in.

"Eve?" She knew she sounded frightened.

There was a barely perceptible rustling from the other side of the bed. She circled it, surveying her surroundings, a spooked animal on the alert for danger. She stared at the heaped mound of bedclothes. Nearly paralyzed, she somehow managed to reach and take hold of the quilt and the sheets, and she yanked the tangle of fabric. Eve's body laid under it, contorted, her neck twisted at an impossible angle. Her unseeing eyes stared wide into Anne's, and there was no question whatsoever that she was dead. Not thinking, Anne backed into the bathroom, overcome with terror.

"Eve...Eve...God, no..."

She sobbed, aghast with grief and terror. All at once the darkness behind Anne, the black shower curtain, came alive, expanding, wrapping itself around her and clutching her in a death grip. Anne screamed, struggling in a panic and determined not to be another victim. She relaxed her body, shrank into herself and jerked downward to the dirty linoleum. Breaking free and rocketing away, she bolted from the apartment and down the stairs.

A thought occurred to her on the bottom floor just inside the building entrance. She hurriedly looked to see if she was being followed as she jammed both hands in her jeans pockets.

"Oh, God, please!"

She pulled one hand out to reveal her keys and the other, her cell phone. She cried with relief. She moved to the door, peeked into the deserted street, then after a quick glance over her shoulder, disappeared into the darkness outside.

It was late morning. Anne slept fitfully, lying fully-clothed on the front seat of her car, parked in some innocuous middle-class neighborhood in Echo Park. There was a faint, intermittent buzz. After a few seconds, Anne came awake and realized her cell was ringing. She took the phone from her jeans pocket and, hoisting herself by grabbing the steering wheel, sat upright. She looked at the number view window, pressed a button, held the cell to her ear and shouted, "What the fuck happened to you?"

Lisa ignored the question. "Anne, are you okay?"

"No."

"Why? What's happened?"

"Someone killed Eve in my apartment. Not to mention Steve."

"Oh, no..."

"Oh, *yes*...I was out on the stairs for a minute because I heard a noise. When I came back in, I found Eve with her head nearly twisted off, then they tried to kill me, too. Some-fucking-how I got away. What the fuck, Lisa! Do I have to go on the run now?"

"I know this will sound empty. But I'm so sorry."

"'Sorry' doesn't cut it."

"I know." Lisa paused. "Can you meet me in about half an hour?"

"Why the fuck should I? If I had any brains, I'd be a couple hundred miles from here."

Lisa was ashamed and obviously trying not to cry. "You're right. You shouldn't ever talk to me again. I'm poison. I just want to say thank you for helping me. It's meant alot."

Anne was too angry and hurt to say anything for almost a full minute.

"Are you still there?" Lisa timidly asked.

"What happened to you up in the mountains? You vanished into thin air."

"I walked a few yards down the highway. Then all of a sudden, Del pulled up –"

"I thought so..."

"I ran and got back into your car, but he stopped alongside. He said if I didn't leave with him that he'd kill you as soon as you came back."

Anne made up her mind, despite her better judgment. "Where do you want me to meet you?"

"No, you're right. You should get out – "

Anne lost her patience. "Christ, Lisa, let's not go through this again. *Where do I meet you?*"

"Do you know where that park is off the 110...off Via Marisol?"

"I think so. It's part of that long stretch of Arroyo Seco, right before you get into South Pasadena."

"That's it. Meet me there in half an hour. Del's gone for the afternoon. I shouldn't have a problem getting there."

"Okay...half an hour."

"Yes."

Anne hung up, letting her hand with the phone fall to her side. She stared off into space, thinking. Then she noticed her bare feet from the night before.

Even though the park was only an eighth of a mile from the freeway, butted up against the hills on the other side – which reflected sound – the traffic was virtually inaudible. There weren't too many people about since it was a workday afternoon. One lone Chicano woman pushed a baby stroller across the lawn almost a hundred yards away.

Anne rapidly walked from the parking lot across the grass, watching for Lisa. She also kept on the lookout for any odd, out-of-place characters. The problem was she knew gang kids from neighboring Mount Washington, Eagle Rock and Highland Park would often stop in this shady refuge to smoke weed. Interlopers, either dangerous or harmless, could show up at almost any hour of the day or night.

Time passed. Anne glanced at her watch, then around the park area, scanning for Lisa. The woman with the stroller was leaning against one of the few cars in the lot, talking on her cell. Even further away, Anne saw what seemed to be a big man in a T-shirt and overalls lumbering across the lot to the public restrooms.

She stretched out, lying on her side and propping her head in her hand with one elbow pressed into the moist lawn. She spotted something in the grass that caught her attention and picked up a leaf. She maneuvered the leaf closer to a furry black caterpillar, coaxing it to climb on. Unconsciously, she smiled, forgetting for a few minutes all the horror and stress of the preceding hours.

Remembering why she was there, she finally set the leaf down and raised her head again to search for Lisa. There was no one in sight, and all the cars in the lot were gone, except for hers.

When she looked back down, the caterpillar, too, had disappeared.

She sat up, crosslegged, a troubled expression spreading across her face. Suddenly, a large, hairy arm descended, pinioning Anne's neck in a strangling chokehold. She opened her mouth to scream, but only a gutteral chortle escaped. She clawed at Bennie's muscled forearm, desperately trying to dislodge it, to no avail, and she felt as if she was going to black out. Bennie diligently concentrated on the task at hand, chomping his upper lip with his hideous underbite, squinting down at the helpless, kicking girl.

Anne pressed three fingers of her right hand together and jabbed Bennie in his one good eye. He dropped her, gasping and groaning with pain and clasping his face. She tumbled free, face-first onto the ground, coughing and gagging and trying to crawl away. Bennie was on his knees, holding his sore eye with one hand and reaching out to feel for Anne with the other. She scrambled backwards, making a vain attempt to stand. She was too dizzy and short of breath, still coughing and seeing starlike patterns swirling in front of her.

Turning over and pulling herself along the grass in sporadic fits, she edged ever further from Bennie, who swept the ground to find her. Finally she regained her footing and ran toward the lot. She glanced behind her once and saw that Bennie had gotten up. He awkwardly stumbled after her but tripped.

She reached her car, unlocked it, jumped in and started the engine. She rammed it into reverse, then drive, careening out of the lot, racing away from the park. Once she was on the freeway, she pulled out her cell phone and dialed Lisa. The area was rife with piss-poor reception, though it seemed to gradually improve the closer she got to downtown. At last, her call went through.

"Hello?"

"What the fuck, Lisa! Did you set me up?" Her voice was hoarse from Bennie's chokehold.

"Anne?"

"Yeah," she coughed, "Surprised to hear my voice?"

"Listen, Del came back in the house and overheard me. He took off for the park with this big retarded guy, Bennie -- "

Anne sarcastically interrupted. "Yeah, I think Bennie and I were just introduced. Why the fuck didn't you *call me, warn me!*"

"I *did* call you. But it went straight to message..."

Anne started to calm down. "Yeah, the signal does suck over there..."

"I'm so glad you're okay. What happened?"

"What do you think happened? Bennie tried to crush my fucking larynx. Was he the one in my apartment last night, the one who killed Eve?"

"I don't know. Probably. He's the one who killed Shingo."

Anne was constantly checking her rear view. "What? I thought they were on the same side."

"Bennie's on whomever's side Del tells him to be. Or not. Del had Bennie kill Shingo *because Shingo killed Steve*. Del had told Shingo to leave Steve alone. But he didn't. Shingo knew one of Steve's friends, some guy called Manny, and tracked Steve down through him. When Del found out, he said he just couldn't tolerate Shingo's 'insubordination' any longer."

Anne was appalled. "Jesus Christ. Lynch told you all this?"

"Yes. He loves to boast. He knows it scares me and that I can't do anything about it, that I'm powerless."

"So why did Bennie kill Eve?"

"Who knows. Bennie's brain-damaged. He probably thought Eve was you."

"So much for Del not wanting stuff to blow up in his face. I don't know how he's going to put the lid on all this."

"He's not worried. This means nothing to him."

"He seems a little worried about me."

"You're a loose end. He ties up loose ends."

They were both silent for a few seconds. "Where are you now? It sounds like you're driving, too."

"I am. I took the gardener's car. Del was over-confident. He just left me at the house when he drove off with Bennie. He thought he had me scared enough not to run again. But, at this point, I'd rather die than stay there."

"Where are you headed?"

"Remember the place we went? Way up past Zuma, halfway to Santa Barbara?"

"Yeah. I'll meet you there."

"Give me a couple of hours. I'm going the long way round. I want to make sure there's no way Del can track me."

"Okay. Two hours. As soon as I get there, we're driving north as far as we can go."

Lisa turned into the same semi-wooded area near the empty beach that she had visited before with Anne, parking the car under an overhang of shady trees. She got out and came around to the passenger side, opened the door and sat, tilting her seat back to stretch and relax. As she exhaled deeply, she sighed, and she closed her eyes. After about five minutes, there was the sound of another car. Lisa was immediately alert, smiling at the thought of seeing Anne. But then she anxiously grabbed the rear view mirror, angling it to see who it could be, intuiting that it wasn't Anne who was driving up. She thought she recognized the sound of the soft, purring motor. Her crestfallen expression drained her face of blood. There was the soft tread of shoes on gravel.

Del stopped at the open door. "Hello, dear."

"It's impossible. I never saw your car behind me. You couldn't —"

"You shouldn't express everything in absolutes. Of course I knew." He crouched, pulling something out from under the chassis of the gardener's car, what looked like a small electronic device. He displayed it proudly. "I've got one on all the cars that regularly come to the house. Even ones I don't own. You never know when they might come in handy."

Del sat on the edge of the seat beside her, which caused her to go rigid.

"You never want to admit you need what I give you."

"You're not capable of giving me anything. You've had the same effect on me that you had on my mother. Except unlike her, I never ever wanted it. Never."

"Don't lie."

"It's not a lie. You snared me when I was too young, too stupid, too weak to put up a fight. Too overcome with grief. I didn't know then how much you were a cause of that grief."

"Your father and mother were made for their fate. I did very little to tip the scales."

She spat in his face, shouting. "Liar. You pulled them down with you into your cesspool."

He smiled ruefully. "My gutter." He withdrew a spotless handkerchief and wiped the spittle from his face.

"Yes, your stinking corrupt gutter."

He moved his face close to hers, and she turned her head away. He murmured close to her ear. "But there is elegance in corruption. It's a cliché to say it, but the corruption caused by indulgence, by that abject consummation, holds rare beauty." His mouth undulated obscenely. "Decay and corruption, the debris left behind by death, is the breeding ground for life."

"For parasites. For flies and vermin."

"But they are the most enduring forms of life. Like the weed, they need little nourishment. They can flourish in a world of concrete and stone."

She turned to give him a look of abject hatred. "How I loathe you!"

"You little idiot. You still don't understand those are the words I live to hear."

She slowly nodded, knowing it was over and she couldn't win; at least not the way she'd hoped. "Each time that I've felt I couldn't sink any lower, I surprise myself. Killing real feeling with sensation."

"The senses are feeling."

"Jaded, dead senses."

Del smiled. "Sad, but true..."

"Dead."

"I was made to dominate. You must understand, you were made

to submit."

Del inched even closer, turning her head with his hand and mashing his lips against hers. She squeezed her eyes tightly shut. Del moved to the other side of her face, ravishing her neck and ear. She gasped for breath as if she was suffocating.

The Santa Ana winds had picked up again. They made the tree branches sway and sigh with whistling and rustling sounds.

Dell got out and stood by the car, looking out to sea. "I'll expect you back at the house."

She shamefully turned her eyes away and nodded.

"Of course, you can stay here for a while. Relax. Think about what I've said. How I'm right. But remember – "

Lisa looked up at him.

"– your friend can't save you. Nobody can."

She looked away again, dead inside.

"If you want me to leave this Anne girl alone, you won't try to run away again."

Lisa closed her eyes and listened to the sound of Del walking away, of his car door opening and shutting and his high-grade engine starting, purring with sinister life. He pulled away down the dirt road, through the lot and turned back up onto the highway.

She stared at herself in the rear view mirror.

"Nobody can save me from myself."

She absent-mindedly reached for her purse beside her, and, without looking, pulled out her straight razor.

About half an hour later, Anne pulled up behind Lisa's car. She got out and walked along the passenger side but stopped abruptly as some smeary red writing became visible to her on the front window. Anne quickly opened the door, and one of Lisa's lifeless arms fell limply out, dripping blood on the ground.

Anne went stiff with shock. It hit her like a blast of icy wind, and she realized that she had been in denial, that she had intuited days before that this was a very real possible outcome to Lisa's impossible situation. She slowly sat down on the seat beside her, oblivious to the blood.

Lisa had slashed both her wrists. Before she had slit her throat, she had written on the window in scarlet: *"Anne, I'M SORRY"*

Anne shook her head in disbelief and stared at dead Lisa's pale white face. She reached out with quivering fingers and shut Lisa's half-open lids. Anne scrunched her own eyes shut as tears poured down her cheeks, her whole body wracked with uncontrollable sobs. Finally, she was able to control her weeping and tenderly clasped Lisa's face in both of her hands. She pressed her lips to Lisa's lips, lingering there for a full minute, stifling a sob as she at last pulled away.

She stood up with difficulty and firmly shut the door. Then she walked to her own, got in and, with very deliberate motions, started the engine, shifting it into gear and pulling away.

After a half hour of hit or miss guesses in the Silver Lake hills near the intersection of Esplanade and Gentry, she found what she was positive was Del Lynch's old mansion. She angled the Buick to the curb and parked, then just sat there, solidifying her resolve.

She didn't have a weapon, so she got out and went to the trunk to retrieve the tire iron.

It was early evening. In another hour, the sun would start to go down.

She didn't bother to scan the block to see if anyone was looking, just went directly to the six foot high stone wall, hauling herself up and easing over it. Immediately, she saw she was in the garden. Approximately ten yards away, on the other side of a large goldfish pond, Bennie sat on a stone bench with his back to her. She burst into a loping run, splashing through the pond and, lightning quick, coldcocked Bennie with the tire iron, just as he was turning his head. He fell onto all fours, and she bashed him again. She thought she had knocked him unconscious, but as she walked by his prone body, he reached out, caught her ankle and pulled her to the ground beneath him. He gripped her around the throat with one hand and with the other yanked the tire iron from her grasp, throwing it behind them into the pond. He mashed her face sideways into the dirt.

Suddenly something tumbled from Anne's top jacket pocket – it was the furry little dragon doll that Lisa had left in the car in the mountains. Without warning, Bennie stopped, loosening his grip, and Anne, for a brief second, flashed on Steve with his hand around her throat. One of Bennie's enormous fists picked up the tiny stuffed creature.

Anne's eyes darted in panic. Bennie was completely distracted. He climbed off her but remained in a kneeling position, studying the little toy. She regained her feet, choking, gasping and rubbing her throat. Once she was standing, she stared down at Bennie, incredulous.

Instinctively, she knew Bennie's reverie wouldn't last, and she looked frantically around. There was gigantic stone beside the pond. She wasn't positive she could lift it, but she tried anyway. It wasn't quite as heavy as she had thought, but still probably weighed a good fifty pounds. She clumsily maneuvered it, hefting it aloft, approaching Bennie from behind. She grunted, raised the stone as high as she could – which was about shoulder level – then let it go on top of Bennie's head. He made a comical "oomph" sound and was knocked flat. She hoisted the rock again. Bennie was face-down, his breathing rapid and shallow, the back of his head bloody. His left leg shuddered and spasmed. She raised it once more, then let it go. His skull split open, pulverized with a deafening crack that almost sounded like breaking glass.

Anne stared in disbelief, resisting the psychotic fugue state into which her mind was trying to pull her. An enormous gout of gushing blood and brain tissue poured from the squashed head. It was like a roaring river, soaking the ground and grass crimson.

She forced herself to snap out of it.

Two enormous French windows were open directly before her, revealing the mansion's sitting room. She drifted into the house through billowing curtains, and it felt as if she was floating.

When she came into the center of the mansion, she was stunned into immobility with the recognition. The foyer was identical to the one in her dream. Something made her stop at the table against the wall.

It was the vase of yellow flowers.

So far, she had seen no one else besides Bennie.

She turned her head slightly, as something else attracted her attention. Just as she had done in the dream, she walked to a closet door that was beneath the staircase. The door was ajar, and she swung it open. The black leather raincoat was hanging there, and the sawed-off, double-barreled shotgun was leaning against the wall. She picked it up and cracked it open. Both barrels were empty. She picked up a box of shells, but it was empty, too.

Then she remembered the flowers.

She slipped into the raincoat and carried the gun with her to the table with the vase. Methodically, she pulled off the yellow petals from their stems and loaded them into the barrels. When they were all gone, jammed snugly into the gun, she snapped the barrels shut.

"Can I help you, miss?"

She whirled and saw the butler, Elias, stiffly descending the curved staircase. She was at his side in a flash, meeting him halfway, then hauling him by his collar down the rest of the steps till he was prone on the floor in front of the open closet.

He was terrified. "Good God, what do you want?"

"Where's Lynch?"

"He's not back yet. Probably won't be for another couple of hours."

"Where the fuck is he?" She rested the end of the sawed-off barrels between the old man's eyes.

"I can't tell you."

"If you don't, you've got only a few minutes to live."
He gulped, but he had trouble swallowing and started to gag. Anne waited for him to calm himself.

"*I mean it.*"

"I can't. He's like my own *flesh and blood.*"

"Say your prayers, motherfucker. "

Elias' eyes rolled back into his head, but he forced himself to relax.

"I've told him so many times that his transgressions would eventually catch up with him."

"Stop beating around the bush." She cocked both hammers.

"He's at a dinner party at Maxim's downtown."

"Address?"

"Figueroa just north of 4th Street, if I'm not mistaken."
She brutally jerked him into the closet, summoning a strength she didn't know she had. Quickly, she went through his pockets, pulled out a thick ring of keys and started fingering them.

"Which is the closet?"

With a palsied finger, he pointed to one key with its grip lined with pink rubber. She shoved him against the wall, then slammed the door and locked it.

Once she was downtown on Figueroa, she found the restaurant quite easily and pulled into the half-full parking lot. She asked the valet if she could park the car herself, as long as she still paid the fee. He hesitated, but she went into flirt mode, and he finally acquiesced, smiling moronically.

She found a place as near to the entrance as she could, then tucked the gun under the long leather raincoat as she got out and strode confidently across the lot.

When she trotted through the entrance, the maître d' saw she was barefoot and disheveled, and he tried to run interference, but she wouldn't stop.

"I'm sorry, Madam, you can't stay. You aren't dressed properly."

He started to follow her.

She kept on going.

"That's quite all right. I'm just making a delivery. To Mr. Lynch. Then I'll be leaving."

"I'm sorry, Madam. He cannot be disturbed. I can deliver it for you."

"My instructions are to deliver it personally and see that he signs for it."

The maitre'd was sweating profusely. He was a small man and intimidated by Anne's determination.

The restaurant was only a third full.

Anne felt a wave of relief and anticipation wash over her as she spotted him off to the right, seated at the head of a table with six other men and women. The table was butted up against an enormous, tinted picture window that overlooked Figueroa. Without hesitation, she strode right up to Lynch. He was in deep conversation with the lady on his right, and he didn't notice Anne until she was almost standing on top of him. The buzz of conversation at the table suddenly ceased, and Lynch slowly turned. He pretended not to recognize her.

"Miss, I'm afraid you are interrupting a private dinner. How may I help you?"

Then he noticed the raincoat.

"Lisa killed herself. Slit her throat. Because she just couldn't stand living with you any longer."

One of the women gasped.

Lynch tried to remain stoic, but, little by little, his face was draining of color.

"Bennie's dead, too."

Anne withdrew the gun from the inner lining of the jacket and pressed the end of the barrels against Lynch's chest.

The guests at the table were struck dumb.

"I wanted you to see it coming. To know you were going to die."

She pulled the double trigger and, for a couple of seconds, nothing happened. Lynch nervously laughed, relieved. Then the barrels exploded, and he was slammed back onto the floor, his head breaking through the glass of the window. All at once, the unsupported weight of the crystal pane crashed down on his neck, decapitating him. There was now a large, ragged red cavity in his chest where his heart and lungs had been. Blood had spattered onto Lynch's dinner guests nearest him. The women screamed.

Anne turned and resolutely pressed forward down the aisle between the rows of tables. The gun hung limply at her side. Patrons rose up, stunned, and backed away as she passed. But she ignored them, her eyes fixed on the front entrance. She dropped the gun on the floor as she passed the maître d's station.

And then she walked out the door.

THE GLIDER

c. 1998 & 2001, Heathknell, UK

First of all, let me explain that I'm writing this for Audrey, because I know she would have wanted her story told. The real story, not what you might have read in the papers or on some news website. And, by that very admission, you might judge correctly that Audrey is no longer around to tell the story herself – although, in a way, she will be telling it.

I worked with Audrey in the local police department at Heathknell, a small community you've probably never heard of, that is in the south of England near Dover. I'm still working there. I was Audrey's replacement after she died.

Audrey was a Detective Sergeant and had come up through the ranks the fabled hard way. Of course, not only was she fighting the glass ceiling of gender prejudice, but also that she'd been born into a large, poor family in East London. By some miracle, she had excelled at school, helped no doubt by a near-genius IQ. She had been a bit of a tomboy in her teen years during the 1970s, although she had not been a lesbian as some of her rigidly conformist classmates had guessed.

She was tough, but her looks and demeanor softened in later years. In the early 1990s when I met her, she had taken to wearing the kind of dresses and fashion accessories that had been popular in the 1960s, and which have since become popular again since the turn of the millennium with a retro vengeance.

Audrey's favorite colors were sky blue and black, and we could usually find her attired in tight, sleeveless sheath dresses of one of those colors on any given day of the week, including her one day off. She also liked to sport a pearl necklace, a slender silver wristwatch and almost microscopic diamond earrings.

Her hair was auburn and done in a moderately short, wavy bob that stopped just at the bottom of her neck. She wasn't beautiful in the cliché traditional sense of the word. But I always found her eextremely attractive, despite her gangly, sometimes awkward carriage. She looked like a bit of a cross between British actress Anna Massey and American actress Audrey Totter, who had starred in numerous 1940s noir films.

For a short time during the first year I knew her, I had a huge crush on Audrey. We'd ended up in bed together and, at the start, it seemed we might really make a go of it. But little things in our personalities – especially my immaturity, since I was ten years younger – and the fact that we were both in the police served to sabotage things. Our love affair slowly, inevitably had the rug pulled out from under it. However, we remained close and were good friends up until the day she died.

It was in 1996 when Audrey really hit her stride as an absolutely spot-on, brilliant detective, and she was constantly being ridden hard for it by our boss, Superintendent Bill Mallory, a white-haired, by-the-book martinet with a florid complexion and the reputation of being entirely too cozy with local politicians in the surrounding villages. Anytime Audrey hit pay dirt and made an arrest, he would get flustered and resentful. The television show "Prime Suspect" was enormously popular right then, and he would often quip to Audrey, "Who the fuck you think you are, anyway? Fucking Helen Mirren?"

She would always narrow her eyes demurely and give him a sly, feline grin, something which drove him right round the bend. She had so many successes: the apprehension of the Palestinian business-man who had killed his mistress when she found he was smuggling opium in Indian-made sporting goods; the arrest of a notorious band of football hooligans who'd been responsible for the torture-rape-murder of a young African exchange student, to name just two examples. These

were arrests that made not just local news, but headlines across the
nation. Mallory couldn't do anything in the end except promote her to
Detective Sergeant. It rankled him horribly that she was a woman with
the highest success rate of any of the subordinates who had ever had
the misfortune to serve under him. Nevertheless, Mallory knew that,
despite Audrey's humble modesty, her glory reflected back on him,
and her successes were his as well. They had had a few set-tos when
Audrey had refused to toe the line and go easy on ruffling the feathers
of certain influential shitbirds in our insulated community. But I had
been there to support her, so things had settled into an uneasy truce
between them. Most likely she would never have risen above the rank
of Detective Sergeant, but she didn't care. She was doing what she was
good at, and she loved it.

It was in the late spring of 1998, when I was on a much-
delayed three-week vacation, that Audrey's final case came to a head.
While I was gone, she left me a detailed account of what was
happening with her – and to her – and what I was to do if she did not
end up ever seeing me again.

I am going to quote virtually all of it below, interjecting my
own insights and conjectures once or twice to put the puzzle together.

As preface, during the four months before I had left on
holiday, we had had two horrific murders in the adjacent villages,
Galmoor and Reddingshire. Both were single, attractive, young women
in their early thirties, found strangled and sexually assaulted. One had
been an Irish secretary from Dublin on holiday by herself. The other
was a popular Reddingshire shopkeeper, about to be married to a well-
known barrister in Dover. Audrey and I were assigned to the cases and
soon learned from tireless research that there had been a string of five
similar homicides in neighboring counties just north of us during the
past year. The ages of the girls ranged from 16 to 35. By accident, we
discovered through Interpol – just before I left – that there had been
two similar killings in Belgium, one in Ostend near the ferry departure
point at the port, and another in a suburb of Brussels two years before.
There were some obvious forensic similarities in the majority of the
cases that led Audrey and I to believe they were linked, and that one
person had done them all. Audrey describes these similarities in vivid
detail late in her account.

I'd been reluctant to go on holiday and leave Audrey in the hot
seat, which the case was fast becoming. We'd had no leads except for
the tenuous Belgian link; homicides that Mallory was far from
convinced were connected to our killings. There was growing political

pressure, especially from the Dover barrister whose fiancée had been a victim, to appeal to Scotland Yard. And, in fact, a man from the Yard had come down, though only in an advisory capacity. So far, Mallory had been lucky; the killings having taken place in different counties, except for our two, the national papers had not yet connected the dots to generate a Yorkshire Ripper-style panic.

I offered to postpone my trip, but Audrey wouldn't hear of it. She knew I was burnt out and had been running on empty for months, my last holiday having been almost two years previous. My then-girlfriend, Janice – now my wife – had coaxed me to take her to visit her family in the Scottish highlands and, though not looking forward to interaction with her rigid parents, I was most assuredly looking forward to a break from the relentless grind.

I left on May 1st for three weeks. While I was gone, close to the end of the third week, I received an odd phone call from Audrey. Getting a call from her like that was unusual enough, but her demeanor made it doubly so. She was cryptic, and I later realized her voice was tinged with loneliness, a resigned sadness that chilled me, more so later when I knew the details of what had transpired.

She told me she was leaving me a document on my desk, a letter she had written with specifics of the case that we had been working, and that I was the only one she completely trusted to know what to do with it if something happened to her. Needless to say, this greatly alarmed me, but she adamantly, finally angrily, refused to broach the subject of my early return. She said she was operating under an excess of caution and anticipated no real danger. "After all," she exclaimed light-heartedly, "We're in police work, and one never knows the unexpected twists and turns such a life can take." She wouldn't go into any greater detail, but told me where to find the letter when I returned. She strongly asserted that I would never have to read it if things went as smoothly as she hoped. There was a faint undercurrent of doubt in her tone that spooked me, and no manner of reassurance she could offer would put my mind at ease. I agreed to do as she wished, after much cajoling on her part, and wait to return to work at the appointed time.

This is the letter:

"First of all, Phil, let me say that I'm writing this as more of a personal letter than as a police document. Though you will certainly be able to enter it as evidence if things go wrong and not according to my plan. My handwriting should be easily verifiable and, if I'm not around

to testify, it should give the rest of the case more than enough added
weight.

At first, I was hesitant to put all this down in a letter, feeling it
would certainly shock and embarrass you, not to mention the
department. My initial shock, shame and horror at my own behavior
quickly dissipated when I realized that if something happened to me
before I could wrap up the investigation – or perhaps you would agree
after reading this, 'affair' would be a better word – I would be beyond
caring what people thought.

The main thing is – and I want you to promise me this – all of
this must come out, the whole story, if I am not around to tell it. And I
mean every sordid, perverted detail. Mum and Dad are dead, and whom
am I fooling? They never gave a damn anyway. I couldn't give two
shits what my brothers think.

It started a couple of days after you left; May 3rd, I think. I
had been driving back to Heathknell through the countryside, the sun
poking from behind the clouds, dappling the fields in that idyllic way it
can sometimes do after scattered spring showers, when the car
shuddered several times, then abruptly died. Luckily, I was able to
maneuver it to the side of the road. But try as I might, I could not get
it started again. I was in a dead zone, so my mobile was of no use. I
resigned myself to waiting for a Good Samaritan to roll along. In the
meantime, I was studying the Dover case file – rather the Reddingshire
case file. I keep thinking of it as Dover because the victim's betrothed
is that obnoxious, heartless bastard barrister from there.

I was standing outside, leaning against the car with the hood
up, grateful it was no longer raining. To my surprise, several lorries
zoomed by without even slowing. After about half an hour, a Daewoo
Lublin III minivan with Belgian plates approached. He pulled up
behind me on the shoulder and got out. He was a guy of about thirty
years of age, handsome in a heavy way, looking a bit like a young
Gerard Depardieu. He spoke perfect English with a slight accent and
immediately set to work trying to get my motor started, to no avail.
After ten minutes of futility, he offered me a ride into Heathknell. I
grabbed my coat and my falling-apart accordion file, locked the car up,
and we were off.

We made small talk, and I learned his name was Yves, and
that he'd been in southern England about eighteen months, just driving
around, although he'd recently taken a cottage outside of Dover. His
mother had died a little over two years ago in Brussels. Apparently her
death had shaken him up quite a bit.

Astonishingly enough, what with all the Belgian connections, the time frame and his transient character, alarm bells had not yet started to go off. Knowing me and my suspicious nature, you might well ask, 'Why the hell not!' Even after he found out I was police and gave me a self-satisfied smirk and a raised eyebrow, I didn't think it unusual. I joked with him that he had a guilty conscience. He used the hoary cliché of, 'Ask me no questions, and I'll tell you no lies.' Even that stupid maxim didn't put me off. I suddenly knew that I fancied him in an overpowering, impulsively unthinking way. My mind was clouded – 'flooded' might be a better word – with raging hormones, and just the sound of his soothing, fluent voice aroused me. When his arm accidentally brushed mine as he opened the glove box to reach for cigarettes, I realized that I was sopping wet between my legs.

That shocked me a bit, and I braced myself to sober up, as if I'd had one too many pints. I nervously turned in my seat to survey the inside of the van and noticed an odd contraption in the back that thankfully distracted me. He explained it was a glider; that he was into hang-gliding and that it was the perfect country for it, what with the winds coming off the sea in the channel.

It shows how far gone I was as I'd always considered men who went in for hang-gliding to be a bit light in the loafers, poofs to be blunt. But it didn't deter me, didn't even cross my mind at the time. I know now I was falling under what some might charitably describe as a spell. That shames me as much as some of the worse things that happened later, because I let my guard down, something you know very well it is almost impossible for me to do.

We made a bit more small talk. I tried, but I'm afraid I was no good, pretending I wasn't interested in him. My nervous chatter undoubtedly made it all too plain. You know me, Phil…all work and no play? You might be surprised, but I hadn't been laid since you. And what is that? At least two years? We keep coming up with that two-year mark. Not to be too vulgar, but you and I never held anything back from each other. I needed a session between the sheets, and it was obvious the effect he was having on me.

He dropped me off at the station but didn't ask for my number. I was disappointed, to say the least. I hadn't been flirty, but I hadn't acted uninterested in him, either. I gave him my card, joking that if he ever got into trouble he could give me a bell.

The rest of the day was uneventful. Mallory was gone already, nothing was happening, so I phoned the garage and got Fred on the line right before he left for home. He was cross at getting an emergency

call right then. I coaxed him, and he begrudgingly drove me out to my
car in his tow truck. He couldn't get it started, either, so hooked it up
and we brought it back into town. He checked it more thoroughly once
we were at the garage and figured immediately it was the solenoid. He
asked if it could wait until next mid-morning as he'd have to drive to
Reddingshire first thing to get the part. I acquiesced.

Just as I was leaving Fred's, my mobile rang, and I didn't
recognize the number. It didn't even occur to me that it might be him –
Yves. I'd forgotten that I'd scrawled my private number on the back of
the card.

He said he was still in the neighborhood and asked if I'd like to
go for a drink. Of course, I was thrilled and said yes. About five minutes later, I was in his van again. He asked if I minded a jog into Dover;
there was a pub there that he fancied.

It was an appallingly provincial little place, though I
gradually warmed to it; I liked its dark, warm, cozy atmosphere.
Unfortunate coincidence of coincidences! Who should I see there but
Richardson, barrister boyfriend of the strangled Reddingshire girl. I
didn't think he was going to notice me at first, and I'm afraid I rather
obviously turned my head towards Yves as Richardson passed by us on
his way out. He was nearly through the door when he did a cartoonish
double take and stopped dead in his tracks.

'Well, fancy seeing you here! Hard at work, I see,' he quipped,
his pocky face bent down close to mine.

I smiled and said nothing.

His tone got more sarcastic. 'I don't suppose that there is the
remotest possibility there's anything new?'

I shook my head.

His face went from crimson to purple.

'No breaks, no leads in the case? At all?'

'I'm afraid not. At least that I am at liberty to discuss in public,
Mr. Richardson.'

'What is that supposed to mean!'

'There is nothing significant, if that gives you any comfort.'

He turned quickly without saying goodbye, and I gave the two-
fingered salute to his back. Which, I suppose, was not the brightest idea
that I ever had as Drury, the head of Dover Council, was just coming
out of the gents not ten feet behind him and saw me. He passed by and
exited without acknowledging my presence.

I wasn't surprised that Yves was curious. I wouldn't know till
much later just how curious. I filled him in on – superficially, of course,

just stuff that had already been released to the local papers on our two homicides. Which seemed, in retrospect, to have disappointed him a bit. I explained that Richardson was the betrothed of the dead Reddingshire girl. Yves made the appropriate tongue-clucking sounds and comments of disgust that such could occur in a country like England. At the risk of coming off as unattractive, I quickly disabused him of that notion, pointing out that, after the States, that was one of the only things that England was good for, as a stomping ground for sexually fucked-up serial killers. He went slightly pale and finished off his whiskey and ordered another one for the both of us.

Soon, talk of serial murder was far behind us. We gabbed on and on about things of not much consequence, though I was impressed with his intelligence. He was witty, well read and, as the drinks had their effect, seemingly much more interested in maneuvering me back to his cottage.

As you probably had guessed during the past year, I've been depressed. And now I was getting good and pissed. Drink was the fuel for my detonation of all decorum. There was a palpable mist of lust between us, but I think he was somewhat shocked when I suggested we retire to his home. To my surprise, he seemed reticent at first, but warmed to the idea once we were hurtling recklessly through the fog to his neighborhood.

The location was remote and not too far from the cliffs. There wasn't another house for at least half a kilometer in either direction. It was hard to tell in the darkness, but I verified the impression later in the daylight.

It was furnished in boring American contemporary style. Actually, that's not really accurate or fair. It was really more in the Scandinavian mold; spartan, functional chairs, sofa, tables and appliances in a dead-looking Danish Modern. After his rather impressive acquittal of himself in the pub, I found his two-bedroom cottage startlingly dreary. However, it was dreary in a cheerful, sunny, characterless way. There was something else about the place I couldn't quite put my finger on at the time, though I realized what it was later. More about that presently.

I'm afraid we made a rather zigzagging stagger of a beeline to the bedroom. Although drunk and as much in the moment as I could possibly be – you know how hard it is for me – I was prepared to be disappointed. An hour or so later I remember feeling how absolutely marvelous that I wasn't! He was dynamite, amazingly tender, yet aggressive, rhythmic, potent and long lasting. There seemed to be real feeling underneath, and now I wonder what that was. In light of what I subsequently discovered, could it have been even remotely possible that it was genuine? Or was it poor, manic-depressive me supplying it for the both of us?

The next thing I knew, it was dawn, and I had to forcefully coax him out of bed, hangover and all, to drive me to Heathknell and my appointment at Fred's. He dropped me there around 8:00 AM, and we made tentative plans to see each other again very soon.

Fred was late getting back from Reddingshire, so I walked the two blocks to my place to shower and change and, by the time I returned, so had Fred. Still, it took Fred a while, and it was just past 9:30 when he finally had the new solenoid installed. A bit late, and I was reminded of this straight off with my mobile jangling, Mallory on the other end wanting to know where the hell I was. I told him I'd be in directly. He started shouting, 'Don't come to the goddamn station. We're not there. Come straight out the main road towards Galmoor till you see us. There's been another fucking one!'

He didn't have to say anything else.

My sixth sense kicked in before I was even out of town. The further I drove and the closer I got, a tingling apprehension took hold of me. I dreaded coming upon the crime scene. I had a sinking feeling I knew where it would be, but I wouldn't let my conscious mind acknowledge how or why I knew. Sure enough, just a quarter kilometer beyond where my car had broken down, I spotted Mallory, Sherbourne and the others. They were over to the left, about fifty meters off the main road in an idyllic meadow of golden grain. The sun was shining and the sky a gorgeous powder blue, but the air had a clammy, chilly feel to it.

I tramped up to them, and Mallory let go with an expected, "About bloody time, in' nit?"

I didn't look at him and, instead, lit a cigarette. I strolled around the scene as Sherbourne made his measurements and took his photographs. Bergier, from the Yard, had gone to London for a couple of days and wasn't due back till Monday.

The girl looked no more than 17. None of us knew her right off by sight, but once her identification was found about ten meters closer to the road, we all recognized her name: Amy Latimer, the daughter of the Heathknell school principal. You undoubtedly will remember her. You ran her in once for being a runaway and in possession of pills. As we later learned, that's what her mother had thought she'd gone and done again. Given her punk reputation and penchant for dirty denim and black leather, I was astonished to see her dressed immaculately in a pale, sky-blue pinafore with matching navy-blue mini-skirt, trimmed with a blue speckled white lace. Alive, it's the kind of outfit she would not have been caught dead in. Except here she was, dead and wearing it. I had a gut feeling that the killer had outfitted her after doing the deed. Her dyed black hair, with inch-long chestnut roots, was brushed back in perfect waves, lying pastorally against the smashed-down grain – just like the two others you and I saw in Galmoor and Reddingshire. A copious stream of blood, already blackening with the hours passed, had run down the inside of Amy's right thigh, pooling on the ground. There were bruises around her neck in the shape of dark purple and blue finger marks. Really, you could all but see the twin palm prints of the killer pressed into the stiff flesh of her throat. Her eyes were half open in a kind of sleepy surprise.

Of course, Mallory hadn't been there at the Galmoor and Reddingshire scenes and, as you pointed out at the time, Sherbourne's pictures left a bit to be desired; naturally Mallory was his predictable self and skeptical about my impressions of similarities to Amy's death."

Audrey's letter had a break here, with photocopies of selected pages of forensics reports from the coroner and from her own astute observations. Then she picked it up again...

"You will see the pattern even more clearly if you refer back to the unexpurgated Galmoor and Reddingshire files. I'm now convinced 100% that the killer dressed his victims after murdering them. I brought this up to Mallory, but he claimed the blouses and skirts were different colors. It didn't seem to bother him, though, that both the Galmoor and Reddingshire women wore blouses and skirts that were also brand new from the same designer, had a similar cut to Amy's death clothes and were also trimmed with blue-speckled white lace. Although I'm still waiting for full reports from the other northern counties where there were similar murders, I've made preliminary calls to the different offices and have had it confirmed that lace was also present on the clothes of those victims. I haven't bothered to bring it up to Mallory. It seems altogether too complicated for him.

Anyway, I'm getting a bit ahead of myself. That night – the night of the day Amy was found – I hadn't yet put it all together linking the skirts and blouses. At that stage, it was just intuition. When I knocked off work at 9:30 that evening, I was preoccupied and not thinking of Yves. Then I got a call from him on my way home. I was tired, and I very nearly begged off his invitation. But I suddenly remembered how fantastic he'd been, and I decided I'd meet him at his house.

Well, Phil, this is where it is going to get seriously strange, and I must warn you straight off you're going to be wondering, 'What in God's name was she thinking?' No excuses. When I got there, I threw caution to the wind. I was no longer thinking of the case. Any trepidation I had about Yves was neatly tucked away in some dark corner of my brain. I rationalized I was seeing goblins in the woodpile, as my dead and drunken Da would have put it.

Yves and I got resoundingly wrecked on some American bourbon. Before I knew it, he was telling me a sad tale about his lost first love who had died a tragic death in Liege ten years ago, and how the only person who had been there for him was his mother. He showed me a photo of his mother that was apparently taken about a year before her sudden heart attack, and I must say she was strikingly beautiful, not looking anywhere near her sixty-five years. She was blonde and had a voluptuous, Amazonian stature as well as that Aryan sexual arrogance I've come to associate with the few female SS officers that 'served' Germany during WWII.

The next thing I knew, I passed out in his bed. When I woke up, it was extremely dim light, and the illuminated clock beside the bedstead read 3:10 AM. I wasn't sure where I was. Then I remembered. I could feel Yves moving beside me. I turned over and got the shock of my life. At first, I thought that there was another woman in bed with us. Yves was wailing away, fucking the daylights out of what seemed to be a gorgeous twenty-something girl with enormous, staring brown eyes and parted, full lips, wavy, lustrous brown hair, large breasts and well-developed abdominal muscles. Even though I was still quite drunk, I was incredulous with shock and anger. I leapt out of bed stark naked, and proceeded to cut him a new asshole, swearing a blue streak. He was shocked that I was so shocked. But I went speechless when I realized that the other woman was no other woman at all, but a life-size and exceedingly realistic doll! Down to every anatomical detail.

I began to get dressed without hesitation. Then he was at my side, imploring me to understand and not to judge him. Astonishingly enough, Phil – and believe me, I am as astonished now as you must be reading this – I gave him a hearing. There was something so deviant and decadent about it, something so wrong, and I was so drunk, I have to admit that it was starting to turn me on! I know with how wild we occasionally got when we were going out, perhaps you'll understand. I know sometimes, when our guard is down, we can all find ourselves in strange places where we would usually be loath to tread. He convinced me. Though he had been with other women in the intervening decade since his girlfriend's death, in those first couple of lonely years the only thing that had kept him sane, kept him from suicide, was having this doll custom-made in her spitting image. I've since learned that there is a company in America and also ones in Germany and Japan that make these lifelike, realistic and anatomically correct facsimiles. Very high-end and very expensive.

I'm ashamed to say that I drank some more, falling into a depressed, debauched abandon. I gave into the sickness with him, and I did things with him and the doll, going down on it while he fucked it and more. I will spare you further gory details.

The next thing I knew, it was 7:00 AM, and I was alone in his bed. The doll was gone, and I wondered if perhaps I had dreamed it all up, that it had not really happened. I then noticed a note on his pillow saying he'd gone out to pick up croissants and coffee, since he was out of both, and that he would return directly.

Putting the note back down, I noticed a strip of something poking out a few centimeters from beneath the pillow on the far side. I tugged it out and caught my breath. It was a ripped swath of the same kind of blue-speckled white lace that had lined dead Amy's dress. And it was stained by what I surmised was seminal fluid.

I immediately got dressed, fighting down nausea not only from my discovery but a wickedly vindictive hangover. I peered out the window which gave onto the drive to see if Yves was anywhere in sight. No Yves. I had time – perhaps only a moment – but enough to make a quick search. I began methodically going through his bedroom, pulling things open with a handkerchief to not leave any more prints around than I had already. There was one top drawer in a low bureau, on which was perched a large television and VCR, that was locked. I left it for the time being and adjourned to the loo, going through his medicine cabinet. Of all the luck, I found a key amidst the pill bottles and, sure enough, it was to the locked drawer. I moved at the speed of light, despite my throbbing cranium. Videotapes and a video camera with cables attached were in the drawer. All the videocassettes were unlabeled, except for one called 'Mother.' I quickly popped it into the player, simultaneously switching on the telly. I was immediately greeted by gross cries of female orgasm. I turned the volume down to a whisper while I glanced nervously between the curtains on the window. When I turned to face the screen, I was horrified to see his mother, nude, in the throes of ecstasy. The quality of the recording was not the best, but it most certainly was her. And she was in bed, straddled atop Yves! It was obviously in Belgium, in a different house in some time past. I hit 'eject,' and frantically plucked up the next tape in line.

I was beyond being shocked at that point and was not surprised at what I saw. Yves was in bed with Amy, and it was the bed there in the room, the same bed in which I had just slept and... 'made love.'

The images on the screen held me rapt. Somewhere in the back of my mind, I knew Yves would return soon. But I could not stop, not yet. I found the remote and fast-forwarded the tape. Then, as I hit 'play' again, there it was – Yves strangling Amy, throttling the life out of her delicate throat as he fucked her.

I switched off the TV and VCR, replaced the tape, closed and locked the drawer and brainstormed what to do next. I didn't have a gun with me and, at that time, I didn't think that was the best way to take him. Something occurred to me, and I opened the closet door next to the telly and bureau, and there she was on her private throne, the love doll. She sat serenely on a chair with purple velvet upholstery, and I noticed with disgust that Yves had not cleaned her up. There was semen seeping from her realistic, hairless vaginal opening onto the fabric.

A flash went off in my head, and I ran to the loo, returning the key to the appropriate place in the cabinet, then withdrawing two cotton Q-tips from a metal canister sitting on the top rear of the toilet. I opened a new roll of tissue so I could take the plastic wrap, made for the closet, swabbed what passed for the doll's 'genitals,' folded the Q-tip swabs into the plastic, then jammed them into my purse as I slammed the closet door. Out of the blue, I realized what was odd about Yves cottage. No sounds were penetrating from outside – I could see an elm tree in his front yard with the branches violently swaying, yet could hear no noise from the wind. Which meant that the house was sound-proofed. If one was outdoors, even on the doorstep, no sounds could be heard from within, either.

Abruptly, I was sick and had to run to the loo again. I vomited prodigiously, gagging and spluttering. Perfect timing, for sure enough, I heard the front door open. I was overcome with disgust and self-loathing, but I could not cave in just yet.

After a couple of minutes, Yves found me crouched by the toilet.

'Too much to drink, I'm afraid,' I muttered by way of

apologizing, as I wiped the puke from my lips. I bent down and washed my face with cold water. Yves poured out a litany of sympathetic phrases, massaging my shoulders and kissing the nape of my neck as I straightened and shuddered.

Phil, it was all I could do to keep from attacking him. He was not who I thought he was. He hadn't even particularly misrepresented himself. He was too sick for that. His schizo compartmentalization was in full flower. Somehow I held it together and gave a sterling performance.

'Is that coffee I smell?' I asked, as I steered him into the kitchen and slipped on my boots. I switched on my cell as he poured the coffee.

No mention of the doll, the weirdness.

I quickly downed my cup when he handed it to me, begging off a full breakfast. pleading work and voicing how I absolutely could not afford to be late two days in a row. He then did something that has haunted me these past few hours. He reached out and gently ran the back of one hand down my right temple and cheek. A tear welled up in one of his eyes. He admonished me to take care, saying he knew the case I was working on was dangerous, and he didn't want any harm to come to me. My heart was in my throat, and I felt as if I couldn't swallow. I gave him a sad smile but could not bring myself to kiss him, instead giving his caressing hand a quick squeeze.

He stood in the doorway, framed by an ivy-covered stone arch I had not noticed before. As I backed out and turned the car around to head for the motorway, I glanced over at him and noticed that his smile had evaporated, his face becoming neutral and blank.

That's it so far, Phil. Now you've got this. I have been pondering for hours just what to do. It's not like me, I know. I've already dropped off the swabs with Sherbourne for DNA comparison to what was taken from Amy and the other two victims. I labeled it with Yves' name and address. You've got the rest in the files. I don't trust Mallory not to bollocks this whole thing up. If you were here, or Bergier, it would be different. Sherbourne's no help, except in the lab and, besides, he has no training or experience for this kind of thing. I don't get on with the Dover bunch or maybe I'd call them in for back-up. They've always been downright pricks regarding anything to do with me, and I know they'd take the whole thing over. Perhaps I'm not being professional, taking that attitude. As you know, that's one of my problems, being the lone wolf.

In any case, I've decided to confront Yves with what I've

found, telling him it's no use killing me, that a detailed report has been left for the proper people – you! – and that DNA comparison of his semen to that found on the dead girls is in motion. I don't know what effect it will have, this approach. He may be a genuine split personality and not know what his right hand is doing from his left. God knows how long his mother was having sex with him. If it was from childhood, it's more than possible he's a full-blown schizophrenic. That's what I surmise from his behavior with me. But then again, he could just be an incredibly sick, sane monster who enjoys raping and strangling young women.

I'd tell you to wish me luck, but that's no good, is it? If you're reading this at all, it's after the fact, and things did not go as I had hoped. I am going armed.

The thing I must tell you...all of this is tormenting me, tearing me apart in a way I've never experienced before. What kind of person am I, what's wrong with me that I could have found this monster attractive, in fact, been on the verge of falling in love with him? And is this some kind of death wish, that I'm going at it alone? I know it is probably ill-advised. But truthfully I see no other way.

Love to you, Phil, and to Janice..."

That's the end of Audrey's letter.

You may have read in the papers how it ended, but even those generalized "specifics" didn't tell everything.

Audrey had gone out to Yves' house the night before I got back. So, when I found her letter on my desk at noon the next day, when I came in on that Sunday, meaning only to just take a few minutes to check my mail, I read it straight away. It was immediately obvious upon finishing it that something had gone wrong.

I notified Mallory and Sherbourne, and they accompanied me with some local constables and Dover's Inspector Lanyon to Yves Delacroix's cottage.

The place was open. Before we even had a chance to enter, I spotted Audrey in the garden, off to the left side of the door. She was curled up in a fetal position amongst rosebushes, her revolver still in her hand. Three bullets had been fired. She was lacerated and bruised as if she'd been in a violent struggle. The coroner later counted eleven stab wounds in her body, any three of which could have proved fatal. She had bled to death.

We designated the cottage a crime scene and immediately sent out an alert for Yves since he was no longer on the property.

Undoubtedly she had made good with at least one of her shots. The coroner reported that at least a third of the blood we found at the scene – there was a lot of it – was not Audrey's. And we soon found it matched Yves' DNA.

That same afternoon, almost simultaneous to our finding Audrey, Dover police received an odd call from a young couple who had been picnicking on the cliffs. They had encountered a strange, bloody – and naked – man. He'd driven up in a Daewoo Lublin III van and, with difficulty, had unloaded a hang glider. The male of the couple apparently knew something about hang-gliding, and had recognized the machine as an older 1980s model, without the safety cocoon fabric that came later to encase the lower half of the pilot's body. It was a crude, rudimentary device.

Something had seemed very wrong, to say the least, and they had watched in awe as the man dragged the glider to the cliff edge. He had taken a long time to get the apparatus ready and had faltered several times before he was prepared to cast off. The billowing sail and the folded control steering bars gave him problems in his compromised condition. He had been bleeding from what appeared to be wounds in his lower left abdomen and left arm.

The couple had been understandably fearful at the man's appearance and irrational behavior. It had not occurred to them to offer him assistance or even ask what was wrong. Just before he made his leap, he abruptly turned to the pair, who were several meters away, and they noticed he had a long butcher knife in his left hand. He then had said, "The sun's about to go down. I guess I should have listened to her advice."

With that, he had launched off the precipice on the glider. The air currents had caught him up for a good couple of minutes, and he had soared out over the ocean. The couple had noticed him doing something with his left hand, apparently still holding the knife, first between his legs and then at his throat. What looked to be spray trails of blood had cascaded downwards, though it had been hard for them to tell for certain. They had lost sight of him a few seconds later.

The next morning a local fisherman discovered the body about a half kilometer away, washed up on shore with the dawn tide. Yves must not have flown too far when he came plummeting down. Surprisingly enough, the fish had not really been at him. But, in addition to the two bullet wounds, there were horrific cuts where Yves had mutilated himself. His genitals were gone, having been cleanly sliced away and his throat had been slashed.

It has been an ongoing tug-of-war within me whether to release Audrey's unexpurgated text. All natural inclinations to protect her memory have been swept aside because I know in my heart just how badly she wanted the whole story told. She was a truth teller, and she valued truth – the unvarnished, de-politicized truth – above all else. She hated hypocrisy. I know that by leaving the letter she had hoped to mitigate her own faulty judgment and perhaps prevent the future mistakes of others. And to remind us all that every human, no matter how monstrous or hideously alone or seemingly inhuman, is connected to the rest of us, even if by the most tenuous of threads.

JACK'S GIRLFRIENDS

CHERIE'S PAYBACK
(Ladies of Perpetual Sorrow)

c. 1970-1971, Riverside, CA
and 2010, Highland Park, CA

Jack hadn't thought of Cherie MacInnes in a long time. Then he got an email from out of nowhere saying that she was dead. Killed in a car accident. She'd been drunk and had gone off a cliff somewhere in Tennessee.

Back when he'd known Cherie, the last year he was in high school and his first year in college, there obviously hadn't been emails or the internet or any of that. It was 1970, so you had to call someone up or write them a letter to get in touch. Jack was 17, and she was a year or two younger. They had both grown up in Riverside, California, and hadn't gone to the same high school because they lived in poles-apart neighborhoods. But even if they had lived closer to each other, they would have gone to different schools. His parents didn't hold with public institutions of learning, instead sending him to a Jesuit-run, all-boys place. Which was actually out in the styx near where Cherie lived with her mom and her younger brother and two baby sisters.

Cherie had gone to Ramona High, on the south side of town. It was not toney like Poly (short for Polytechnic), which was in the center of the city, or as lowdown as Rubidoux High to the west, which was definitive slum territory. But Ramona High was known for being more drugged-out than either Poly or Jack's school, Our Lady of Perpetual Sorrow. A lot of reds were consumed, in addition to weed, wine and beer.

He couldn't remember exactly where he'd met Cherie. He was driving, by then, and his parents were letting him use the family's backup car, a 1962 Ford Falcon station wagon. It could have been one of three places – either a party or a free concert at Fairmount Park; or downtown at the mall on 3rd Street, the block next to the Mission Inn, where longhair street kids used to hang out in the early evenings. Once every couple of weeks the cops would come to roust everyone out, then, after a couple of days, a steady stream of teens would trickle back. Most of the kids were white trash from Rubidoux and west Riverside. But some came from the downtown neighborhood, some trekked from as far away as Jack's district to the east, near the University where his father was a professor, and some hailed from Cherie's area to the south, where there was a smattering of isolated houses amidst a lot of orange groves.

Cherie was a tiny thing, only about five feet tall, mischievous, with an infectious deep-throated laugh. She wasn't beautiful, but the combination of wildness and innocence existing side by side in her made her attractive. She enjoyed drinking and smoking pot and occasionally popping pills, and Jack had guessed – correctly – she was sexually uninhibited. However, at the time, she still had an innocence and a vulnerability that was touching. Despite her wild side, she was a good girl and often had to look after her younger siblings, since her mother worked part time to support them. Though they certainly had very little money, Jack supposed that they owned the old house they lived in off of Victoria Avenue on the edge of the orange groves; they never seemed in danger of losing it. But he never got a true picture of what was going on with the father. He was never at home and, as far as Jack knew, he hadn't been there in a long time. Jack didn't know if he was in prison, dead or just working and traveling on the road.

The couple of times Jack went to visit, the mother stayed in the house. Jack and Cherie would adjourn to the large garage on the other side of the backyard, which wasn't used for cars and was kind of Cherie's clubhouse, with old ripped-up sofas and big, empty wooden spools made for cable storage that served as tables. She had a small PA with a microphone and stand just inside the door, and she occasionally invited friends over to play music. She was a huge fan of Janis Joplin, and she let loose one afternoon when he came over. He was awestruck at the power of her voice. It was startling to hear that kind of naked intensity coming from her. Cherie was of only average intelligence, but she was immensely talented and should have been fronting her own group. Jack knew first-hand how hard it was to do. His own lone attempt at getting something together in high school lasted precisely two months, then splintered under the strain of everyone's divergent musical tastes. And the seemingly unanimous opinion of everyone playing with him that his singing sucked.

He only visited Cherie a couple of times. He remembered sitting with her in the garage clubhouse, sharing a joint, then kissing. He was still a virgin himself, and he had the impression, despite her indiscriminate proclivity for make-out and petting sessions, she may have been one, too. He knew she had a crush on him, but he was infatuated with another girl, Laura, who also, coincidentally, went to Ramona High. So he was not interested in letting his affections get too far along with Cherie. He liked her, she was a nice, attractive girl, but he didn't want to get in deep enough to hurt her.

Things never really worked out with Laura. They had a number of torrid, nocturnal make-out sessions lying in the back of his station wagon, both of them naked to the waist, but it never went farther than that. Which was probably just as well. He was just a little too interested, and Laura grew tired of his ardent, aggressive attentions. He had another steadier girlfriend, Cecile, in mid-summer of 1970. She was a sweet, 16-year-old mulatto emancipated from her parents and living with her tall, longhair Okie husband out in the west Riverside slums. She was in and out of juvenile hall, so despite their fondness for each other and many discreet dates, the welter of complications tore them apart.

Jack had another good female friend, May Turner, who he hung around with a lot and who he was half-in-love with. She was striking, darkly handsome, with a raw, high-cheekboned face, short shaggy black hair and large breasts. They made out on occasion, but she never let things go too far. He knew she preferred girls to boys. They used to joke about going to bed together, but it never happened. There was something she found repellent about male sexuality, undoubtedly from what – he found out much later – her own father had done to her when she was little. Nevertheless, even if they went for months without seeing each other, she remained one of his best friends. The last part of that summer he went to Europe on a student tour and headed straight off to college in Los Angeles within a week of returning.

He didn't see Cherie for a while. Plenty happened to him the initial couple months away at school, dropping acid for the first time and finally losing his virginity. It was early in November 1970 when he came home to Riverside for the weekend and ran into Cherie at a party far out on the south side, in La Sierra.

He tried to recall who was there, conjure up a mental picture of the night. It was a cheap tract house in a semi-wasteland of low-income families, a three bedroom place with hardly any furniture, dirty beige walls decorated by psychedelic DayGlo posters, with several black lights providing the sole illumination. The house couldn't have belonged to some kid's parents, unless they were "heads," as they lamely called them; more likely it was someone's big sister or brother who was old enough to have a job and rent.

Various sounds emanated from the crappy stereo: "St. Stephen"-era Grateful Dead, The Velvet Underground with Nico (surprisingly!), Steppenwolf's first album, Jefferson Airplane's "Surrealistic Pillow," The Doors, Jimi Hendrix, Big Brother and The Holding Company with Janis, The Steve Miller Band…

No one he was really close to was there. He was positive that May and his high school buddy, Russ, were not in attendance. But he had a nodding acquaintance with almost everyone. There were several girls he had gone out with once or twice or, at the very least, had made out with at some other party: Vickie, a heavily made-up brunette who was always overdressed, even when the weather was sweltering; Vickie's more innocent, little blonde sister, Connie; Jonelle, whom he knew the best; the low rider Mexican pair, Doreen and Dolores; Mary Miller and her sister, Betty. As far as guys, his memory was fuzzier – he instinctively paid more attention to the girls – but he thought Mary and Betty's brother, Billy, was there, a well-meaning, ne'er-do-well wannabe folksinger who knew every Dylan song by heart and who would eventually wear out his welcome if he was in close proximity to an acoustic guitar; there were the amateur-criminals-cum-musicians, Marshall Dixon and Davey Scovilli, two scumbags who always seemed patronizing and made Jack feel uneasy; and last but not least, Bobby Morton, a much older, full-bearded hippie who was looked on as a kind of wise, venerable elder and who, most nights, held court at downtown Riverside's 3rd Street mall. He said little, and Jack could never recall having a conversation with him. His girlfriend of record was Mary Miller.

None of the girls were from St. Francis, the all-girls high school where Jack's mother worked as secretary. None of the kids were from his school, Our Lady, or from Poly or from North High (the public high school up in Jack's university neighborhood). All of them were either from Ramona on the south side or Rubidoux on the west. Or, like Jonelle, drop-outs in and out of foster homes.

And Cherie was there. He didn't see her until he had been wandering through the rooms for an hour or so and was starting to get bored. They shared a joint and a beer, and then he mentioned to her he was heading home. She asked if he could drop her off at her house, since it was on the way. She was so cute, always smiling – at least when she was with Jack – and talkative, though he couldn't recollect anything they talked about.

Cherie was shy with most people but not with him. When he pulled his 1962 Falcon station wagon up onto the dirt shoulder that was the curb, all the lights in her home behind the chain-link fence dark, she scooted closer and kissed him. They opened their mouths and made out for a few minutes before she pulled away and sheepishly asked a startling question.

"Can I give you a hand job?"

Jack had never had a girl be so sexually forward, and he was flattered and thrilled. She laughed embarrassedly at his smiling, dumb-founded expression.

"I always wanted to jack you off when we went out before, but I never had the nerve to make the move. But I'm kind of stoned..."

She let the sentence trail off. Jack was speechless, and when he smiled and faintly nodded, she quickly unzipped him and had him out, grinning broadly at how hard he was already. Unlike other girls her age who might be branded "loose," Cherie had an exuberant innocence about sex that was exhilarating and, in retrospect, charming. She never stopped laughing softly as she stroked him and kept saying, "Wow... wow... wow..."

When he finally climaxed, she exclaimed, "Oh, my God, you came so much! That was so exciting!"

They kissed for a minute, and then she smiled impishly as she opened the door.

"I always wanted to do that."

All Jack could get out was, "See you soon."

She nodded, shut the door and was off.

He tried to rearrange himself as he drove back down Victoria Avenue through the orange groves. It was a big mess with a wet spot in the crotch of his jeans. He knew his mother would still be up when he got in; she always was, even if it was 4 AM. His mind raced, trying to figure out what he could hold in front of him as he walked in the house. Luckily for him, she was already in bed, reading. His father had gone back to work at his university lab, finishing up his experiments.

Even though Jack thought it would be great to see Cherie again, he knew he had to go back to Los Angeles on Sunday to make a Monday morning class. As frequently happened back then, a girl Jack would have a crush on one week would soon be forgotten and usually replaced by another a couple of weeks later.

Things went along well at school, and it was Christmas break before Jack got to come back to Riverside and hang out. One Friday night he went to a concert with his friend, Russ, in Russ' MG. He wasn't sure who they'd seen – Led Zeppelin? Steppenwolf? When they got out, it was a little before midnight, and they headed from the Swing Auditorium in San Bernardino to one of the local Riverside cruising hangouts, the Jack in the Box parking lot on Central Avenue a few blocks from Poly High.

A lot of kids from the concert were already there, sitting on the hoods of their cars with the doors open and their 8-track stereos cranked. Distorted Grand Funk Railroad blasted through the lot, the sound waves bouncing off the littered asphalt. Russ lit up a joint, and they sat there sharing it, keeping an eye out for black-and-whites.

There was a tap on Jack's window, and he jumped. It was May, and he rolled it down.

"Busted."

"Very funny."

"I thought so, the way you flinched."

Russ reached across Jack and handed May the roach. She finished it off, then crumbled it between thumb and forefinger, letting the ashes flutter to the ground. May was clad in black T-shirt and black jeans and had the punk rock look years before the term came into anyone's vocabulary.

Billy Miller, drifting by holding hands with Cherie, caught Jack's eye through the windshield. Billy was staring straight ahead, so didn't notice them, but Cherie locked stares with Jack, looking red-faced and mortified. Then they were gone.

"She is such a cutie pie."

Jack smiled at May's remark, and said, "Yeah."

"What was that way she looked at you?"

"She looked unhappy," was all Jack said.

"She seemed embarrassed that we saw her with Billy."

That's what Jack thought, too, but he didn't want to volunteer his opinion to May. But it made his heart ache for some reason.

"She has a crush on you, doesn't she?"

Jack didn't answer Russ' question, and May smiled, poking him knowingly in the shoulder.

Jack had a date with Jonelle for a movie at the drive-in the next night, and they decided to still go, even though it was raining. A couple of years before, Jonelle had been one of his best friends, right around the time he'd first started driving. She'd been living with foster parents then, and she didn't go to the Catholic all girls' school, so Jack couldn't remember how he had met her. But her foster parents lived near Poly High in an upscale middle class neighborhood. They were extremely nice, respectful of Jonelle's privacy and always left the two of them alone when he visited. Jack and Jonelle never got to the boyfriend/ girlfriend stage, though they occasionally made out.

Jonelle had straight, long black hair, pale white skin, thin lips and mascara always heavily applied around her big moon eyes. She was at least a quarter American Indian; Jack wasn't sure what tribe, and she was also a little flaky, having dropped acid numerous times. But she had a kind of wistful, sad charm about her that Jack found attractive. They had a strange, easygoing bond that was intuitive and mysterious.

She had just started living with her real parents again in the boondocks of west Riverside, not too far from the drive-in. He'd never met them, but he knew they were bad news. Jack thought it was a terrible idea that she had returned home, but he kept his mouth shut.

The house was a rundown crackerbox. There were a few scraggly patches of grass for a front lawn, strewn with the broken toys belonging to her younger brother. The place gave Jack the willies as soon as he approached the front door. Jonelle answered the bell and let him in.

"I can't leave just yet," she rolled her eyes, "They want to meet you."

"Great," he whispered sarcastically, "I can't wait."

She led him first into the kitchen on the right, a hellishly tiny, harshly-lit room where her shriveled-up mother gazed coldly at him as she hovered over something indefinable frying on the stove top.

"Mom, this is Jack."

She nodded curtly and went back to staring at the frying pan. Jack knew she was a devout Jehovah's Witness who enjoyed beating Jonelle with belts and brushes.

Jonelle took his hand, giving it a quick squeeze as if to say "steel yourself!," then pulled him down a narrow hall to a rear den illuminated by a black-and- white TV. The room had hardly any furniture. A giant, potbellied bear of a man with a crewcut, dressed in shirtsleeves and dungarees, grinned at Jack from a rocking chair. Jack glanced at the TV and saw Porter Wagoner introducing a stoned-looking Jack Palance to his country western studio audience.

"So yer the one takin' out my lil' girl tonight, hunh?" He stood up, towering over Jack. He rubbed his left hand through the grey fuzz on his perspiring, close-cropped head and, with his right, hefted a can of Hamm's beer to his lips, taking a large gulp.

"Yes, sir."

The man laughed and stared hard at a blushing Jonelle.

"This boy's got manners. You hear that, girl? He called me 'sir.'"

He shuffled closer, leaning forward and down, bringing his face mere inches from Jack's.

"Where you takin' my lil' girl tonight?"

"The drive-in movie."

"The drive-in movie, hunh? They do all kinds of things at those drive-in movies besides watch the movies. That's what I hear anyway." He guffawed, elbowing Jack in the shoulder.

Jonelle was grimacing, turned halfways away, watching Jack Palance mutilate a country song at low volume.

Jack was 5'11", but her father stood a good four inches taller and was a foot wider. His breath smelled like a cross between a brewery and a sewer. Jack tried not to show he was breaking out in a cold sweat.

"You gonna get yerself a piece tonight?"

Jack played dumb. "A piece of what?"

"Ha! That's a good one! You know, a piece!"

"No, I don't think I know what you mean."

His laugh faded and his shit-eating grin grew smaller. He finished his beer and waved them off. "Go on. Get out of here."

Jonelle and Jack started into the hall. Jack nearly jumped as her father's huge paw grasped his shoulder. The burly boozer bent close to Jack's ear and whispered, "Don't do anything I wouldn't do."

He hee-hawed a braying laugh as Jack faintly nodded.

The two left the house, trotting through the rain to the muddy, curbless street. Jonelle said nothing, even after they were inside the car.

The drive-in was about five minutes away and, about halfway there, Jonelle whispered, "Sorry about him."

"You don't have to apologize."

"It's so embarrassing."

"He's scary."

She said nothing for a minute, then finally, "Yeah."

"Are you safe there, the way he is?"

She turned in her seat to look at Jack, her straight black hair dripping from the rain, "We'll see."

Jack steered them into line at the drive-in; there were only a couple of cars ahead of them at the drive-thru box office. She reached out and squeezed his hand.

"Let's not talk about him tonight. I really don't want to talk about my family at all."

He nodded to her as he handed the attendant the money. They pulled into the lot, the rain pouring down now in sheets. Since they were in the station wagon and wanted to lie down in the back with the rear seat folded flat, he put the car in reverse and backed into their spot. Once they were comfortably settled with a couple of blankets, and he had hooked the speaker through the passenger window, he cracked the window on the rear pull down gate so the glass wouldn't fog.

It was a British picture about witch-hunting in the time of Cromwell, starring Vincent Price. The American distributor had changed the title to *The Conqueror Worm*, referencing an obscure poem by Edgar Allan Poe. Though it had been a good ten years since the first Price/Poe effort, *House of Usher*, the company was still obsessed with wringing every last box office dime they could out of the ever more tenuous Poe connection.

Jonelle and Jack snuggled for a bit, frequently making out and only sporadically watching what was happening on the screen through the bleary rivulets of water. Suddenly the horrific images, Price's character ordering his flunkies to set fire to several crucified witches, registered with Jonelle. The next thing Jack knew, she was flailing against him, screaming, trying to get out of the car. She yanked herself away, kicked open the back gate and plunged stumbling into the deluge.

He leapt out after her, grabbing onto her arm about ten feet behind the car as she slipped to her knees. He pulled her up and enfolded her in his embrace. Both of them were sopping wet.

"I'm burning! Burning! I can't watch!"

"What are you talking about?"

She refused to look at him. "*I'm burning!*"

"Jonelle!" He shook her.

She wouldn't meet his eyes, just moaned, with her face averted towards the dark, overcast sky of falling rain, her eyes tightly shut. At his wit's end, he slapped her. That sobered her a bit, and she lowered her face, looking at him.

"Get in the car."

People from the surrounding vehicles were rolling down their windows to stare.

Jonelle did as she was told and sheepishly crawled onto the open back gate of the car. He followed and pulled it closed. She refused to look at the screen and threw herself, sobbing, into his arms.

"What made you do that?"

At first, she wouldn't answer.

"Come on, Jonelle. What-the-fuck? Tell me what made you go crazy like that."

She raised her face from where she had been nuzzling against the wet shirt plastered to his chest.

"I'm a witch."

"What?"

"My friends and I – " she saw his expression and immediately added, "Nobody you know. We're into witchcraft. When I saw those witches burning, I felt like I was burning, too. Like I was on fire!"

"But that isn't real. It's a movie." Jack's observation did little to comfort her, but she did not freak out again. She couldn't watch the rest of the film. Her inner tumult subsided, and she clung to him, half asleep in his arms through the remainder.

He didn't see that much of Jonelle until about nine months later. She came to stay with him for a couple of weeks at a house where he was temporarily living in Torrance, right at the start of his second year in college. Ironically, she and one of his roommates – a brainy guy from Texas who played electric guitar – fell in love, ran away together, had a baby and, after doing too much strychnine-laced acid, became fanatical Jehovah's Witnesses.

The crazy stuff that happened with Cherie had made him think about

Jonelle.

To understand what happened to Cherie and Jonelle, one had to understand the fucked-up, dysfunctional subculture of a lot of Riverside teenagers back then. Many male role models – both young men and teenage boys in the Inland Empire – were not nice guys. For every one guy like Jack, or Russ, or Jack's other friend, Chip, there were ten other guys who were cruel bikers, ruthless drug dealers, treacherous addicts, racist jocks or self-obsessed, egocentric musicians. Many of them regarded women as things – objects to be dominated, used and discarded when done.

Both Marshall Dixon and Davey Scovilli were from large, poor families transplanted from East Texas. They both lived on the west side and, when they bothered to show up to school at all, it was to Rubidoux High. Jack considered them to be white trash and, as he was soon to find out, some of the worst of the worst. They wore their hair long like him, but they weren't peace-and love hippies or idealists or "socially-engaged-for-change" individuals. They were petty criminals, probably sociopaths, who burglarized, dealt drugs and enjoyed beating people up whenever the spirit moved them. Their one redeeming quality was that they were both pretty decent guitar players. Occasionally, they liked to rent a generator, get their amps and some people together and go set up late at night out in the brush-choked wilderness of Pedley, a rural west Riverside suburb. They would rig a huge, thick sheet of plywood as a makeshift stage, then would play loud-as-fuck, getting wrecked on weed, wine, whiskey, beer and pills till the wee hours. The cops never showed up. Jack was at a couple of these parties and, because he knew something about amps and PA's, he sometimes helped with the cables, wiring and sound set-up.

Maybe a year and a half before that, around the time he first got his driver's license, he had known Marshall slightly. Several days running, they had double-dated a couple of pill-popping French-Canadian sisters named Millicent and Mandy.

Jack didn't really have any reason to feel one way or another about Marshall and Davey. He didn't like them, he didn't trust them, but he didn't hate them. Not until after he heard Billy Miller's story.

Jack ran into Billy one night, just before Christmas vacation break was over. It was down at the 3rd Street mall in the first week of January 1971, a couple of weeks before his 18th birthday. He hadn't seen Billy since the night Billy had been with Cherie at the Jack in the Box.

"How's Cherie?"

He gave Jack a weird look.

"I saw you with her at the Jack in the Box two or three weeks ago."

He smiled nervously. "Oh, yeah, didn't see you, I guess.

"She okay?"

"Unh...unh, yeah. I guess so."

"What does that mean?"

"Nothing."

"You don't seem sure. You haven't seen her lately?"

"No, no, I've seen her. We've been going out."

"Well, what's the matter?"

Billy hemmed and hawed, not sure if he should tell Jack.

"You didn't hear what happened, did you?"

"What do you mean? To Cherie?"

"Yeah."

"When?"

"Unh, it must have been a few days after that night at Jack in the Box."

"I haven't heard anything. I haven't talked to her."

Billy kept looking away from Jack.

"Will you stop beating around the fucking bush and tell me?"

"I guess it's okay I tell you. I know she likes you, and you guys were kind of tight."

Jack frowned.

"You know, as friends."

Jack just stared at Billy, dreading his unknown secret.

Billy gulped. "She and I went out with Davey and Marshall to the orange groves one afternoon. Out where no one was around, maybe a half mile from her house. There was this other guy with us, too. Friend of theirs. I'm trying to remember his name. He's in jail now, up at Wayside."

Billy's eyes were getting a little wet. "Anyway, when we got there, Marshall broke out the weed, and we toked up. Man, it was strong shit. Gold, or something stronger. So, Davey and Marshall say, 'We're going to go pick us some oranges.' Right then, this guy – you know what? I think his name was Darryl. Yeah, now I remember. His name was Darryl – he fires up another joint and passes it to me right off the bat. Same time, Davey reaches out to Cherie, who's in the front with him and Marshall, and says, 'Come on.' Me, I'm in the back with Darryl. Before I knew it, she was giggling and going with them. I took another drag, and Darryl looked at me and goes, 'Suckers! More for us.' I handed the joint back to him. I noticed Davey and Marshall and Cherie had gone out of sight. I made a move to get out, and suddenly I felt Darryl's hand clamp around my wrist like a vise."

Billy was sweating, not relishing telling the tale. He took a deep breath.

"I knew then for sure something was up. Darryl goes, 'You stay here, you don't want to bother those three.' My imagination started going crazy, picturing all kinds of things happening. I can't believe Cherie didn't have enough sense to stay in the goddamn car."

Jack's face was white as a sheet. He sat down on a birdshit-encrusted mall bench, and Billy plopped down beside him. Billy gently placed his hand on Jack's arm.

"You okay? You look kind of sick."

Jack didn't answer.

"I guess it is the kind of thing makes a decent person feel sick. I still feel sick. I got sick to my stomach having to sit in the car with that goon. He looked like a fucking caveman. Had a tattoo right here…" Billy pointed to the v-shaped web of skin between his left thumb and forefinger, "…it said 'Fuck It!' And there was a tattoo of a harpooned whale right next to it."

Jack found his voice. "How long did they have her out there?"

"I don't know. It seemed like maybe…what? Half an hour? It seemed like more than that, but I think we got there around 4, and the clock on the dashboard said it was 4:30 when Davey and Marshall came back. The assholes were done. I flashed on all kinds of horrible things, like maybe they even killed her. The pricks – they were laughing, really stoned. They couldn't get their pants zipped up all the way. Then Darryl reached across me, and shoved open the door and kicked me out into the dirt. There was a cloud of dust when I looked after them, the car racing down the road."

"Jesus Christ."

"I walked maybe ten minutes before I found her. She still had her jeans down around her ankles. She was crying but, you know, silently – there was no sound coming out of her. She had blood between her legs.

"How could those bastards have done that?'

"Yeah, I know. I known those guys since I was little. They've always been mean, and I knew they did it to some other girls – "

"You knew they did it to others?"

"Yeah."

Jack exploded, standing up, towering over Billy. "What-the-

fuck were you doing getting into a car with them with Cherie, going out
to the orange groves to get stoned?"

Billy looked meekly up at him, red-faced and hurt. He slowly
nodded.

"Yer right. I'm an idiot. I just never…I just never ever in a
million years thought they'd do something like that to Cherie.
Especially with me around."

"Why not?"

"I dunno." He stared at his feet, shamed, then looked back up,
tears on his cheeks. "I guess because, you know, she's so cute. So tiny.
And you know, I'm not very strong, but they knew she was my
girlfriend."

They didn't say anything to each other for a couple of minutes.
Billy sighed at last and went on. "We walked back to Cherie's house.
It wasn't that far, but she could barely make it. She was still bleeding.
When we got back, her mom took her to the hospital. Cherie wouldn't
tell her who did it. And she told me not to tell her mom, either. The
doctor told Cherie she'd never be able to have kids."

Jack stood again and took a few steps. He was afraid if he sat
there any longer beside Billy, he'd punch him in the face.

"Where you going?"

Jack didn't answer him and didn't look back. He walked the
block to his car, got in and started driving. He drove for at least half an
hour, so angry he was unable to see straight. There were all kinds of
revenge plots swirling through his head. He kept thinking about Cherie,
wanting to go tell her that he had heard what had happened and that he
cared. In the end, he came to the conclusion it was a bad idea. She'd
want to know how he knew, then he'd have to tell her, and she'd be
ashamed and hurt all over again. He was torn, but he thought it was
better to think it over before he said or did anything.

Jack got home a little after midnight, and his father was still up,
watching Johnny Carson. Soon he went to bed, and Jack went to the
liquor cabinet beneath the kitchen sink. He pulled out the bottle of Jim
Beam and poured himself a glass three-fingers-full. Alone, with
everyone else asleep, he sank down onto the living room sofa and
started watching an Italian horror movie on channel 13 called *Death
Smiles on a Murderer*. It was a dreamlike tale set at the turn of the
20th century with an almost stream-of-consciousness narrative about a
young girl who had died after being made pregnant by her older lover.
She came back from the grave to get revenge on the man and his

family, as well as her own incestuous brother. Jack nursed the whiskey while the images on the TV spurred all kinds of vengeance scenarios. He imagined tampering with Davey and Marshall's brakes, causing a terrible accident, impaling them each on the steering column and front axle respectively; tying them up and letting a hungry, rabid cat claw out their eyes while they screamed for mercy; walling them up behind an inescapable facade of rock solid brick and mortar.

After the movie was over, and he had finished his drink, he went to bed. Before he fell asleep, he figured out that he could rig their instruments and amps so they would both be electrocuted the next time they played one of their boondocks jam sessions.

The next day he felt antsy about getting the ball rolling, lowering the boom on Davey and Marshall. He was going to have to be back at school in a few days for the start of the spring semester.

Jack went with May to the drive-in that night and saw more horror movies, *Twins of Evil* and *Hands of the Ripper*. In the break between the two films, Jack told her what happened to Cherie. May was disturbed by the story and even more so by Jack's determination to avenge her.

"Don't be stupid. Electrocuting them while they're playing guitar? That's harebrained. It'll never work. You might even end up killing or maiming someone innocent. And if things go wrong, which I'm sure they would, they'll know it was you. At the very least, you'd get your ass kicked. I know those guys. They've fucked with a lot of girls I know. They may have even killed some people."

For some reason, that hadn't occurred to Jack before.

"Killed people? But they're so young."

"So what? They both come from families of criminals. It's like a diseased litter of feral animals."

They didn't talk for a few minutes. Horns were starting to honk because people were getting impatient for the second feature to start.

"Promise me you won't try anything stupid."

Jack wouldn't look at her. She grabbed his arm.

"Promise me."

He finally turned and nodded. "Someone's got to do something."

May smiled. "Don't worry. They'll get theirs."

They embraced each other as the movie came on. Jack tangled his fingers in her short mane of hair, massaged the back of her head and gently caressed the nape of her neck.

"That feels good." She pulled her face back to look him in the eye. "Don't mind my saying this, but sometimes when I'm with you, you make me feel what it's like when I'm with a woman. You're so tuned in to me."

He didn't say anything, just let his lips brush hers, and they opened their mouths and kissed. The rest of the evening they barely paid attention to the Victorian grand guignol images on screen.

When he dropped her off, she paused before getting out. He could tell that she was thinking of Cherie again.

"You've got to promise me you won't do anything."

Jack looked away into the darkness, then turned back and nodded. "I promise if I decide to do anything, I'll give you plenty of warning."

She grimaced. "You better, Jack. You just fucking better talk to me first. I've got some ideas, but I don't want you to spoil what I have in mind."

"What?"

"No, I'm not telling. Not till I'm sure."

"Okay."

She bussed him on the cheek and suddenly was gone, disappearing into the shadows of the yard in front of her apartment house.

He didn't go in right away when he got home, just sat in the car in the dark. At last, he climbed out as if he had the weight of the world on his teenage shoulders. He propped himself against the still warm engine hood and gazed up into the inky blackness of the sky. There was no moon, and the stars were sparkling, microscopic splashes of light above Box Springs mountain.

For the whole next week he was haunted by images of Cherie being violated. But he stayed at home, avoiding his parents and brother and sister.

Then, on Sunday morning right at dawn, the day he had to drive back to Los Angeles, there was a tapping on his bedroom window. He pulled the curtain and found May staring in at him. He slid the glass open.

"Get on out here as quick as you can. I want you to come with me. I've got something to show you."

"Give me a couple of minutes."

He knew his mother would be up within the hour to make coffee and would freak out if she found him not at home. He left her a note saying that he'd gone out already to have breakfast with a friend.

Outside, May grabbed his arm, pulling him close to whisper in his ear.

"Take your car and follow me. I don't want to have to come back in this direction. It's a half hour out of my way, and I have to go into work later."

Jack did as he was told and, before too long, he was tailing her south, then southwest on Victoria Avenue. After ten minutes, they passed Cherie's family's house on the left, all quiet with the curtains drawn. Another couple of minutes, and May turned left onto a narrow road through the orange groves. They stopped after another few minutes.

May met him as he got out.

"This should be okay."

"Okay for what?"

"I've figured when the local deputies patrol through here. Nothing on Sunday until a lot later."

That kind of talk made Jack nervous.

"We have to walk a bit through the trees."

"Where we going?"

"You'll see. Leave your boots in the car and put these on." She handed him a pair of flip-flops similar to the pair she was wearing.

Jack followed behind her in silence as she threaded her way down a dirt row with fruit-bearing trees lining either side.

She continued talking in a low voice.

"Last night I ran into Davey and Marshall at Fairmount Park. Some kids were having a beer bust down there. I acted friendly. They knew I'm not real fond of guys, so it kind of surprised them when I started flirting. I asked them if they had any pot. The motherfuckers looked at each other and smiled, just like lightbulbs were going off in their heads. They said, 'Sure, May, get in the car, and we'll go for a little drive.'"

Something about the way she was telling the story made the hackles rise on the back of Jack's neck.

"And where do you think they brought me?"

As if on cue, Jack saw another narrow road up ahead and the tail fins of what looked like Marshall's maroon Chevrolet. Another few steps, and Jack almost tripped over something. When he looked down, he saw an outstretched hand coming from beneath an orange tree.

Then the rest of the body came into view. It was Davey, lying on his stomach with his mouth and eyes open, a deep gash in his throat

right at his jugular vein. The ground around his head was muddy with
dark brown blood. Flies were buzzing. His ripped blue jeans were down
around his ankles, exposing his pimply bare ass and scrawny legs.

May reached out her hand and gently took Jack's, pulling him
away towards the road.

"They took me here. This was their spot. Where they did
Cherie."

After another ten yards or so, as they got closer to the Chevy,
Jack finally caught sight of Marshall. He was splayed against the open
front passenger door, his back turned, with numerous stab wounds
pocking his olive green T-shirt.

"They tried the same thing with me, just the two of them. I'm
lucky they didn't bring any of their other stoner buddies along, because
I wasn't going down without a fight. And I had this."

May took a very long Mexican switchblade out of the rear
pocket of her black jeans and flicked it open. She had shown it to him
once before. He was speechless.

"C'mon. We can't stay here."

The sun was high enough so that it was getting hot. It was
January, but Riverside was a semi-desert town in the midst of an
unusually warm winter. The smell of the damp earth and myriad
rotting oranges on the ground mingled with what Jack imagined to
be the metallic odor of blood.

He followed May single file back the way they had come.
Where it had seemed like minutes before, it now seemed like hours.
Once they got back to the cars, she turned nonchalantly and asked if he
felt like breakfast.

"Not really. But I can't go home right away after seeing that.
Let's go to the Denny's on Arlington."

She nodded.

"Oh, hey." She pointed to his feet. "Give me those first."

He sat down sideways on the station wagon's front seat and
stripped off the flip-flops, handing them to her. She promptly dumped
them in a brown paper bag along with hers as he pulled on his cowboy
boots.

At Denny's, she threw the brown paper bag into the trashcan by
the parking lot entrance.

Once inside, they slid into a booth.

"Didn't think I had it in me, did you?"

He tried to smile but couldn't.

She laughed softly. "There were a few minutes last night, with

Davey on top of me, where I didn't know if I had it in me either."

"And you came through it without a scratch."

"Not quite." She grinned as she raised her black T-shirt, exposing a bite mark on her left breast and bruises beneath it on her ribs. A straight-arrow family, either on their way to, or coming from, church, was seated across from them. Only the ten-year-old son, his eyes wide and mouth agape, glimpsed May's tits. She turned and winked at the boy, then smiled impishly at Jack.

"You were lucky, May."

"Bullshit. I make my own luck."

"You ever hear about being in the wrong place at the wrong time?"

"Sure. Those two dumb bastards were at the wrong place at the wrong fucking time."

Jack didn't say anything.

"Besides, you know me. I dig taking chances."

They didn't do much more talking. He supposed that beneath his shock and surprise, he was proud of her and glad she was his friend. They each had coffee, bacon, eggs and toast, and before they got into their separate cars to drive away, they hugged each other.

"I won't see you for a while. I'm leaving town."

"I'll miss you."

"Maybe for a little while. But you always have plenty of girlfriends."

"Not girlfriends like you."

"Stay in touch?"

"Of course."

"I'll mail you my new address whenever I get to where I'm going."

He watched her get in her 1960 Buick and drive off, her hand trailing out the window, waving like the Italians do, her fingers and palms flexing and pointed the other way.

He was already back at school in Los Angeles when it came out in the papers a few days later, all put down to a drug deal gone bad. Almost a pound of pot was found in Marshall's trunk. He called Cherie right away in between his classes and made a date with her for the following weekend.

They went out for tacos in downtown Riverside at a drive-thru called Taco-Tia. He told her what had really happened to Davey and Marshall. He felt that she needed to know, but he didn't reveal the identity of her avenger. She couldn't eat anymore after he'd told her. The fact that someone – a girl Jack knew, a friend of his – had put themselves in jeopardy knowing how crazy Davey and Marshall were, someone who could take care of herself, someone capable of dispatching them both in self-defense…that such a girl existed was overwhelming to Cherie. She just sat beside him on the stone bench for several minutes, staring at the sparse nighttime traffic drifting by on 14th Street.

"I'm trying to figure out who would do something like that. And the only girl I can think of, who can maybe handle herself well enough and has the guts, is May Turner."

Jack didn't say anything.

"I know you and her are tight. You can tell me. I would never ever fucking tell anyone or, fuck, you know, go to the cops."

Jack stayed mute.

"Jack, I *idolize* May. I'd *never* rat on her."

He nodded.

"It was her?"

"Yeah."

"Wow…wow."

She inched closer to him on the dirty bench. He put his arms around her, and she put her head on his shoulder.

That was the last time that he saw Cherie.

In the intervening years, a lot of crazy shit had happened. Most of the street crowd he'd known from Riverside back then had left behind a legacy of tragic, "This Ain't the Summer of Love"- style wreckage. A prime example was elder hippie statesman, Bobby Morton, who had pulled off a Manson-wannabe plot, creepy-crawling his own family, killing his father and leaving his kid brother crippled. He had gotten 30 years to life in San Quentin.

May was the person who sent him the email about Cherie's death. They had apparently been living together off and on in Nashville for the last thirty years. The email hadn't said much beyond that. But May had included her work phone number and had asked him to call her. He hadn't talked to her since the late 1970s.

She answered after only a few rings.

"This is May."

"Hi, May. Long time."

"Fuck! Jack. I know. Long fucking time."

"I'm sorry about Cherie."

"I'm sorry it took something like that for me to get in touch. I'm sure you're wondering how she and I got together."

"It's none of my business."

"It's okay. I want to tell you."

There was a few seconds of silence.

"When I left town in '71, I went to San Francisco for a while. Then in 1978, I headed east. I guess the last time we talked I was still up in northern California. A musician friend got me a job as a bartender here in Nashville. I would play music, too, just for fun. I still tend bar and sometimes jam with people, but now I manage this club part time."

"I'm teaching college part time."

"That's something I can see you doing. Still playing music?"

"No. Not at the moment anyway. Diminishing returns."

"Yeah, I hear you."

The conversation petered out for a few seconds.

"Anyway, in 1980, out of the blue, Cherie called me. I'd barely known her before. I thought she must've found me through you… but it was someone else. Another mutual friend of ours I barely know. Jonelle."

"Jonelle. That is really fucking weird. She still a Jehovah's Witness?"

"I don't know." May paused. "Jack…did you ever tell Cherie about…you know?"

"Not in so many words. I told her a girl I knew had set those two up, knowing what would happen. She guessed it was you. She knew you were the only girl in our crowd together enough to pull off something like that and not get herself killed."

"You know what? She never let on that she knew the whole time we were together. I couldn't figure out, though, any other reason why she would have called me out of nowhere. But I was never sure."

"You guys never talked about it?"

"No, I could never bring myself to say anything. I kept thinking, what if she really didn't know? I grew fond of her pretty fast and didn't want to take the chance of losing her. It was good timing for me. I'd split up from another relationship about six months before and had been going through a bunch of depressing one-night-stands. We didn't become lovers right away. She'd been staying with me for about two months. I'd helped her get some temp work waitressing. One day she told me she was grateful for all that I'd done for her, putting her up, finding her a job, but she felt like she was taking advantage of me, and she should move on. I asked her where she was going to go, and she couldn't say. I told her it was okay if she stayed. We just looked at each other for a few minutes not saying anything, and suddenly we were in each others' arms."

"I'm glad."

"It was good for a while. But it wasn't perfect. She always drank too much and still did pills. When she was drunk, she'd sometimes disappear for a few days with some guy. She'd been with a girl or two before me, but she never really got men out of her system. We used to talk about you, you know. Usually when we were both really crocked."

"Fuck."

"No, I wish we'd gotten in touch." May took a deep breath and sighed. "It wasn't even that I minded that she occasionally needed to be with a guy. It's just when she was drunk, her judgment was really lousy. I would always worry about her. This last time, she was gone for almost a week. Then she called me from the road to let me know she was all right and that she'd be home soon. That was the last time I talked to her."

"Christ."

"She was driving by herself in the country, in the hills. Drunk, of course. And she went off the edge, down a steep 90-foot slope into a ravine. It was all overgrown. She probably wouldn't've been found for a while, except the car caught fire, and some truck driver saw it from above."

They didn't say anything for almost a full minute.

"Well, I guess that's it."

"I miss you, May."

"I miss you, too, Jack."

They hung up.

A few weeks later, for days on end in the month of May, there were torrential rainstorms and unprecedented flooding in Nashville. At least thirty people died. Jack was worried after hearing the news reports, and he tried to call May's number. An elderly man answered, who turned out to be the owner of the bar where she worked.

"We're still closed. The floodwaters fucked us."

"Oh, hey, I'm not really a customer. I'm a friend of May Turner. I'm out in California, and I was worried about her. After what I saw on TV."

There was an uncomfortable silence on the other end. Jack

could hear what sounded like a shovel scraping against cement in the background.

"Hello?"

"Yeah…yeah, I'm here."

Jack could hear the man breathing heavily.

"May…May didn't make it."

Jack couldn't speak.

"You there, son?"

"Yeah."

"Sorry to be the one to tell you. When you look at how many people live around here, it ain't really like that big of a percentage, you know, number of people drowned. If she hadn't been driving on that damn low road, she would still be alive. But she wasn't feeling well and asked me if she could leave early. You know, the weather and all. I tried to get her to lie down in the back. Was kinda worried about her driving with what was going on. But she was stubborn. I guess you know that, if you was friends."

"Yeah, we were friends." Jack tried to keep his voice from breaking.

"Anyway, they found her right off. Not like she went missing or anything." He paused, getting a bit emotional. "As I said already, son, sorry to be the one to break the news."

"That's okay. Thank you."

Then the man hung up, and Jack set down his phone.

NIGHTS IN VENICE

c. October, 1977
Venice, CA and Hollywood, CA

Venice Boulevard lay inert and comparatively quiet outside. Jack looked at his watch, loosened his tie and sat down at the beat-up old dining-room table that was pushed up against the picture window. That was one good thing about his teaching job – getting home by 3:30, before the rush hour started. Only a few cars drifted lazily back and forth on the east-west lanes, separated by a mound of slightly raised earth supporting unused rail tracks. Gravel swathes on either side of the endless span of iron bars supplied parking for all the apartment dwellers unlucky enough to be without a carport. His 1969 Falcon was out there, jammed in at an angle. He studied the dirty, peeling white paint and grimaced.

He finished rolling the joint, then took a sip of beer. His stare fell on the scattered notepaper on the cluttered tabletop, the pile of 11th grade essays next to his journal. Beside these was a short, but precarious stack of 45s, singles he needed to listen to again before he reviewed them for the punk rock magazine he wrote for without pay.

He struck the wooden match and touched it gingerly to the

end of the reefer. Taking a deep hit, he held it and exhaled. The as-yet
untouched newspaper lay folded face-up directly in front of him. More
death and destruction. It looked as if at least three serial killers were at
work in the Los Angeles area. The media had just dubbed one of them
the Hillside Strangler. And the police thought there were at least two
different maniacs – the Trash Bag Murderers – leaving parts of
dismembered gay men along the sides of southland freeways. Jesus
Christ!

He shook his head at his own fascination and pushed the paper
away in disgust. Everything seemed to be falling apart. He took another
hit and gulped some more beer, and his thoughts drifted.

About a month before, he'd accomplished one of the stupidest,
most thoughtless things he'd ever done in his whole life. No use for it
now, he couldn't turn back the clock. An obsessive attraction for
diminutive but voluptuous Larissa May, one of his estranged wife's
best friends from high school, had sprung seemingly out of nowhere.
It had mushroomed during a sojourn of separation from his spouse,
Honey B., while they tried to sort out their relationship. Honey had
been camping with her parents in their upscale San Pedro digs while
he'd moved into the apartment eight blocks west of Lincoln Boulevard
in Venice, right before his new job started.

Larissa was the only person he knew in the neighborhood,
living about a half mile south on the cusp of the marina. And,
coincidence of coincidences, she was teaching school, too. It had begun
innocently enough, going over for a drink late one afternoon. But his
still developing young libido and liberal imbibing of spirits and
marijuana had stripped away his inhibitions, had made him not
recognize the unreality of the situation. Smoking pot with Larissa and
watching her exotic animal eyes, the fullness of her lips as she voiced
her fierce intelligence, watching her very ample bosom expand and
spread on her small frame as she stretched and yawned after
handing him the joint, had spurred him to say something totally
spontaneous. "You know, every time I look at you all I want to do is
make you come." It had been sincere and innocent the way he'd said
it. He hadn't been leering or reaching out to grab her. He had just lain
there on the couch watching her as she sat cross-legged a few feet
away. What was strange about it all is she hadn't seemed offended.
She had actually smiled and blushed slightly. At least that's the way it
seemed at the time. Had he been wrong?

He knew she wasn't happy with things in her life either. She'd
been tentatively engaged to this macho jock guy who'd graduated from

USC and was now almost out of law school. But she wasn't sure it was what she wanted.

     She and Jack had talked until the sun went down, for at least an hour after he'd made the remark. They'd spoken on the phone a couple of times later in the week, then on a Thursday he'd gone over around 6:00 PM. They'd gotten a little drunk but hadn't really done anything. Even though it had only been a few weeks since, he couldn't remember for sure if they'd ever made out, ever even kissed. But he'd proposed to her that she run away with him the very next day, that they just hit the road and leave everything and everyone else behind. She'd seemed confused, but surprisingly had been impressed by his firm conviction about the rightness of it all and had finally – tentatively – agreed.

     There had been no rational, logical questions asked about how they were going to make a living in the meantime, where they were going to go. Before he'd broached the idea, he hadn't even considered how hands-on controlling her bourgeois parents were. He had given no thought to what it might be to live with her, day in and day out in the far-flung future. He had been overcome by the obsessive need to live life to the fullest, which was what she represented. He could vividly imagine spending hours on end in bed with her. It had been an idyllic, adolescent fantasy that he'd been determined to fulfill, no matter whom he hurt in the process.

     But when he'd called her the morning they were supposed to run off, one of Larissa's girlfriends had answered, telling him that she'd gone to Las Vegas to elope with her wannabe-lawyer-sometime-boyfriend. It had come as a tremendous shock. She hadn't even had the courage to get him on the phone herself to tell him his idea of scampering away together was a childish notion – imprudent, irresponsible and impossible. Or that it was something she just could not do to her longtime friend, his wife, Honey. She had just run in the other direction as fast she could.

     He smirked to himself as he deeply inhaled another hit. Well, that marriage was certainly going to last! Then he stopped smiling. A couple of days later his wife had called. Larissa had not only scurried off the other way but, before doing so, she'd gone and told her parents about his inappropriate proposal. And they'd called his wife's parents. And Honey's parents had told her.

     How gutless. Like a goddamn narc, not having the courage to tell him to his face to fuck off, not being brave enough to even tell one of her best friends that her husband was a two-timer. She'd had the two sets of parents do it! He felt so stupid, so naïve. Not to mention the agonizing guilt that had welled up inside at the painful humiliation he'd caused his wife. He'd apologized to Honey, but he knew it was a pathetically impotent, hollow gesture.

Jack suddenly walked over to the ancient, high-powered stereo he'd set up on the hardwood floor and picked up the ragged copy of The Stooges' *Funhouse* album. He flopped the vinyl on the turntable, switched on the amplifier and cranked up the volume. The loud sexual "oomph!" and angry grinding of the guitar groove hit him with a palpable wave of force. He glanced at the ceiling. Was the guy upstairs home yet? Who cared? *Fuck him!*

Jack surveyed the nearly empty living room. A torn and over-sized stuffed leather chair sat in the middle of the floor a couple of yards from the entryway to the anemic half-kitchen. He turned back in a circle as the music surrounded his body in an invisible blanket of warmth.

A dark-haired woman clad in a black sweater and an off-white dress was staring in at him from the sidewalk outside his window. He shuffled to the edge of the table, gazing at her through the huge oblong pane of glass. She seemed fairly young and was good-looking in an emaciated way, with very pale skin. He stared right back, but she didn't flinch at the unbroken eye contact. There was only a narrow, clumpy strip of ivy separating his building from the walk, so they were no more than eight feet apart. He took a few steps and opened the front door, intending to speak to her. But as she went out of sight for the few seconds it took him to come outside, he heard a car starting up. By the time he stood on the doorstep, she was history. There was an early sixties model Chevy disappearing down the boulevard towards Lincoln, apparently just having pulled from the curb.

The phone began ringing inside.

It was strange, that way she'd been looking at him.

He didn't want to go back in to answer the phone, fearing it would be only more bad news. Finally, he capitulated to the insistent *bbrrr-iingg, bbrrr-iingg* screaming over the stereo. He was surprised he could hear it. He lifted the receiver with one hand as he lifted the turntable's tone arm with the other.

Sure enough, it was his landlord telling him to turn his music down, that the upstairs tenant had lodged a complaint. Jack explained how he'd just now turned it off, then quietly apologized and hung up. He was pissed. He'd talked to the guy upstairs when he'd first moved in, asking him if his downstairs antics ever got too disturbing to please talk to him first before going to the landlord. The fucker hadn't bothered. Just called the goddamn owner right off the fucking bat. Wasn't there anyone anymore who had any guts? If the guy had phoned him directly or even pounded on the floor, he wouldn't have gotten mad -- all he would have done is turned the volume down a bit. He'd told the stupid guy that, hadn't he? He found the prick's number and called him. The guy's voice was tentative as he picked up. Jack let him have it.

"What-the-fuck? Didn't I tell you I'd be glad to turn my music down if you asked? Didn't I!"

The guy stammered out something, but Jack rolled right over him. "Fuck you, calling the landlord. I wouldn't have done that to you. Fucking asshole!" He slammed the receiver back in the cradle. He felt as if steam was coming out of his ears. He yanked his tie from around his collar, whiplashed it over the straightback chair at the table, then grabbed what was left of his beer as he headed into the bathroom to take a shower.

It was Friday night, so he didn't have to work the next day. Albert and his tiny Mexican wife Adele, two refugees from the Inland Empire and both writers for the same punk rag, had just moved to Venice a couple of blocks from the beach. They'd invited a few people over for dinner by way of a housewarming.

When he arrived, he realized the dinner was smaller than he'd expected. There was only one other person present besides Albert and Adele, an attractive but melancholy blonde who already seemed slightly hammered. Al made it clear no one else could come, and Jack tried to fight down the feeling the couple, knowing vaguely of his love life's immolation, had matched him up with this misanthropic girl whose name was Carol. They immediately sat down to eat, for which he was grateful. He felt awkward and shy, and he was glad there was the distraction of eating to cover up lulls in the conversation. But it was more fun than he'd imagined it would be. His three dinner companions had a withering sense of humor which they employed to tear down everything and everyone in the national news as well as the local music scene. They drank about as much as they ate, so when Carol asked him if he'd give her a ride home to her apartment in Hollywood, he hesitated.

"I was in Hollywood this afternoon," Al chimed in, "I gave her a ride down here because her car was in the shop."

Jack nodded tentatively. "Yeah, okay. I'll give you a ride."

"Think you can manage?" Al asked, smiling.

Jack colored slightly, and Carol repressed a laugh.

"Yeah, sure. I'm fine." He raised his coffee cup and finished it in a gulp as he stood.

They talked mostly about mundane things, getting to know each other as they made the pilgrimage through West L.A. Below the surface in Carol, Jack detected the same kind of stifled resentments he had himself, and he thought he glimpsed a ferocious intelligence that had been frustrated at every turn, as much by her own quirky personality as external forces. It made him like her. By the time he dropped her in front of her place on a side street off of Fountain, he was ready to ask for her number. She beat him to the punch, scrawling it on a matchbook and handing it to him.

"Call me when you're in Hollywood."

He didn't want to wait and, on a strange impulse, called her when he got home.

She answered with an annoyed tone. "Yes?"

It wasn't even midnight yet.

"Don't tell me you're asleep already. It's only been half an hour."

"Jack?"

"Yeah. I was going to be in Hollywood tomorrow tonight. I want to see the bands playing at the Masque."

"Hhmm…I was going, too. Why don't you swing by and pick me up around 9:00?"

"I'll be there."

"Good night."

"Good night."

He hung up the receiver and glanced around his empty apartment. It had gotten terrifically cold. The warm feeling he'd gotten from the sound of Carol's voice growing friendly when she'd realized it was him suddenly dissipated. The light ocean breeze from earlier in the evening was gone, replaced by a wind of growing intensity. It was seeping under the front door and the edges of the kitchen and bedroom windows, wrapping its icy fingers around him, making him want to go to bed in his long leather jacket. He picked up the quart bottle from the big table, unscrewed the cap and took a healthy swig. The bourbon coursed down his throat like a stream of hot coals, and he shivered involuntarily.

He was exhausted from the stressful week. There was nothing on TV so he decided to go straight to sleep.

The next thing he knew he was waking up with the overhead
light on, crashed out on top of the bed still in his clothes. He rubbed
his eyes, glanced over at the clock and saw that he'd been comatose
for nearly two hours. He was so groggy he decided to forego
brushing his teeth and stripped off his boots, pants, jacket and shirt
in that order. The clothes fell in a heap on the hardwood floor as he
crawled under the meager set of blankets. Shit! He hadn't turned the
light out. It was freezing, and he'd be damned if he was going to get
up to do it. Grabbing the nape of the leather coat, he expertly lashed it
out at the wall switch, and the room was plunged into darkness. The
faint glow of streetlights fought to penetrate the dirty muslin curtains.
Damn, the blankets were worthless. He didn't remember it getting this
cold during the previous October down in Hermosa. Then again, he
and Honey had had a decent heater in that apartment. He stretched and
groped along the floor, picked up his jacket again and spread the leather
over his feet.

The wind was moaning and sighing outside, occasionally building to a roar then subsiding. Tree branches gesticulated wildly in faint
shadows beyond the curtains, and there were the sounds of things
falling and tumbling down the street end over end -- wood, paper and
tin cans. The streetlights flickered.

He slept a deep sleep until about an hour before dawn, when he
suddenly had the distinct sensation there was someone in bed with him.
He sensed that he was awake, but he couldn't open his eyes, and he
wasn't sure if it was because of something physically wrong with him
or if he was too petrified with fear. The wind had not abated.

It was even colder than earlier, if that was possible, yet a thin
sheen of perspiration covered his entire body. There was definitely
someone or something lying right alongside him. Abruptly, he suffered
a paralyzing horror as that something clamped onto his chest like a
vacuum, zeroing in on his torso with a perpetual upsurge of suction. He
felt as if it was trying to leech out his very essence, and he battled in a
seeming trance to prop open his eyelids and fearlessly stare the thing in
the face – if it had a face. Somehow, after what seemed like an eternity,
he managed, but his blood froze when he realized nothing was there. At
least, nothing he could see. But there was something writhing beneath
the covers, something holding up the blankets in a hollowed space of
empty shadows.

He must still be asleep, that had to be it. It was the only
explanation. He'd had sensations before in dreams of being rooted to

the spot and unable to move, unable to run or even to walk. Yet this was too real. He'd never experienced anything like this. Then there was a horrible shrieking, like the whole windstorm was suddenly inside the room. An invisible membrane of resistance suddenly burst within him, and – thank God! – he was at last able to move. His arms and legs thrashed against the thing that was siphoning away his soul, and the momentum of his violent rush of adrenaline propelled him backwards out of bed onto the floor with a muffled crash. He immediately straightened up and slapped on the light.

There was nothing there. The limp bedclothes lay in a tangled mound in the center of the mattress. Not letting his gaze stray from the bed, he reached down and, lightning quick, slipped on his black jeans. He elbowed his way into the corduroy shirt and grabbed the sheet and blankets with both hands and yanked them away. Hesitating for only a few seconds, he darted his hand over the faint depression in the mattress where he'd been sleeping. Nothing! He swept his arms over every inch but, try as he might to find evidence of the thing, whatever had been in bed with him was now gone.

He didn't dare try to go back to sleep, he was still too freaked out. After taking a long piss, staring at himself in the bathroom mirror, he puttered into the kitchen wrapped up in the leather jacket and put on some coffee. While he waited for the water to boil, he pulled out a cigarette and lit it, sucking in a long drag. He hacked through a sudden coughing fit and spit into the cluttered sink.

The rest of the morning he spent in the living room at the table, reading the newspaper, taking in all the sick things going on in the world and then grading his 11th grade students' assignments. He went for a long walk in the afternoon and ate at a hamburger stand on Washington at dusk. By the time he got home, it was dark again.

He listened to a few singles at low volume. Time zoomed by and, before he knew it, it was time to leave to go pick up Carol. He made sure all the windows were locked and pulled the drapes closed in the living room.

When he arrived at her 2nd story apartment around 9:30, she invited him in since she wasn't quite ready. There was an echoey dub reggae album on the primitive little stereo.

"Want a drink?"

He nodded.

"There's a bottle on the kitchen table and glasses in the cupboard." She already had a tumbler of straight bourbon in her hand

and took a swig as she returned to the bathroom.

She kept up the conversation. "We better do our drinking here. Hell will freeze over before the Masque ever gets a liquor license."

He poured himself a stiff one, then gravitated to the sound of her voice, leaning against the doorjamb and watching her do her hair and put on her make-up. She smiled wryly at him as he studied the fine old vintage bathroom.

"I love your place. I've got hardwood floors, too, but your place is in much better shape." He let his gaze wander over the layers of purple and green tiles that lined the bottom half of the wall.

"You ever lived in Hollywood?"

"Not yet."

"This is a great building." She put down her empty glass on the floor as she abruptly pulled down her tight sharkskin pants and unashamedly sat on the toilet. They smiled at each other as she peed.

When they went outside, he saw the cold wind had kicked up again, and leaves were scattering down the pavement and sidewalk between the streetlights. She suggested they take her car, an old Peugeot with a peeling, rusty red paint job.

The club was in the disconnected basement of the Pussycat adult theater on Hollywood Boulevard. You entered through the back alley off Cherokee, a dimly lit side street. As they walked up from where they'd parked the car, he noticed shadowy figures down on the corner of Selma Avenue, the next cross street down.

She followed his gaze to the slouching, languid young studs a half block away and laughed. "That strip right there's a heavy cruising area. They're turning tricks all night long."

"Yeah, somebody told me that that coffee shop over by the newsstand on Las Palmas is a big chicken-hawk hang out."

"The Gold Cup."

They took a few more paces as the wind whipped around them. "You know who Elizabeth Short is?"

He glanced at her, digging his hands into his coat pockets to keep them warm. "The Black Dahlia?"

She nodded. "See that crummy hotel we just passed?"

He looked over his shoulder at the shabby building with its nondescript illuminated sign advertising rooms for rent.

"That's the last place she was living when she got murdered."

The whole neighborhood seemed to be steeped in a history of depravity, and he had to admit it gave him a perverse thrill of pleasure.

He could tell it did the same thing for her. The very bricks and mortar of the buildings and the asphalt of the pavement gave off an aura of moral corruption.

They were suddenly at the door. He paid the $5 admittance fee for them both, and then they descended down the stone steps into the echoey cavern. A band was already thrashing away on the tiny, slightly raised wooden stage. There was a good crowd of perhaps a hundred people milling around, crushing forward to either study the spectacle or participate in the general melee of mauling in the front.

Jack had only been there a half dozen nights, but each time he enjoyed it more than the last. And this evening was more exciting still because there obviously was an electric charge of sex running between him and Carol. They stood there watching the band until the last song. Carol looked over, smiled and took his hand leading him back up the stairs to the cold outside.

"Where we going?"

"For a drink. I've got a bottle."

They walked back by the Black Dahlia's lonely, rundown old hotel. Carol pulled a pint of bourbon from under the front seat when they got to her car. She looked up and down the block to make sure there were no black-and-whites about, then quickly upended the bottle, letting it bubble till a quarter of it was gone. She handed it to him. He grinned and did the same. As she reached again for the liquor, she brushed her lips against his, letting them linger there as she screwed the top on. After a few seconds, she tucked the glass flask away under the seat, and they headed to the club.

Inside the darkened basement, there were even more people, and Jack could tell the club owner was worried that the fire marshal might show up and shut the place down. The sound was louder than before and, if Jack hadn't been half in the bag, his ears would have hurt. He wasn't sure, but he thought the frenzied band upfront was called The Skulls.

The club was a warren of ruined rooms that reminded him of catacombs, and he pulled Carol off into one of the side passages. They wandered into a nearly empty chamber where only one other couple sat huddled in the far corner.

They each leaned a shoulder against the dusty wall, and their faces slowly met. Jack took her chin in his hand and held it, kissing her. They dawdled there in the shadows, making out in a luscious, stupefied languor. There was something he could feel seething inside of her, something that gave into their mutual desire with a contemptuous abandon. Whatever that sinful something was, it turned Jack on, and he bent further into their kiss. They suddenly pulled away from each other's lips by mere inches, in total synch, and locked stares. He broke eye contact, letting his eyes rove over her delicate, yet cruelly beautiful features. Raising one index finger, he traced it gently along the surface of her moist, pouting lips. Abruptly, he crushed her to him again, slipping his tongue deep into her mouth. He heard her moan over the din, trailed his left palm down to clutch her full ass and cupped the back of her graceful, tapered neck with his other hand.

Their dreamy, self-contained absorption in each other continued until closing time. They were still half-crocked as they walked to the car. They weren't actually conscious of the plummeting temperature, but the staggering cold sobered them a bit.

Jack told her about his strange, frightening experience in the early morning hours.

She laughed. "Wow. I was going to ask you to stay the night, but maybe I should invite myself over to your place instead."

"I guess you dig the idea of restless spirits."

"You guess right! But it probably won't dare fuck with the two of us together. They only come out when you're all by yourself."

"Maybe so…You need to go back by your place?"

"No."

"You okay to drive?"

She nodded vigorously. He held the door open for her after she unlocked it. Once she was ensconced comfortably, he made his way to the other side, jumped in, and they were off.

When they angled into the parking area in the middle of the street in front, she leaned forward to gaze out at the baleful yellow structure.

"God, it looks just like the kind of anonymous building where there would be murders."

She was right. He realized that's what had been lurking in the back of his mind. It was the type of place you'd see on the TV news, surrounded by crime scene tape, slightly out of focus and serving as the deceptively humdrum background for a homicide cop answering a nosey reporter's lurid questions.

He laughed it off. "Hey, I have to live here…at least for the time being."

As they waited for an out-of-service bus to whoosh by so they could cross, they both stared down toward the coast a half mile away. The wind had died down, and a gentle, icy breeze was blowing a thick fog in from offshore.

The deadbolt clicked under the turning key, and they tumbled into the room, laughing. Jack switched on the table lamp, and she closed the door.

"Make sure it's locked."

She did as she was instructed, then peeked out the side of the curtains while he lit a joint.

"Jack, did you know that used to be a police station across the street."

"Yeah. It's the one they used for exterior shots in *Assault on Precinct 13*."

"Yeah."

"A great movie." He handed her the joint. "I saw it up in Hollywood at the World Theater."

"That place is insane." She took a deep drag and held it.

"99 cents for three movies. You can't beat that. And the stuff they show is almost always wild exploitation stuff. They're always playing obscure, trashy European films as well as drive-in type pictures."

"It's a lot of fun if you're with people. But it's horrible for a woman to go there by herself."

He took the joint from her, reached out and pulled her to him by the lapel of her black leather jacket. "You mean there's guys like me trying to do stuff like this?"

She laughed. "If only! The jerks trying to pick you up at the World have pee stains on their pants and drool coming out of their mouths!"

She leaned into him playfully, and they kissed. He backed away but kept his eyes locked into hers as he laid the joint down in the ashtray. He lifted the half full bottle off the table and walked backwards, slowly drawing her into the bedroom.

Once they were in the sack with their clothes on the floor, they unhurriedly explored each other's bodies by candlelight. Gradually they inched closer, as if a fever was mounting, mashing together the contours of their flesh. Despite the chill in the room, the liquor had them sweating, and they surrendered to a ravenous hunger. Jack would later retain an almost psychedelic memory of the night, images of two bronze figures coupling, the flicker from the candle flame gleaming on their wet skin.

They stayed in bed until nearly 3:00 PM on Sunday, only rising to make some coffee. When they finally got up for good, they decided to swing by Pancho's, a joint known for the best chile relleno in Los Angeles, and which, coincidentally, turned out to be the favorite Mexican restaurant of the both of them.

By the time they made it back to her neighborhood, it was nearly 8:00. He declined to come up to her place since he had to wake early the next morning to be at school. She strolled with him to his car, and they leaned against it for a few moments, making out.

"It was fun, Jack. We should do it again soon."

"Yeah, I had a blast. I'll call you."

She smiled broadly and waved as he got in and started the car.

He was nervous about lying in that bed again all by himself, and it was only 10, but he decided to crash as soon as he got home. He'd been in the sack with Carol for nearly twelve hours, but only a few of those had been devoted to slumber. He was dog-tired and immediately fell asleep, snoozing dreamlessly without interruption until the alarm roused him at 7:00 AM.

The small charter school on the border of Westchester and Inglewood where Jack was employed was a strange place. A middle-aged couple who used to work at Jefferson High ran it. The morbidly obese husband and wife had found a niche catering to upper-middle-class blacks and lower-middle-class whites, parents who were horrified at the gang activity rife in Inglewood's public institutes of higher learning. A month or two before he'd been hired, the husband principal, Mr. Harmon, had had a debilitating stroke and was paralyzed on one side of his body.

Jack taught English grammar to approximately sixty kids divided into grades 8, 9, 10 and 11. The majority were in the two higher grades – 25 in the 10th and 20 in the 11th. The scariest and worst behaved were in the 10th. But the 11th was nearly all female, and most of them were intelligent, funny, sexy and eager to work, if occasionally too talkative. There were three or four girls who were close to being beautiful, and he had to keep reminding himself they were still – just barely – under eighteen. Jack was only 24 years old, so the age gap sometimes seemed non-existent.

Despite his misgivings, Jack had felt things were going okay for his first month there. If any student got too out of hand, he'd send them to see Harmon, and whatever the overweight, crippled principal said or did to them in his office was startlingly effective. They'd always come back perfectly behaved, at least for a few days. But when Jack arrived that Monday morning, he was chagrined to learn Harmon had had another stroke and was in the hospital. Things didn't look good.

As the week progressed, things went steadily downhill.

That Monday night was parents' night, and he was shocked at how few attended. There were several single mothers, all black, and one of them was provocatively flirtatious, straightening his tie, smiling wickedly and gazing longingly into his eyes. At most, she was only five years older than him, and it was all he could do to keep from asking her to meet him later at a local bar. Another mother was dirty and disheveled, her jaundiced junkie eyes peering out at him from beneath lids at half-mast. She was the mom of the most frightening kid in the school, a hostile sociopath who rarely showed up and who, when he did, would play sarcastic word games when called on and who seemed constantly shermed-out – dusted to the gills. It didn't surprise Jack that this poor lost soul was the boy's mother. But what amazed him was that she cared enough as a parent to show up at all.

He was vaguely depressed as he drove back to Venice. He thought about calling Carol but resisted the temptation, lest he seem too eager. It was 9:00 PM when he pulled into the parking area across from his place. He wasn't hungry because he'd eaten a hamburger earlier, but he decided to pick up a sixpack from the tiny liquor store that sat next to the abandoned police station across the boulevard. The Mexican owner thought it was funny seeing him in a tie. Jack sighed and smiled as he paid and grabbed his beer.

When he came out, he noticed that the pale, black-haired girl he'd seen on Friday was sitting on the steps of the darkened precinct house. After hesitating a few seconds, he strode across the dried-out lawn in front of the intimidating façade, working up the nerve to address her.

"Hi, I live in the building across the street. The yellow one."

She looked at him with a vacant stare as he sat down beside her.

"You were looking in at my window Friday afternoon, weren't you?"

"Was I?" She was pretty spaced out.

"You don't remember?

She turned back to survey the block.

"I used to live in that building. I often come to look at it. I don't remember if I did last Friday or not."

Jack abruptly noticed her left arm, which sported a welter of needle tracks. She was clad in the same off-white dress, but without the black sweater, and her tangled black mane fell partially over her fine-looking face. If he'd had to describe her, he would have said she had a vaguely aristocratic air and aquiline Spanish features.

"My name is Jack."

She tilted her head and peeked at him through clotted hair strands. A barely perceptible, strangely haunting smile formed at the corners of her thin lips. "I'm Mañon."

Suddenly a bright light shone on them, and Jack jerked around to see a black-and-white pulled to the curb. Two cops were getting out. He stood up.

"Come on down here."

Jack gingerly walked towards them.

"You got any ID?" asked the one who aimed the flashlight in his eyes. His older partner circled behind him. "Maurice, check out where the girl went." The older one nodded in assent and started a loop around the deserted precinct house.

Jack quickly glanced over his shoulder as he fished his wallet from his pocket and realized Mañon had vanished. He handed the license to the cop.

"It says you live in Hermosa Beach. What're you doing up here?"

"I live right across the street. That yellow building. I just moved in about a month ago when my wife and I separated."

"What's with the tie? Just get off work?"

"Yeah. It was parents night up at the school where I teach in Westchester."

The cop grunted, his suspicions subsiding. He returned the license to Jack.

"How well do you know that chick you were with?"

"Not really at all. I just met her. I've seen her around the neighborhood."

"She good looking?"

Jack thought it was a weird question to ask. He shrugged. "Yeah, in a strange sort of way."

"Just wondering. I've seen her around, too, but never closer than we just got. She's a slippery one. You should be careful. She's probably homeless and messed up…you know, strung out."

Right then his partner returned.

"Any luck?"

"Nawwh, she disappeared into the woodwork, as usual."

"Hey, Maurice, guess what? Our friend here lives in the building across the street."

"Really? No kidding? The yellow one?"

The young cop nodded, smirking.

"Whew, how do you like it there, son?"

Jack swiveled to look at him. "It's okay."

"A lot of shit's gone down there."

"What do you mean?" Jack asked.

"You know, domestic violence crap and drug dealers getting blown away. But the neighborhood's quieted down a bit in the last few months. Things got kind of nutty at first when they closed the precinct down, like kids let loose in a candy store. But things have settled."

"The last thing was – when was it, Maurice?"

"What? Maybe seven or eight months ago?"

"Yeah, that sounds right. Some chick snuffed herself."

Jack swallowed. "Which apartment?"

"Not sure. Maurice and I weren't on that night. But it definitely was in that building. Speaking of buildings," he gestured to the deserted police station, "You should stay away from here at night. We come down hard on vandals, and some of our buddies on the force aren't as friendly as us. You might get roughed up."

Maurice chimed in. "The place is getting taken over by some artsy-fartsy non-profit over on Washington in a month or so. What's the weird name of that place?"

Jack knew the organization he meant. "Beyond Baroque?"

The younger cop laughed at Maurice's surprised reaction. "Our friend here's a teacher. He would know something like that."

Right then an emergency call came over the cruiser's radio. The two scrambled back into their squad car, slamming the doors. The younger one grabbed the radio mike, "10-4. We're on our way." He glanced at Jack as they peeled out. "Take it easy, kid."

Wednesday, they got word Mr. Harmon had died. Thursday, two of the more unstable 10th graders threatened to kill Jack if he followed through on his threat to flunk them on their mid-term report card. Jack tried to let it all roll off his back. After the hyper melodrama he'd been through in that last two months, his senses were getting a touch jaded. But the surplus of negativity in the air was starting to get to him.

Thursday night, he ate dinner at Carol's, and they drank beer and whiskey, playing cards with a very literate punk musician couple who were in a band that often played at the Masque. Even after the game ended around midnight, and the couple had gone home, Jack and Carol stayed up late, talking. He didn't have to go to work the next day because the school was closed due to Mr. Harmon's funeral – which he wasn't expected to attend – and Carol was in between temp jobs. Before they went to bed, she mentioned something to him that he was hoping to follow up. A friend of hers lived in a building on Fairfax between Melrose Avenue and Santa Monica Boulevard, and an apartment had become vacant.

They fell asleep having sex and woke around 10:00 AM on Friday. They drove over to breakfast at Oblatt's, a small, old-fashioned studio restaurant right next to the Paramount lot. The two of them did nothing of consequence in what turned out to be an intermittently rainy afternoon, hitting a couple of bookstores and going to an early movie.

Carol knew a lot about films – she was a frustrated film student, just like him. Later in the evening, they talked for hours about various hard-to-see European and Japanese movies. Because Halloween was right around the corner, there were vintage horror pictures on TV that night till dawn. They brought the set into the bedroom so they could watch in between bouts of fucking.

Earlier that evening they'd almost gone to the Masque, but the next morning they were glad that they'd been lazy. The Saturday morning paper described how some nutjob had shot off an Uzi on the corner of Cherokee and Hollywood Boulevard around midnight -- fortunately no one had been killed.

After Carol fixed their breakfast, she told him she needed some time alone. They'd originally talked about going to see some bands at an auditorium down on Olympic Boulevard that night. Now she wasn't so sure. Jack was picking up schizo vibes but played it cool. He didn't push it, telling her he'd call her later.

He unlocked the door of his apartment to the sound of the phone ringing. It was Carol, sheepishly apologizing and saying she'd just been feeling claustrophobic – if he still wanted, he could pick her up around 8:00 to go see the bands. He said sure, and they said their goodbyes. But the phone immediately rang again. This time it was Honey, telling him that her father wanted to come by Monday after Jack got off work to take back the big double bed. She didn't say much else, even after he asked her how she was. She told him he'd be getting divorce papers in the mail, then abruptly hung up on him. He was expecting it. She had been his best friend since midway through college, but nothing had ever quite clicked with them as a couple.

They should never have gotten married in the first place. Nothing like 20/20 hindsight.

He sat there for a good five minutes, staring at the floor. Frustrated with himself, he suddenly jumped up, snagged the nearly empty bourbon bottle from the table and grabbed some 45s with his other hand. He put one on, cranked up the stereo and upended the bottle. He hadn't had much to drink on Friday, but now he was in the mood. Fuck that guy upstairs! He was going to play the music LOUD! It was Saturday afternoon. If the guy didn't fucking like it, he could go for a goddamn fucking walk!

His drinking and the fact that the waitress at the Mexican restaurant took forever bringing him his dinner made him late picking up Carol. She'd done an about-face again and was acting like she wanted to be on her own. He tried to remain calm, even when she sprung it on him that an old friend of hers from back East was in town and was gong to go with them. The guy wasn't staying too far from the show, and it was on the way, so it didn't seem like a big deal.

Jack wasn't sure what to make of the guy once they'd picked him up. He and Carol obviously had a history together, but how deep it ran was anybody's guess. Once they got to the big auditorium, Jack immediately lost them in the huge crowd and didn't see Carol again until after the first band was done. She'd sashayed up to him, obviously stoned on pot, and asked if he wanted to come out for a beer. He nodded and followed her. They picked up a sixpack next door at a busy liquor store and went to sit in his car.

"Thanks for not being an asshole about Tony. I used to hang with him in high school. He comes in and out of L.A. on jobs sometimes, and we occasionally still see each other." She took a long swig of beer.

"It's cool." He drank about half of his at a gulp, then cracked the door and drained the rest of it on the asphalt. "I think the next band is going to start."

She nodded, smiled self-consciously and chugged the rest of her drink as she got out.

The same thing happened during the next band's set. She disappeared with Tony, and he had to go look for the pair at the end of the show as everyone filed past him. Try as he might, he could find no sign of them, but he was shocked when he got to his car. Carol and Tony were in the front seat making out, their tongues down each other's throats. He felt as if someone had opened a red hot oven mere inches from his face. He could feel his cheeks and neck flush crimson with hurt, fury and embarrassment.

The two finally noticed him standing outside and sheepishly pulled away from each other's arms.

Jack got in and said sarcastically, "I guess I left my car unlocked."

Carol and Tony said nothing. He switched on the ignition, pulled from the spot at the curb and made an illegal U-turn, heading down Olympic. Luckily, Tony's timeshare pad was close by, so the drive wasn't as horribly excruciating as it could've been. When they arrived, Jack purposely didn't park.

"You guys want to come up for a drink?"

Jack curtly jumped in before Carol could reply. "No thanks. I've got to get Carol back to Hollywood."

Tony nodded knowingly and moved to peck Carol on the cheek. But she grabbed Tony's arm while glancing pointedly at Jack. "I'll walk you to the door."

Jack tried not to watch as the two of them shuffled drunkenly along the stone path to the building entrance. He couldn't help himself and turned just in time to glimpse her twist away from locking lips with her "old friend." As soon as she got back in and slammed the door shut, he roared down the street.

"I've never seen anyone be a bigger fucking baby!"

He glanced at her incredulously. "What-the-fuck? You're incredible. I pick you up to go out, you spring it on me at the last minute your old boyfriend is going with us, you ditch me the whole night and then, after I've given up trying to locate you two, I find you fucking making out with the fucking guy in the front seat of my fucking car!"

"I'm not your goddamn wife! Stop making a mountain out of a molehill."

"I know you're not my wife. You're not even my fucking girlfriend. But if you wanted to spend the whole evening with him, or go out on your own, or whatever, you could have just told me. Instead of going back and forth about it all afternoon."

She gave him a poisonous stare. "I didn't know what to do. It seemed to be *important* to you."

"Look, you know what? Nothing's worth getting treated like you treated me tonight. Wiping your shoes on me like I'm some kind of doormat. If you don't know what you want, baby, okay. Fine. Just don't humiliate me in the process."

They didn't say anything after that until they were almost to her street. She swiveled her whole body sideways to face him just as they veered to the curb in front.

"Look, Jack, I like you. I'd still like to see you. It's up to you. I'm sorry about tonight. I haven't had a steady boyfriend in a long time, and I'm used to doing exactly what I want."

He didn't reply.

"Maybe we should give it a couple of days before we talk. Let each other cool off."

He finally nodded. She bent over and quickly kissed him, then started to get out

"Carol?"

She bent her head back in. He pathetically made an effort to smile at her. She smiled faintly in return and raised her hand in a wave as she shut the door.

The whole night stung him to the quick. It had only been a little over a week, and he was already alarmingly fond of Carol. It made him sick to his stomach. She was another in his "girls who needed to be rescued from themselves" category. There'd been several since he'd started his love life at 17 – Cecilia, Jackie, Emily, even Honey. They all had either self-destructive personalities or fucked-up families, or both. And all needed someone to love them and be there for them, even if sometimes they didn't know it themselves. Things hadn't worked out with any of them. Either he'd grown tired of their bullshit, or they, his, or circumstances beyond their control had intervened. Realizing all this with such clarity made him hate himself. He felt like a presumptuous idiot. Who was he to save anyone? He could barely take care of himself. For some reason he thought of the homeless girl Mañon, that she fell into the same niche. Unexplainably, the realization put him on edge.

He felt lonely as hell on the ride home. He wasn't looking forward to spending the night in his cold, haunted apartment.

Suddenly he realized it was almost closing time for the liquor stores, and he screeched to a halt at the first one he passed. A minute later he was back in the driver's seat, a wrapped quart of bourbon sitting snugly next to him.

"Goddamn pathetic lonely-ass motherfucker," he muttered as he parked.

Women were throwing themselves at him two or three times a week, and here he was having to spend the night by himself. Locking

the car, he suddenly thought of his poor humiliated wife Honey and
realized what an ass he was. He jogged briskly through the mist to his
front door. He didn't spot the black-haired girl on the walk until he was
nearly on top of her – that's how thick the fog was getting.

"Sorry, I didn't see you…Mañon, right?"

She nodded but didn't speak.

"You look cold. You want to come in for minute?"

"No thanks."

He nodded awkwardly, feeling rebuffed and turned to unlock
his door.

"Would you…?" Shy and awkward, it seemed hard for her to
get out the words.

He glanced over his shoulder at her as he twisted the key.

"Would you come for a walk with me? I love walking in the
fog."

"I…I don't know. It's pretty late…"

"I'm so damn lonely, Jack."

He was honestly surprised she recalled his name, and
something about the way she said it melted his heart. The lonesome
tone of her voice mirrored his insides. Against his better instincts, he
agreed. "Okay. Hold on a second. I'm freezing."

He started inside, then hesitated and looked out again at her
forlorn figure on the walk. "Mañon, you *can't* be warm enough. All
you've got on is that sweater."

"I'm fine. Don't worry about me. Get something for yourself."

He smiled at her and dodged into the apartment. He grabbed
the thick-knit, white woolen pullover that sat in the overstuffed chair
and quickly put it on under his long leather jacket. He cracked open the
new bottle and took two healthy swigs of the raw-tasting whiskey. He
poked his head out the door, holding the bottle.

"Want a drink? It'll warm you up."

She smiled faintly. "No thanks. I don't drink."

The remark made him remember her needle tracks. He set the
bottle on the table, exited and locked the door.

Walking with Mañon was a strange experience. He felt an odd
commingling of serenity, peace and trepidation. There was something
about her ageless, unhurried nature that seemed uncanny. Despite the
chill, she had the sleeves of her sweater rolled back to her elbows, and
the very visible evidence on her ruined arms scared him, made him
wonder if she had a junkie boyfriend lurking a couple of blocks further

down, waiting in the fogbound dark of somebody's carport to knock him senseless and rob him. She laughed – just as he was thinking that thought, just as if she knew exactly what was running through his mind, and it sent a chilly shiver down his spine.

Something drew him on. The liquor, the thick mist and the lateness of the hour made him lose track of time. All of a sudden, he realized they were at the edge of the boardwalk that ran along the beach. And in the entire stroll from his place, they hadn't seen a soul.

"Maybe we should turn back."

"No, come on, let's go out on the sand. The waves are so beautiful right now."

She clasped his hand, and her cold, sleek touch sent a premonition whooshing through his head. The conversation he'd had with the pair of cops about his building swooped back, and he involuntarily caught his breath, petrified, rooted to the spot with fear. Slowly he raised his gaze from their two hands joined together, trailing up one junk-wrecked arm to her transcendentally beautiful visage. Her eyes pierced him to the bone. He stared into the fiery blue coals and was suddenly conscious of no longer being afraid.

She tugged at him gently, and he let her, following her onto the shore. They didn't stop until they were a few yards from the crashing surf. He could just spot the waves rolling in and out in the shifting vapor. He automatically stripped off his leather jacket, spreading it like a blanket across the damp sand.

They both sat down, and she immediately came into his arms, pressing her icy lips to his. He leaned back, lying prone, and she edged up to lay partially on top of him. He surrendered drunkenly to her kisses, her lips and tongue intoxicating him like a drug. Their freezing, pliant contact fooled him, sent his senses spiraling until the arctic moisture of her mouth was burning him with a frightening, escalating passion. Her coarse black hair became silky sable under his touch. The strands shone with an ebony luster, and the ocean breeze fitfully brought them to life, wrapping them around his fingers.

Abruptly he felt something clamp onto his chest and, with a horribly dizzying rush of knowledge, he recognized the invisible thing from his bed. The suction was worse than before, like nothing he had ever experienced – a blood-draining, consciousness-destroying, spirit-killing energy yanking at everything inside his corporeal shell. What terrified him even more, there was a deep-seated part of his psyche that wanted to give into her, let her take him out of the insecure, egocentric hell that was his world.

It was like falling off a cliff, being vacuumed up, swallowed by a huge cosmic maw into a bottomless, churning chasm of Nothingness. A siren shrieked in the distance, and the piercing sound was just enough to jar him so he could regain his equilibrium. He tried to move but was paralyzed. Unlike that first Friday night, his eyes were already open, and he looked fearlessly into the two azure flames that were her eyes. Unexpectedly those blazing sapphires were extinguished, leaving twin black holes that were windows into other universes. The stars obscured in the sky were startlingly visible there in her sockets, hundreds of them blinking like demonic pinpricks punched in almond-shaped ovals of inky velvet. Something snapped audibly inside his chest, and he was able to thrust her to arms' length. As he did so, she vomited a huge gout of black blood on him, soaking his sweater. He raised and flexed one knee, then kicked.

He nearly passed out as he struggled clumsily to his feet. The next thing he knew, he was standing erect, staring at her as she wobbled in place a couple of yards away. She moaned softly, blood dripping in a copious stream from one side of her mouth. Tears flowed from her eyes, and he found himself thinking odd, dreamlike thoughts, that those gleaming drops of sorrow were really fractured crystals of broken Time. As she turned toward the sea, he glimpsed what looked like a gaping bullethole in her left temple, the dark orifice oozing a thick, crimson pus.

He was shocked to find himself still thinking of her as beautiful – a lovely lost soul, heartbreaking in her eternal death throes. She slowly drifted toward the waves. The fog and sea finally enveloped her, and he thought he heard her faintly whisper his name in a spellbinding coda of mourning.

His white sweater was hideously stained. Oblivious to the cold, he snatched it off and threw it after her. Shuddering uncontrollably, he slipped into his jacket, then turned and ran as fast as he could. He didn't stop until he was inside the comparative warmth of his apartment – her apartment.

When he got back, it was just after sunrise. He couldn't stop shivering. He felt as if he had been in one of Wilhelm Reich's fabled orgone accumulators. Except instead of a surfeit of sexual energy, all he had accumulated was fear. It seemed to be his motivation for everything. It was why he drank so much and did drugs. It was why he'd married Honey. It was the reason that he'd taken the first gig that fell into his lap – that stupid, half-ass teaching job – instead of beating on doors and braving rejection trying to get into the movie business. He was perpetually afraid that no one could relate to his skewed, downbeat vision of 20th century life. That's why he wanted to obliterate himself, cancel out his feelings while still somehow balancing on the tightrope and not falling off into the everlasting darkness below – a living Death.

All of these painful realizations made him almost want to see Mañon one more time, ask her what it was like to be a junkie, ask her what had driven her to blow a hole in her beautiful head. But he knew instinctively that if he ever did see her again, he would no longer be part of a flesh-and blood universe.

He looked around the living room. There was no way he could continue staying there, waiting for the other shoe to drop, waiting for Mañon and all that she represented to return some night to suck every last bit of redeemable life out of him.

Things with Carol didn't seem quite so bad now – although he couldn't help wondering if deceptive rationalizations like that were what had started Mañon down her own path to self-destruction.

Knowing that any relationship he developed with Carol would be rocky, he still decided to call her. As he dialed her number, he said a silent prayer to a God he didn't really believe in that the apartment in her friend's building on Fairfax was still available.

ASSUMPTA

c. 1982 – 1989 Hollywood & Long Beach, CA
& 2009 Highland Park, CA

Jack hadn't thought of Assumpta in months. Then came the two
dreams. Really just the one dream with her. The other one had been
about his latest ex, Linda. However, both came one after the other on
the same night, conjuring a double whammy of psychic violence. He'd
gone to bed in the wee hours of the morning, no more troubled nor
neurotic than usual; truth be told, probably less so. Then early the next
afternoon when he had awakened, fresh from the Assumpta dream, it
was a different story. The problem was, the dream didn't seem to end.
Of course, it had to have ended. He'd woken, gotten up, brushed his
teeth, dressed, checked his emails and had had something to eat. But
over the course of the next few days, there were fleeting moments
when he still felt inside the dream.

Back in late 1982, when he'd lost hope of Roslyn ever returning his
affections beyond mere friendship, Jack had remained obsessively in
love with her for nearly another two years. It had dragged him through
the next two records he had made with his band, supplying him with
plenty of eloquent, angst-ridden and sometimes monotonous material.

It had tortured him every waking hour while he was at his day job at the independent record label. He had drunk countless liquid lunches – invariably two double Margaritas on the rocks without salt – on workday afternoons at the nearby Mexican restaurant, El Coyote. Virtually every song he had written during that period was about Roslyn in some way, and it was still painful to remember it, so many years later. But in the present, it was a different kind of painful – painfully embarrassing that he could have once been so obsessively in love with someone who was not in love with him and, at most, had had a momentary crush. Painfully embarrassing that he could have been that obsessively in love with *anyone*, when he no longer believed in "being-in-love" that way. It was too self-reflexive, too needy and self-negating.

That kind of love was based on adolescent daydreams, pop songs, old black-and-white movies, 19th century literature – things that all held currency for him. Ultimately his previous experiences of "being in-love," for the most part, manifested themselves as self-deluding fantasies. It was true that at least a couple of his relationships were based on genuine mutual feeling. But even from those starting points in reality, he and even his closest mates had had unrealistic expectations of the other and a surfeit of romantic projections.

He often thought about these things because he was still self-obsessed, but in a more objective, once-removed fashion. When he found himself in lazy, idle thought, he would sometimes try to figure out just where he had gone wrong. Then, over and over again, he would have to tell himself that that was too judgmental, too shortsighted a way to look at the past. He was "changed" now. He didn't feel himself totally incapable of being-in-love anymore, that's not what it was. It was that now being in love meant something different. Something cultivated over a long period of time. Something that was not a one-sided idyll.

He longed for that all-consuming fire he had once felt, not just for Roslyn, but for several other women, including his second wife, Janet, in the late '80s and his ex-girlfriend, Tina, in the early '90s. He had become so rational in the last decade, really out of an urgent sense of self-preservation, it seemed as if there was nothing that could burn him to the ground like that anymore. Jack laughed ruefully at the thought. Most people would define wishing for a scorched-earth love as being willfully self-destructive.

When Linda had left him at the end of May 2009 for someone

else, after eight years of being together, he had not been feeling that same kind of obsessive love. Yet what he had felt at their parting was worse than anything in the wake of the non-consummation of his love affair with Roslyn or at the end of his marriage to his second wife, Janet. First of all, he had never even been close to having another eight-year-long bond with anyone, a relationship where the other person had become even more family to him than his own flesh-and-blood. It was also the only relationship in which he had been completely off liquor and drugs. And then, when the end came seemingly out of nowhere, he realized that all the complacent things he had sworn to himself he would never do again, all the emotionally lazy places he had told himself he would never go, he had in fact been doing and going to, day-in-and-day-out, for the last couple of years of the relationship. And so had Linda, despite what he knew was her determination not to do so. It had been a horrible realization. Like having your head held under for suffocating, end-over-end minutes in a bathtub full of ice water. When you came up, you were gasping for air and desperately searching for even some faint memory of what it was like to live alone with no one at your side as a mate.

Many things constantly sparked these futile memories, but the latest was an email from a girl named Assumpta, someone whom he had not seen nor spoken to in years. Jack tried to figure out when it was she had just completely dropped out of his life – he thought it must have been sometime in 1989. And she wasn't a girl anymore; she was a fifty-four-year-old woman with a ten-year-old daughter.

The email had actually come over a year before, in late October 2008 – a little more than six months before he'd gone through his break-up with Linda. When he had seen it in his inbox, it had dredged up a startling residual sexual charge. He had thought Assumpta would never speak to him again. And then, with her email, there was a chance to make some kind of anemic amends for his large part in their destructive on-again, off-again relationship that had started in 1982. The sexual thrill of getting to call and talk to her on her cell – she'd made the suggestion in the email – after so many years, threw him for a loop. He didn't want to think about her that way anymore. He only wanted to tell her some things that might help, in a feeble way, to ease the memories of hurt and anguish she must have carried. Thinking that way made him feel arrogant and self-important, automatically assuming that he had meant that much to her. But then when he'd talked to her, he realized it had been true.

They had talked for almost an hour. He had taken a break from work, going out to call her from the parking lot of the repertory cinema; the place where, little did he know then, in seven months time would no longer be his workplace.

Assumpta was married, had been since 1991, and had even been on the verge of divorce just before the turn of the millennium when she had unexpectedly found herself pregnant. Having the child had brought her and her husband back together.

Getting in touch with Jack, she had not wanted to re-establish a relationship or even a friendship that could eventually lead to physical contact. She had just been curious to see how he was doing. They didn't articulate it, but it was obvious that they didn't quite trust themselves or each other, despite their devotion to their current mates. Their lust for each other had dragged them through degrading humiliation and frustration before.

Then a couple of months after Linda had left, Jack had emailed Assumpta to let her know what was going on with him, not to try to get together or to suggest anything "improper," but just to be able to talk to her once more, to hear her voice. She had never responded, and he let it drop.

Months had trickled by, and then, at the end of 2009, he was thinking about her again. He realized there had been many other women he had written songs about in his nearly thirty years of playing music, but he had never written about her. He had been in denial for a long time because he was so ashamed of how he had treated her; not that she hadn't had her own part in their unhealthy dynamic. Nevertheless, she had surely shaped his world and his outlook as much as May, Roslyn, Janet, Tina and Linda.

He remembered the first time that they had gone to bed together. He and his best friend, Burton, had gone to a punk rock Halloween concert way out in the Valley somewhere. He recalled that The Cramps had been the appropriate headliners. Burton had taken mushrooms and so had a lot of other people. Jack hadn't, just sticking to a few beers.

Most of the audience was in lame costumes, but not Jack and Burton. Their attitude was "Fuck that!" They just came as themselves. Jack saw Roslyn with her on-again, off-again boyfriend, and they were stoned out of their minds. It was painful to watch them together, but he shrugged it off, the alcohol having put him in a philosophical state of mind.

Assumpta was there with a couple of her girlfriends. Jack had seen her around before at shows, had talked to her, but had never seen her look the way she looked that night. She was decked out in a Marie Antoinette-style dress that made her look like a rare Creole jewel from New Orleans in the late 1700s. Her ample bosom was prominently displayed to full advantage on her small frame, and the dress made her seem as if she'd stepped from a dream in another age. She was slightly drunk, as was he, and the heat in the big room gave her brown Latin skin and faintly Indian/African face an oily sheen of sweat that drew him to her like a magnet.

He couldn't remember what they talked about, but the gist was that they both wanted to leave together. Burton wanted to stay and said he was fine getting home on his own; he knew plenty of people there. Assumpta hadn't been the one to drive, so it didn't matter to her friends.

Driving back to Hollywood, she sat across from him in that dress, barefoot, with one leg bent and splayed on the seat, smiling mischievously. They kept looking at each other with stupid grins on their faces, knowing the fun they were going to have when they got to his place. He couldn't remember the last time he'd gone home with a girl who was every bit as eager to jump in the sack as him and not inhibited about showing it.

When they were finally in his bedroom, the only light from two botanica candles, he felt a rush of overwhelming euphoria. He sat on the edge of the mattress, her leaning back against him, cradling her slightly upturned face into his neck, her eyelids at half mast and her smiling lips apart. Her breath came quick and expectant as he slowly peeled down her low-cut lavender bodice, setting free her golden flesh.

"You are so beautiful." He took in a deep breath, and the spicy fragrance of her long, curly, oily black hair filled his lungs and made his head feel light. They fucked all night long. The next day was Sunday, and they dawdled in bed for hours until they finally got up for him to drive her to her friend's house in Hollywood.

Jack didn't see her again for a few days, but they made a date for the following Friday night. She came over around 9 o'clock. They sat cross-legged on the skanky carpet of his living room in the old, pre-WWII building, playing records at low volume, drinking beers and smoking weed. He loved the raspy, smoky quality of her voice, which contrasted with her little-girl laugh. Finally when he reached down between her legs and under her dress, his fingers came away wet, and they both laughed, getting up to go into the bedroom.

It went on that way for a couple of weeks, her usually coming over late after they went to see bands play, getting into candlelit showers together in the ancient bathroom before falling into bed.

She knew he was hopelessly, stupidly and futilely in love with Roslyn, but she seemed not to care, and she let herself fall in love with him. She bought him a luxurious, vintage scarlet bathrobe with pink stripes. She gave him little Mexican "worry" dolls, microscopic figurines of hard paper folded and twisted into inch-high human replicas, tiny things he was supposed to burden with his anxieties so he would not be weighed down by them himself.

Gradually he became antsy at how attached she was getting to him. He found himself comparing her to Roslyn, an unfair and impossible thing. She couldn't win. Jack knew he had no rational perspective on the situation, and it spooked him. He started to find her wanting in various ways. He knew he couldn't love her the way she wished and needed, so he began to call her less, see her less. He always had excuses: he was busy with his work at the label, busy producing some new band or rehearsing with his own band. Most times the excuses were true. Still, in spite of his inability to love Assumpta, he felt unbridled sexual desire for her. He felt guilty about the lust and about his impossible infatuation with Roslyn. All of this made him drink more, made him look for pretty, new faces and bodies to conquer when he was out prowling at night in bars and clubs.

His pulling back from her made Assumpta's longing for him worse. One afternoon she told him over the phone that she had thought about killing him and herself. She was *that* crazy about him. It was scary, even though he was reasonably sure she would never go through with such a thing. She may have had only a handhold on the roof ledge of rationality, but it was a firm handhold. He stopped calling her, though he'd sometimes see her out at gigs.

One rainy weeknight his band played at the Anti-Club on Melrose Avenue near where the street hit Normandie and the 101 Freeway. It was an off night at the very small club, only half-full, and Assumpta was there. He was polite, but he had plenty to do, so he didn't hang out too much with her. Afterward, once they had played their set and had been paid, he took off to go home alone.

Almost as soon as he arrived, he got a call from Assumpta. Her car, parked about a block north of the club on a residential side street, had a flat tire. She didn't have a jack, and she had no one else in the neighborhood to call. Could he come to help her change it? He thought she was living only a few blocks further east on Manassas, right next to the freeway, but he held his tongue and agreed to help.

When he got there about ten minutes later, the humid spring rain was coming down in sheets. It was too warm to wear a jacket and, by the time he walked from his car to hers only a few cars away, his white long-sleeve shirt and black jeans were soaked. She looked the same, her hair plastered down around her face, and her blouse and dress molded to her body. She was sexy as hell, but he was in a bad mood, angry at her because -- rightly or wrongly -- he couldn't help but think that she'd cooked up the situation so she could spend some time with him. Which probably wasn't true.

He didn't say a word, just went back to his car, opening the trunk to get the jack and the lug wrench. A minute later he was on his knees in front of her flat tire, applying the tool to the wheel. But none of the nuts would loosen, no matter how he strained against them. Unfortunately, he didn't have one of the four-pronged "Maltese Cross" style lug wrenches that gave better leverage, just a single spoke one that came to a tapered, crowbar-style tip on the other end. The rain was pouring down around his face, running in rivulets behind his ears and into his eyes. He shouted in frustration, knowing he was not going to be able to get the wheel off. The lug nuts had been machine-tightened by whoever had last changed the tire. His Triple A road service was expired because he'd forgotten to pay the bill, and she didn't have the service, period. There was no one to call.

"I'm not going to be able to get the tire off. It's screwed on too tight. You're going to have to have someone else help you or get it towed to a gas station."

She frowned. "I hate to ask you, but could I come spend the night at your place?"

He wasn't sure why he was so mad, but he was fit to be tied. He hated to feel as if he was being forced into something.

"I thought you lived just down the street now, on Manassas."

"Not for another few weeks. The other tenants haven't moved out yet. I'm still down in Long Beach. I can't stay with Marion, she's out of town tonight."

He nodded curtly. "Get your stuff."

She eagerly did as she was told and followed behind him as they made their way through the downpour to his '69 Ford Falcon.

Once at his apartment, they stripped and dried themselves off and got into bed.

"We're just going to sleep, Assumpta. It's not fair to you otherwise. You know I'm not in love with you."

She looked at him and nodded.

He hadn't even turned off the bedlamp before she had had her hands on him, fondling him, trying to get him hard and succeeding.

"You know you want to fuck me."

"Of course, I do. But you know it doesn't mean anything."

"I know."

"I'm fucked up. I'm in love with someone else. It doesn't matter that they're not in love with me."

"It doesn't matter to me, either."

Tears cascaded down her cheeks as she climbed on top of him, straddling his lap and forcing him into her. She fucked him wildly from the get-go, as hard as she could. He could feel himself pounding into the front of her womb.

"You're going to hurt yourself."

"I want to."

"Stop it."

But she kept on. He knew he could really be hurting her, and he was of only average size. He finally looked down right before he came and saw traces of blood where their pelvises met.

It had stopped raining by the next morning, and he dropped her off at her car after she had arranged for another friend from Long Beach to meet her. As he pulled away and watched her receding in the rearview, he realized what was really bothering him the most about Assumpta. Seeing her feelings for him and her humiliation was like looking in a mirror; it was exactly the way he felt about Roslyn, though he had not quite gone to such extremes. He felt profound empathy mixed with his desire for Assumpta, but also a push-back, wanting desperately to escape, a determination not to encourage her or to make her feel any worse than she was feeling already.

Three weeks later she invited him to a combination birthday and house-warming party. She and her punk-rock girlfriends had finally moved into the decrepit Manassas mansion.

He didn't promise anything, but he foolishly told her he would try to come after band rehearsal. The early part of the evening with his group crawled by, and he drank a lot. He was halfway smashed when he arrived at her house around 10:30.

She was happy to see him. She looked very cute in her peasant-style dress, and she took him by the hand to lead him upstairs to her bedroom, ignoring the many guests circulating in the foyer between the living room and kitchen. Her bedroom was cozy, lit by candlelight and smelling of marijuana. They were both in different head spaces, Assumpta imagining that maybe he'd softened towards her since he'd shown up at the party, and Jack nervously picking up the mood of her hopeless affection. It brought out the mean drunk in him, something that surfaced rarely, no matter how much liquor he'd downed.

Jack couldn't remember exactly what they said to each other, but it was contentious. She wanted him to stay overnight as a birthday present, and he was unwilling.

Looking back on that night, he was ashamed, and he couldn't understand why he had taken his abrasive behavior to such lengths. Of course, he was conflicted. Remembering it all, he realized that a lot of the anger he was feeling wasn't just at Assumpta but at himself for having such contrary impulses. Mad at himself for being so attracted to her but convinced it couldn't work between them as a real, healthy relationship, knowing that he would hurt her even more deeply if he continued to see her. It had been a mistake to come to the party, at least with that antagonistic attitude. They verbally sparred back and forth for a few minutes before Marion, one of Assumpta's housemates, succeeded in getting her to open the door and to come downstairs to entertain her guests.

Assumpta was understandably annoyed with his stubborn demeanor and mixed signals, wondering why he had even bothered to come to the party at all.

He slowly followed her out onto the landing, but paused as she descended. He sat down on the top step of the stairs to survey the party below.

Loretta, an attractive Mexican girl he knew from shows but had never dated, started climbing up towards him, a drunken smile on her face. One of the reasons he had never asked her out was that he had never seen her sober. Now she had a beer in each hand and gave one to him as she slumped down beside him. They made small talk, and she flirted with him shamelessly, despite Assumpta being one of her friends. He returned her advances, perversely attracted to her debauched behavior, and they abruptly started making out with each other, tongues stuck down each others' throats. When he looked back down after he and Loretta had unlocked lips, Assumpta was standing at the foot of the steps, glaring at them, wounded deeply. There were angry tears in her eyes. In a cruel mood, Jack leaned over and kissed Loretta again. The next time he looked down, Assumpta had disappeared, probably into the kitchen, and he felt a hot flush of shame and guilt reddening his drunken face. He pushed Loretta away, mumbled "good night" and stumbled awkwardly down the stairs, then out of the house to his car.

Jack didn't talk to or see Assumpta for almost six months. Then one night he ran into her at a club. He had started seeing a girl much younger, a college student named Briana, but their relationship hadn't evolved into commitment yet, and she wasn't along that night. Jack thought he had apologized to Assumpta for his cruel behavior at her party, but he wasn't positive. In any case, Assumpta told him she had moved back to Long Beach, living alone in her own apartment. He got her new number but didn't end up calling her for several weeks, feeling guilty at his overpowering desire for her.

He would go through twisted dialogues with himself, trying to decide if it was okay or not to go down to see her, knowing she wanted to jump into bed with him just as much, that they both sparked a sexual bonfire in each other that neither of them had ever experienced with anyone else. The only difference was she was in love with him; he was not in love with her and was not sure if he ever could be. He was fucked up by too much emotional insecurity from his teenage years and, most of all, his residual infatuation with Roslyn.

One Thursday night he buckled, calling her late and asking if he could come down to visit. A few minutes later he was on the Long Beach Freeway south.

It was good seeing her again. They only talked a few minutes before they shed their clothes and were fucking each others' brains out on a lounge sofa that resembled a psychiatrist's emaciated couch. She was sad when he told her that he couldn't spend the night, that he had to get up to be at work by 9, and he left around 2 AM.

Once again Jack was torn with inner conflict, a split right down the middle about seeing her. What they felt for each other was like an addiction, except there were feelings of overwhelming tenderness on Assumpta's part...of being in love. He felt that tenderness, too, and affection – there was no question of that – but most of all, the irresistible lust. What he did not feel was the "being in love" or any impulse to be tied to her as a mate. He just felt in the very pit of his stomach that it wouldn't work. Much later, when it was too late, he wasn't so sure. Nevertheless, it was what it was and now irrevocably in the past.

It was right on the verge of summer, with mostly warm days and nights, and he ended up going to see her two Saturday afternoons in a row, making it a point to leave in the early evening.

The first time he went down during daylight was also the first time he got to clearly see what her building looked like: a two story 1930s structure that was seemingly divided up into six fairly large single apartments. Assumpta was on the second floor in the front. The big main room with a high ceiling had large windows on two sides, with an oblong kitchen and bathroom branching off of it. The old-fashioned double bed folded down out of the wall. She had a dining "picnic" table against one of the windows facing west and an ancient desk and the "psychiatrist's couch" against the windows facing south.

That first Saturday they immediately went to bed, then got up and went down to the beach before it got dark. The fog was starting to roll in. She took him to an old block of WWII army bunkers on a partially fenced-in bluff facing the ocean. The concrete pillboxes had been look-out posts during the early 1940s, scanning the horizon for Japanese invaders, but had been deserted since the mid-1950s. Now they were a refuge for disaffected teens looking for a discreet place to get loaded or laid without being disturbed. They strolled around the ghostly battlements and didn't say much. He took her out to a local seafood restaurant before returning to Hollywood, and they were the only customers in the joint.

The following weekend was sunny and hot, though a strong breeze was coming in off the water. They drove to a deserted stretch of beach. In the intervening months he'd gotten rid of his dying '69 Falcon and purchased a used 1980 Dodge cargo van, a good vehicle to drive if you were in a band. They left the van in a cliff-top parking lot, then walked down a sloping, overgrown path. They laid out a huge beach towel, flopped horizontal on it and talked for a while; about what, he could not remember. Eventually their yen for each other got the better of them. She knelt before him, her back to the sea, another towel wrapped around her shoulders. She stretched it out along the length of her arms. There was what looked like a middle-aged woman and a very young child about 200 yards further down the shore – the only other humans out there. Assumpta pulled the towel tight, shielding her torso from view as a token minimum of modesty, and Jack slid down her tube top. He released her sweat-beaded breasts and cupped them in both of his hands, bending forward to lick and suck her stiffening nipples. She stared at him with a kind of intoxicated rapture. They both wanted to fuck, and there was no way to do it out in the open unless they wanted to risk being interrupted or, worse, arrested.

She pulled her top back into place, and they picked up the

towels and ascended along the path to the cliff-top. Both of them simultaneously got the same idea, glancing at each other by way of acknowledgement, and he led her ten or twelve yards into the dry brush of the sand dune skirting the trail. They found shelter amongst a clump of desiccated reeds, bushes and ice plant, spread the towel and quickly peeled off their clothes, coupling excitedly. Afterwards they lay there for only a few minutes. The wind was picking up, and it wasn't exactly comfortable, stiff branches poking them in the ass if they happened to move too far in the wrong direction.

When they returned to her apartment, they took a bath together, which was pleasant and relaxing. In some ways, he felt that that afternoon was the closest he had ever come with Assumpta to accepting the idea that maybe they could work out as a couple. She fixed him some huevos rancheros after they got out, and they sat at the dining picnic table, eating and drinking beers. Assumpta playfully stretched across one leg beneath the tabletop, planting her foot firmly against his cock, kneading it until he was hard. They stripped again and gravitated to the bed, smiling, going down on each other and fucking.

Once they had both come, they lay there talking and, for the first time, she told him how she sometimes had sex with a couple of her girlfriends. There was one girl in particular who lived in Santa Monica, who apparently was Assumpta's virtual *doppleganger*. Assumpta said, "It's amazing, almost like making love to yourself." Jack was entranced and thrilled by the idea, longing to meet this girl, really to get them both together for a torrid threesome. Now, he couldn't remember if he had ever suggested it to Assumpta. Somehow he thought not. If he remembered correctly, the look-alike girl was a lesbian who was not fond of going to bed with men. And Jack was already guilty about his motives for seeing Assumpta in the first place.

That guilt started to creep into his bones as the sun went down around 7:30, and he got the yen to leave. The feelings that he had had only a few hours earlier, that maybe he should give it a try with her, were dashed as he remembered he had a date with Briana at his Hollywood apartment later in the evening.

Assumpta was unhappy that he was leaving so early and that he had repeatedly refused to stay overnight with her. For him, it wasn't so much that he didn't want to; he just knew what it would mean to her, and he felt that he would be digging the hole deeper for the both of them.

Assumpta had not continued to pursue him as ardently. If she called and left a message on his answering machine, and he didn't call back, she did not try again. He knew through the tangled quagmire of mutual friends she was doing okay. They didn't speak again for at least six months. By then Jack's relationship with Briana had imploded under the strain of his own infidelities and insecurity and Briana's desire to be with someone closer to her own age.

It was Thanksgiving, and Jack made the pilgrimage down to Santa Monica to the home of Burton's mother-in-law, a woman who had, in many ways, been like a second mother to him. They always put together two huge dining-room tables in the living room for holiday dinners, and there would usually be anywhere from twelve to twenty guests. Jack had brought a date to their previous two Thanksgivings, but not this year.

He had a great time, but he was lonely beneath his smiling exterior. He had just broken up his band because relations inside the group had become too contentious, plus the regular onslaught of eardrum-shattering music week after week had taken a toll on his alcoholic nerves. In retrospect, it was probably not the best idea to take mushrooms along with Burton and a couple of other fun-loving guests. When he came onto them quickly, in about half an hour, he not only grew nauseous but increasingly paranoid. Whenever Burton had the least inkling that Jack had smoked too much pot or was stoned on psychedelics, he enjoyed good-naturedly tormenting him. That evening was no exception. At last, no longer being able to stand the constant eruptions of edgy laughter, Jack bowed out, claiming illness. Later, he couldn't figure out how he had driven home to Hollywood from Santa Monica. Thankfully there had been little traffic.

It was only ten o'clock when he got to his apartment, and all he could do was creep into bed, a total wreck. The safety of the bedcovers offered little comfort. He felt the overwhelming urge to call someone. For some unfathomable reason, he called the one person at the time whom he trusted and who he knew – besides his family – really loved him.

Unbelievably, Assumpta was home alone and glad to hear from him. He could not remember much about their conversation, although he knew it was more wide-ranging than usual and – filtered through a prism of psilocybin – of "cosmic" significance. That night he exposed his inner self to Assumpta more than he ever had before and, though he didn't express any kind of suggestion of a relationship, he nevertheless retained the feeling that they were closer than ever. Whether it was his incipient alcoholism or just his usual neurotic self-obsession, by the next morning any transcendental sense of bonding with her had largely dissipated.

A few Saturday afternoons later, after waking up late, he'd found himself still in bed and on the phone with her again, but this time engaged in filthy talk aimed at prodding them both to orgasm. It excited him tremendously. Strangely enough, though he seemed on a trajectory to start seeing her again, he didn't. For the remaining few weeks of the year, his romantic pursuits were diffuse and half-hearted.

In January, Jack and his boss flew back East to check out a couple of Boston bands as prospective signees for their label. Two months later, he was suddenly out of his A&R job, due to their major label distributor postponing their yearly cash infusion. He was also slowly falling in love with Janet, the singer who he would soon partner with in his new band and eventually make his second wife.

He ran into Assumpta a few times in the ensuing four years. Astonishingly enough, he didn't pursue her behind his wife's back. He was determined to be faithful in the relationship, despite his occasionally roving eye. However, the marriage had other problems, not the least of which was Jack and Janet's burgeoning heroin addiction. When Janet got clean in the summer of 1987, and Jack couldn't, no matter how hard he tried, the marriage ended, followed by their band. From then on, all bets were off, and he sunk into the depths.

He remembered that sometime in late 1988, he'd had the audacity to call Assumpta to borrow $50. Unlike others to whom he owed money, he promptly repaid her. In 1989, he re-established contact with her again and went to visit her in her new Echo Park digs, a location much closer than Long Beach, being only about five minutes from his Highland Park home.

He lay on the floor with her in the large single apartment. She had no furniture except a futon, a TV and a bookcase. A kitchenette was part of the main room, with a separate bathroom. She was taking a lot of photos at the time, and a large closet doubled as her dark room.

Sprawled there on the floor on that Sunday afternoon, he filled her in on his break-up with Janet and his pathetic drug-addict existence. They talked for at least two hours. She told him that, for nearly six months, she had been down in Nicaragua, out in the field with the Sandanistas, fighting the American-backed contra mercenaries and being the lover of a Sandanista officer. His esteem grew for her immeasurably. He had no doubt she was telling the truth, with a minimum of embroidery.

She was gently affectionate toward him and soon they were kissing and fondling each other. Jack gradually worked his hand down her jeans, immediately feeling how wet she was, and he suggested they take off their clothes. That's when she put her foot down, telling him she really wanted to have sex but on condition he spend the night and sleep with her. He yearned to do just that and was torn, knowing he needed to leave soon to go downtown to cop. He explained the situation to her, how he was out of dope and how he'd get sick if he didn't make the pilgrimage down to 9th and Hill. What he didn't tell her was that he hoped he'd still be in the mood to see her later.

Inexplicably, he didn't try to call her for several months. Acute, near-suicidal depression about being a drug addict and about the failure of his marriage to Janet kept his mind self-centered and in isolation mode.

He knew Assumpta's birthday was coming up soon. He had actually already bought her a present, a book of photographs of a rural, impoverished Navajo village in New Mexico, something he knew she would like. It had already been wrapped up in the trunk of his car for several months.

Unbeknownst to Jack, he was in for a rude surprise. When her number had just kept ringing and ringing, never picking up, never even going to message, he had driven over to her place on a Sunday night. He knocked repeatedly on her door, with no response. Knowing she had no curtain on her immense picture window that overlooked Echo Park, he circled around her ground floor apartment that was perched precariously on the hillside. He hung onto a wooden railing that jutted out from the southwestern corner of the building and peered into the fully-lit-up place. He was astonished to see her apartment empty, the bright, newly painted white walls reflecting painfully into his pinned eyes.

As the weeks crawled by, he called numbers of several of her friends. Most of the numbers were no good anymore, and the couple that were, the persons answering either couldn't or wouldn't give him any lead on where she had gone.

In the mid-1990s, Jack finally kicked every chemical on which he'd grown dependent, and stayed sober. At about six months, he was out at a nightclub in Atwater, alone, virtually friendless and trying to overcome his overwhelming shyness without the crutch of liquor and dope. He ran into 6'5" Hamish, a Scottish native who'd lived for well over a decade in Southern California and who was close friends with Assumpta. Jack asked Hamish if he'd talked to her recently and, if so, how she was. Hamish unexpectedly went off on him, haranguing him for his "abuse" of Assumpta's affections. He told Jack in no uncertain terms that he'd fucked her up and took advantage of her. Jack meekly nodded, putting up no argument, then walked away as Hamish turned his back.

Two years later, outside the Roxy on Sunset in West Hollywood, a young couple had approached him. They were working on a history of Chicano punk-rock fans and musicians in the 1980s Los Angeles scene, and they mentioned that they interviewed Assumpta in her new hometown of Eureka. Jack asked them to mention to Assumpta that he was asking after her the next time they talked. He saw the couple again about a month later, and they sheepishly explained that she didn't want to talk to him and asked for him not to try to get in touch.

Even though he'd gotten to speak to Assumpta on the phone in late 2008, the break-up with Linda in May of 2009 brought it all back, along with so many of his other relationship failures. Being in touch with her again after so many years: Assumpta's email, then their talking on the phone. And then, when he'd tried to contact her to tell her about the break-up, only silence as a response. At least he'd gotten in some small way to make amends.

     He tried to make memories of her evaporate, just as he had done with so many other women, as he was trying to do now with Linda. And he hadn't thought about her again until very late 2009 when he had had the dreams.

The first dream was about Linda. They were living in a rundown apartment that seemed to be part of an ancient, central California motel, ambiguously located somewhere between Fresno and Bakersfield. It was an awful place where the dominant colors were brown, beige and a dirty yellow. It was dreary, and they both seemed to be unemployed, active alcoholics. They had ratty carpets and ratty furniture (and not much of it). The TV was an old black-and-white model. Most of the time it seemed to be the sole illumination in the living room since they

kept the heavy drapery drawn to blot out the glare of the merciless sun.
The sunlight tried to penetrate around the closed, dusty venetian blinds
in the bedroom and kitchen but had little luck. Then Jack realized that
Linda did have a job, because she constantly took off with a succession
of other truck drivers in an endless, roaring fleet of dirty semis. The
trucks were like growling beasts as they came and went amongst the
awful boxlike bungalows that made up their apartment court.

When Jack was by himself, he watched nothing but old
movies on television. A lot of them were noirish melodramas and crime
films. What astonished him was that he recognized Linda as the star of
several of these chiaroscuro black-and-white programmers. He vividly
remembered one scene where she was dressed in black, her blonde
hair in a bun, her lips pursed as she stared at her off-screen leading
man through cat's-eye glasses. One image was burned into his brain:
the moon and stars were artfully reflected in the lenses. In some of the
movies, she looked a bit like Claire Trevor. But it was definitely Linda;
her name was in the credits. Jack knew that she had been in a sci-fi,
end-of-the-world exploitationer in 1980, something dreadful called *The
Final Apocalypse*, a vanity project of the director. She had even done
a nude pictorial in *Nugget*, a now defunct men's magazine, to help
promote the film. But the movie had barely gotten released, showing
up only on a rare edition laser disc in the early 1990s. These noir films,
though…how could she have been in them? She hadn't even been born
yet when most of them were made. When she came back from her latest
run to Sacramento – or wherever they drove their metal monsters – she
did not want to hear about these strange movies.

The dream ended abruptly, and he woke up in a cold sweat. Almost
immediately he fell back asleep, and the Assumpta dream began. In the
dream, Assumpta was taller and looked more Spanish aristocrat than
Mexican punk rebel. And now she really did resemble her namesake,
Assumpta Serna, the film actress who had been in Almodovar's
Matador, Grau's *Hunting Ground* and Memberg's *I, The Worst of All*.

Jack met up with her for lunch in some strange nether region, a
limbo seemingly located at the nexus of Santa Monica, Brentwood and
Malibu. Maybe it was the Getty Center, because the architecture
resembled an old upscale neighborhood in a southern Italian city.

Assumpta's hair was up, and she was wearing a string of pearls
around her neck and a black, sleeveless sheath dress. Jack had been
sitting waiting for her on the terrace of an outdoor café – a café that
reminded him of the time he'd been to a beautiful, decaying Venice

with his first wife, Honey, thirty-four years earlier. Assumpta pulled away the heavy table in front of him with a casual exhibition of strength and plopped down to sit in his lap, languidly encircling his neck with her slinky brown arms. Her eyes were at half-mast as she nuzzled his right ear, then whispered, "God, Jack, I love you so fucking much." He turned his head and pressed his lips against hers.

"The trouble is, Jack, I have to go back to the Council meeting. They can't finish without me, and the whole damn thing is going way, way over schedule."

Jack grimaced, smiled and nodded. She kissed him on the forehead and pointed to the building where she would be, then got up and trotted away with a sexy gait.

The next hour seemed like endless torment. There in the dream, he was drinking booze again, sipping a brandy with his espresso. Finally his patience broke, and he could no longer bear waiting. He walked briskly over to the building where the Council meeting – whatever that was – was being held and entered between the huge marble columns.

There was an officious, bald-headed bureaucrat sitting at a small table in the foyer beneath a vaulted ceiling that dwarfed them both. The perturbed flunky scribbled away in a large ledger book and refused to look at him, no matter how many times Jack hemmed and hawed and cleared his throat. When Jack had had enough, he sidestepped the reception desk, and the man suddenly materialized in front of him, barring his way.

"I'm sorry, sir. The Council is in session. You cannot enter."

He gave the man Assumpta's name, and things dramatically changed. The man became a fawning sycophant, apologizing for his insensitivity. How could he possibly have not recognized Assumpta's husband? Why, the whole city knew them from their pictures on the society pages. Jack wasn't sure what the guy was talking about. It was the first he'd ever heard that Assumpta's co-workers thought they were married, and he knew they'd never had their pictures published in the newspapers.

He didn't give the man a second thought and bypassed him like the insect he was, barging into a huge circular chamber with Renaissance-era paintings on every recessed panel of its colossal curved wall. The loud, heated conversation within came to a dead halt as he suddenly appeared in the middle of the floor. He was chagrined to inadvertently be thrust into the center of everyone's attention. He did a slow 360-degree turn, surveying the various upper-class men and women who were gawking at him from their raised, amphitheatre-style seats. A handsome, gray-haired woman with glasses shared the spotlight in the cleared circle of marble floor where he stood. She smiled at him.

"Can I help you, my good man?" Her voice echoed in the auditorium.

Jack apologized for his intrusion, he didn't mean to interrupt, but he was growing anxious and was looking for his girlfriend who was participating in their meeting. He couldn't spot her anywhere in the throng of thirty or so people. He mentioned Assumpta's name.

The gray-haired lady's smile grew wider. "Why, she left only a few minutes ago. I'm surprised you didn't pass her. She was on her way back to the screening. You know, of course, she is on the jury?"

It had slipped his mind that she was on the jury of the film festival. They really were in Italy. Was he losing his mind? He had completely forgotten that that was why they had made the trip in the first place. He felt very foolish and knew his face must have flushed a bright crimson. He excused himself. The august body of bureaucrats resumed arguing about money allocated to the arts in their city, specifically the film festival, even before he walked out of the Council chamber. As he came into the foyer, he pushed aside the protesting bald clerk and rushed out of the building.

The cinema was across the square in another ancient palazzo and, before he knew it, he was in the lobby presenting the badge he suddenly remembered that he had in his suit pocket. He asked about Assumpta, and the usherette said that she believed the woman he was looking for had gone in a mere minute or two before.

Jack nudged aside the black sable curtain that separated him from the darkened interior auditorium of the theatre, and he was immediately overwhelmed by the images onscreen. He was shocked to see his and Assumpta's own story unfolding up there in the flickering black-and-white frames. Except the two actors looked nothing remotely like them. The longer he watched, the more familiar the performers became, until he finally recognized a middle-aged John Wayne playing him, Jack, and a middle-aged Simone Signoret playing her, Assumpta. It was a gut punch as it was the most egregious miscasting he had ever seen in a film. His feelings were kind of conflicted, ambivalent about Wayne, but he loved Signoret. That wasn't it – it had nothing to do with their competence or acting skills. They were just totally wrong for the parts. The movie appeared to have been made in the late 1950s, when he and Assumpta had been very young children and, to state the obvious, were years from even meeting each other. The very idea that it was their story being told was absurd, nonsensical. Yet, that's what it was.

Wayne and Signoret embraced and kissed in medium shot on the screen, while, in the late afternoon background behind the pair, a poor neighborhood in Rome went about its business. Jack was struck by the style of the film and recognized the director as Rossellini. It looked so much like those very personal films the director had made in the 1950s with his then-spouse, Ingrid Bergman: *Stromboli, Europa 51, Journey to Italy,* and *Fear.* The bizarre nature of the movie, the fact that he was convinced without a shadow of a doubt that it was the story of his and Assumpta's tumultuous relationship, their long, complicated, often anguished, always white-hot love affair, made him feel as if he was going off his rocker.

Jack turned away from the screen, losing hope of ever finding Assumpta in what, for him, had now become a humiliating darkness where unknown critics and pretentious intellectuals smirked and occasionally laughed, at the white heat of their romance.

He tried to find his way out of the screening, but when he reached the other side of the sable draperies, he found himself not in the lobby, but still in the darkened theatre, watching an endless loop of Wayne and Signoret as Jack and Assumpta going through torrid gyrations in the high contrast black-and-white footage. He tried again to go back the way he had come, but still, on either side of the furry curtain, the same movie was playing.

He awoke in a cold sweat.

And it only took him a few minutes to realize that he was, in fact, not really awake; he had only dreamt that he was awake. He was still slumbering, and he fruitlessly fought for a way out of the dream, out of that screening.

And now he remembered in the present – when he was seemingly really awake – that in his sleep he had given up hope and had resigned himself to the endless loop.

SAN FRANCISCO NIGHT

c. 2010, San Francisco, CA

Jack realized when he was on the plane to San Francisco that there was a hole in his shirt next to the left breast pocket, and he wondered why he hadn't remembered; he'd noticed the hole two weeks before, the last time he wore it. Once he got to the hotel where he stayed for two days every week, he saw that the hole was slowly growing bigger. It was the only shirt he had with him, and he needed to do something about it right away. He had to teach classes the next afternoon and couldn't risk the shirt getting worse. Luckily, the front-desk clerk had some safety pins, so he was able to achieve a makeshift repair as he headed out the hotel entrance for his walk to North Beach.

He made the same trek every Sunday night, heading up from Union Square through Chinatown and, most of the time, eating at a Japanese restaurant on Grant and Pine. Then he'd continue on to the vicinity of Broadway and Columbus. Jack tried to do the walk every week. He felt he just wasn't getting the cardio exercise he needed, and the long jaunt to and from the North Beach neighborhood went a long ways toward making him feel better about keeping up his health.

As he walked, the tear in the shirt came back to haunt him. He started obsessing over the fact that he was in his mid-fifties and was still basically wearing his clothes until they fell apart. The linings in his jackets and coats would slowly rip to shreds, and he'd nevertheless be wearing them two years later. It was the same with his shirts and blue jeans and black jeans, his cowboy boots – his standard issue look; wear whatever it was until it fell to pieces around him. He had been doing it for at least the last thirty-some-odd years, ages before he got sober in the mid-1990s. What made him think anything could possibly change his habits now?

The obsessive, self-deprecating thoughts inevitably led him to think about various women he had known or with whom he had been with in relationships.

Nearly a year before, Linda – someone he'd been with for nearly eight years, someone whom he naively thought he was going to be with for the rest of his life – left him for another man. He was no longer thinking about her, as he had been last summer, in an anguished, traumatized way. Now his thoughts were colored by a resigned sadness and recognition of the overpowering inevitability of Fate. But where had it all come from? How much of it was his fault, her leaving? He knew he didn't have a balanced perspective, because one day he would feel it was totally down to him, his complacency in the last couple of years of their extended relationship; the next day, he would be arguing with himself that it was largely Linda's fault, that he would never ever have done anything like that to her, whatever his feelings might have been for someone else. Loyalty, friendship and surrogate family status were too important – above all else. They had grown a little apart, but they had still seen each other every day – after all, they lived together – and he had made sure that he was always there for her whenever she had needed him, whether it was an emotional, financial or health crisis. It had been true that some of the romance, which had never been white-hot, had gone out of their relationship. But he had still told her almost every day that she had the most beautiful smile and prettiest eyes in the world. There had been an inner glow that always seemed to be coming from her, no matter what – cooking, washing the dishes, grading her online classes or working barefoot in the garden. That beauty was all he had seen, despite her faults and despite his sometimes agonizing one-off desire for the passing girl he'd meet at work or at a party. He had known that he would never act on those feelings, because he was devoted to her. The longer he had known her, the more he had loved her, even though it hadn't been that Technicolor fairy-tale romance-love, that giddy, drunken "in-love-ness" that had fucked him up so many times when he was younger. And he had been glad that he had finally felt that, what for him, was a more "mature" love.

He had still had faults that got on her nerves. He would often mumble when he talked if he was exhausted (which was about half the time) and, in those last couple of years, he would complain about his job when he got home.

He had been working at the repertory cinema for a little over ten years and, for at least eight of those years, he had felt it was a virtually perfect job for him, tapping into his encyclopedic knowledge of movies. But he had grown unhappy at the dwindling audiences, at his own inability to compromise to the extent that "reality" demanded. He had been unhappy that they had had to start playing all the mainstream, easy-to-see, mega-hit crap that brought people in, all the homogenized Spielberg-Lucas thrill machines that mediocre people with mediocre tastes never seemed to tire of, no matter how many dozens of times they had seen the pictures already. He hated the shitty teen movies from the 1980s starring the various lame, bourgeois brat packs, films in name only, packaged "entertainments" calculated to push people's emotional buttons, that made him want to retch; and preview screenings to new films which – 80% of the time – were pieces of shit. He hadn't enjoyed introducing the movies anymore, even films he loved; hadn't enjoyed doing the Q & A discussions, even when the filmmakers had been intelligent and simpatico with his tastes and worldview. He had been frustrated and in a rut, and he had not known how to dig himself out. Linda had gotten tired of hearing about it, had run into the guy from her past by accident (really from her brother's past), had fallen "in-love" and then…BOOM…she had gone, moved out.

In the aftermath, Jack had stumbled through his work, a dazed, numbed automaton on the brink of self-destruction. He hadn't started drinking or using again, but he had immediately gone back to AA meetings to get grounded and regain his equilibrium. It had taken a few weeks to kick in. Then, a month after Linda had left, he had gotten put on unpaid leave from his main job at the repertory cinema until he could "get his head together." It had turned out to be a blessing in disguise. By the end of August, he had realized he didn't want to go back. He knew it would have driven him nuts. So, he had collected unemployment.

He had his job on the side in September, the one class he got

flown up to in San Francisco to teach, and he believed, with some
nose-to-the-grindstone proposal-writing, he could get the university
to expand his work to three or four classes over the two days he was
already there every week. Which is what he had done. Ironically, Linda
had been teaching part-time at the same school for years and had been
the one to put him in touch with the film and TV department in the first
place.

It had been raining a bit this trip, and he had an umbrella with him,
but he had taken the Stockton tunnel because it was dryer and a nearly
three block long stretch uninterrupted by traffic lights. Suddenly he
stopped on his walk as he came back out under the drizzling sky.

     Plastered on the end of the tunnel wall was a poster for the
new album by Sanford Grumacher, the only son of the legendary folk
rock icon O'Herlihy Grumacher – whom Jack loved. But junior was a
mediocre talent, at best. The insipid, melancholic smile on the young
man's face in the black-and-white photo seemed patently phony.

     It irked Jack, and he almost vomited when he saw the
producer's name: Porterhouse Barrett, a charlatan huckster if ever there
was one. Proficient musician, expert technician, yes, but the soulless
music industry equivalent of Lomotil, something the big labels gave
their younger stars or breaking-down older talents to restrain them and
focus them away from the diarrhea of self-indulgence.

     Bitter thoughts.

     He had played music for many years himself and had been
fucked – partly by his lofty expectations, partly by the venality of the
homogenized music business and partly by his own self-pitying vices,
the twin demons of heroin and alcohol.

     He continued walking.

     The thought of music industry Lomotil made him laugh, and he
thought of his new girlfriend, Diana, whom he knew would find it
funny, too. She was a petite, redheaded spitfire, about ten years
younger, with a razor-sharp wit and a stinging sense of outrage about
nearly everything. She was from a hardscrabble working-class New
England town and had grown up with plenty of hard knocks. She had
hauled herself up by the bootstraps, and she had an unpretentious
brilliance that was rare. Cute, sexy, funny, and she was crazy about
him. What more could he ask? But there was something about anybody
loving him that made him nervous. He loved her, too, but he wasn't
sure he trusted or even knew what being "in-love" meant anymore. It
wasn't Diana's fault. It wasn't Linda's fault. It was really due to the

sum total of his experiences since he had hit puberty.

In 1999, he had wondered if he was still capable of that intensity of feeling about women – both euphoric and hellish – that he'd gone through in the 1970s and 1980s. Before 2001, when he'd gotten together with Linda, he hadn't had a real steady girlfriend – at least one who had lasted more than a couple of months – since the early 1990s. He had often felt numb inside, as much as he had wished the opposite. Was it because he no longer stoked the fire with booze?

It had taken him well into the second year of being with Linda to feel in love with her, and even then he wasn't sure what being 'in-love" was. Surely not the delirious, delusionary cinematic fantasies in which he had cast himself when he was in his twenties and thirties. Certainly not the kind of "in-love" obsession he had written about in scores and scores of songs on at least two dozen record albums since the early 1980s.

He finally realized that he had been standing at the end of the tunnel, lost in redundant thought, for several minutes. He didn't re-open the umbrella because it had pretty much stopped raining. He kept plodding down Stockton in the dripping night, turning right, downhill on Clay Street, then doubling back along Waverly Place, an almost alley-like street.

Noxious smells always wafted up from the basement levels of the ancient buildings. Sometimes he smelled rotten vegetables or dead fish, but sometimes – like tonight – he imagined he sensed the odor of Death, decaying meat from unknown, taboo sources. He often daydreamed that some of these backwater, hole-in-the-wall Chinese restaurants were surreptitiously serving up human flesh to unsuspecting tourists.

At last, Jack arrived at the Japanese café.

Waiting for his food, he remembered being a lot younger, way back in 1971 when he had turned 18 and had come to San Francisco for the first time. The Summer of Love had been long over. Speed, heroin, bad acid and teen runaways turning tricks had been the order of the day. But there had still been pockets of "sanity" – or what had passed for sanity compared to the rampant madness. There had been whole blocks that had been relatively tranquil, that had still preserved the most comforting elements of counterculture idealism. Record stores, bookstores, coffee houses, crash pads, restaurants and bars that had still been flush with lingering incense and a kind of hallucinatory magic.

Berkeley across the bay had been like that, too; at least Telegraph Avenue. Then again, maybe it had been dissipating back then, and he just hadn't noticed because he hadn't been living up there, and he had nothing with which to compare it.

Anyway, that vibe, that feeling of gentle euphoria even when you weren't tripping was now gone…long gone.

Still, he preferred San Francisco to Los Angeles. Hollywood, especially, had become a Chamber of Commerce theme park catering to trailer trash. The nickel-and-dime gouging of small businesses and non-profits in any and all ways was the golden rule; raping the hick citizen consumer, the unwritten by-law.

Rents were sky-high in San Francisco, and there was rampant gentrification. But strict laws reining in developers had at least kept the look of the city somewhat intact.

Fuck it.

When he was finished eating, he looked at his watch and saw that it was only 9 o'clock, plenty of time to make it to City Lights, a bookstore he had loved since he was a teenager and had first discovered in 1971. There were fewer and fewer places like it, even in San Francisco.

Once inside the store, an hour passed like a few minutes.

He picked up the last book of the "Red Riding Quartet" by David Peace, the only one he hadn't read, and a collection of love poetry by surrealist Paul Eluard. He leafed through a huge, 700-page biography of Patricia Highsmith he dearly coveted. It cost upwards of $40, but that wasn't what stopped him from getting it. He was traveling light on his two-and-a-half days teaching sojourn every week, and he just didn't have the space for the massive volume in his backpack. Besides, he was sure he could get it on Amazon for at least half the price.

After he had paid for the books, he trudged back into the drizzling night of shiny wet streets. Few people were out, and it was getting colder. He walked up Columbus, stopped at a little coffee house to get a decaf latte to go, then started the return walk to the hotel, down Stockton. He could have caught a bus, but he was paranoid that he needed the exercise. If it really started pouring, he could catch one along the way. The buses weren't like down in Los Angeles, where it was hours between stops; up in San Francisco they ran every ten minutes or so, and it was a prime route with several lines running. Three blocks further, he changed his mind. The puddles of water on the sidewalk were seeping through his worn-out, oxblood leather boots, freezing his already aching feet. He'd had enough and paused at the next stop to sit down and wait.

Once he was seated, he saw that he was right across the street from the Bank of America where he had had trouble with the rude Chinese guy who steam-cleaned out front with a pressure hose early on Sunday evenings. You'd be walking along on the sidewalk, and the guy would see you coming but would refuse to turn off his hose. Two weeks in a row he had made Jack walk all the way out into the street to avoid getting sprayed. The second time, Jack had yelled, "Fuck you! People are walking here!" and he had immediately flashed on Ratso Rizzo in *Midnight Cowboy.*

Of course, the guy was already gone. But there were two other people out in front of the bank's ATMs, an area better lit than the rest of the block. Jack recognized the elderly Chinese street musician who usually played his stringed instrument with a bow – a Banhu, Jack thought it was called – on Grant, next to the dilapidated church at California Street. What was he doing here now? Here where there were only a couple of people strolling by every few minutes? Jack had heard enough of the instrument in-person, elsewhere in Chinatown, and as background score of many Hong Kong films. The guy was pretty uneven in his playing – mediocre at best – even on a good night. When he was off, he was really off, playing the thing out of tune so it sounded like a cross between a yowling cat and fingernails across a blackboard. This was one of those nights.

There was a young teenage boy, also Chinese, in the corner against the ATMs, about ten feet from the musician, smoking crack. When the boy noticed Jack waiting for the bus, he just kept on defiantly huffing the rock. Suddenly he erupted in mid-puff, throwing his crack pipe at the old man, yelling, first in Chinese, then in English, "Shut the fuck up, old man! You suck! Your playing is shit!" But the old man kept on. Jack realized there was a small crowd accumulating around him waiting for the bus, and they were all staring at the boy.

It had turned from drizzling showers to real rain again, and people were foregoing their walking. Everyone casually watched the unfolding drama between the young crackhead and the old musician.

The kid got worse. He would come right up to the old man, shout into one of his ears, then the other, and the old man would act as if he didn't notice. The kid snatched the man's hat and threw it in the gutter. The old man stopped playing and seemed to be gazing at the group at the bus stop across from him. But Jack thought what it really looked like was that he was just staring into space. The kid was getting frustrated, unable to get a rise out of the tranquil musician. The kid pushed the old man's right shoulder, then his left. Finally, he tried to tip the old man out of his chair.

Jack was ready to do something himself to stop the kid's abuse when he noticed that the old man seemed to sigh. He bent down wearily to pick up his coffee can full of coins, drained a little water that had built up, dredged out a few dollar bills and the change and put the money in his jacket pocket. He wrapped up his instrument in what appeared to be a ragged piece of satin cloth and, at last, folded up his flimsy, collapsible stool. He had his back to the kid as he stood up. The kid scrunched up the sleeves of his denim jacket, ran both his hands through his greasy, black mane of unkempt hair. The old man took him off guard, whirling and viciously kicking him as hard as possible in the balls. The kid screamed, both hands ricocheting to his groin as he toppled over, crashing to the walk, his head craned backwards over the edge of the curb as he vomited all over himself into the gutter. A couple of Mexican guys standing behind Jack clapped, and a smelly, fat black drunk laughed. The old man paid his audience no mind. As he picked up his instrument and stool, he tipped a full trashcan over on top of the kid's face. Then he casually walked up the street in the pouring rain.

The approaching bus eclipsed the kid's moaning, and suddenly the sight of him was blotted out, too. It was the Route 30-Stockton line, and Jack was one of the first on. The smelly fat drunk was one of the last, plopping himself down a few seats closer to the front of the bus on the other side. Passengers nearby shrank into themselves, intimidated by his unruly demeanor and pungent aroma.

"Sir, I need the proper fare."

It was obvious that the driver was speaking to the drunk, but the inebriated slob pretended not to hear, looking around him for the guilty party with faux innocence.

"Sir, I'm not leaving until I get the proper fare from you."

The drunk erupted. "Fuck you, motherfucker! I put 75 cents in there! I was born in goddamn 1954. Practically a senior! What you want from me, blood?"

"I need you to get off the bus."

"Fuck you!"

The other passengers were looking at one another with "what-the-fuck?" expressions.

"You don't get off, I'm calling the cops."

"Go ahead, motherfucker! Call the pigs on an old man!"

The bus driver, who was also black, was probably in his early fifties, not much younger than the drunk. Jack was in his mid-fifties himself. The driver stood up and addressed his passengers.

"Folks, this bus is now out of service. I need you to get out and wait for the next one. The Bayshore Express will be along in a few minutes."

No one moved. The drunk was immune to the withering stares from his fellow travelers.

"Shee-it! You makin' a mountain out of a molehill. I was born in 1954. Practically a senior. What you want from me?"

Jack studied the drunk's ashen complexion, his stained watch cap, sweatshirt, dungarees and falling-apart sneakers.

"The cops will be here soon," the driver pointed out.

"Fuck 'em!"

Jack wasn't sure who was going to call whose bluff.

Another bus suddenly appeared behind them, and people got up to get off, including the drunk. But the bus wasn't the Bayshore Express, and it didn't stop. The drunk was already outside, with a handful of other passengers. Only the front door of the 30 Stockton bus remained open, and the driver refused to let anyone back in, despite the weather.

An impatient German tourist, well over six feet tall, sporting a Giants jacket and half in the bag himself, barged on.

"Sir, I need you to step back off the bus."

The German waved his transfer ticket in the driver's face. "But I have a ticket!"

"Sir, I need you to step back off the bus."

"But I have bought a ticket! Look!"

The driver stood and took a step toward him. His voice grew louder.

"Sir, I repeat. You need to step off the bus!"

The tipsy German tourist was really getting angry, and he defiantly went nose-to-nose with the driver.

"I have a ticket!"

Jack almost got up right then to explain to the tourist that the bus driver had to wait for the cops, since he had already called in about the drunk. At least that was what Jack guessed was happening. Except the driver was too stubborn to explain. Or, more probably, he was too stressed out and angry to even think of such a simple solution. Before Jack could pipe up, the tourist shoved the driver.

"Fuck," Jack thought, "I'm outta here."

He made his way quickly to the rear door, touched the bar

release and found himself outside in the light rain, just as the German tourist landed horizontal on the sidewalk. It sounded like the man's head made a cracking sound as it hit the concrete. Jack was shocked that the driver had actually, finally, lost it. Then the driver was straddling the prone, Aryan oaf, his fists pistoning into the dazed man's face.

Right on cue, the Bayshore Express pulled up behind the out-of-service bus, and virtually the whole small crowd disappeared into it as if they'd been vacuumed up. Instinctively, they knew something bad was happening, and they did not want to be caught in the undertow. Jack watched the drunk old black guy's Adam's apple bob in a nervous gulp. The boorish, inebriated slob was genuinely scared at the carnage he'd set in motion, and he jumped up and through the bus's rear doors as a passenger exited. The new driver was oblivious, not only to the drunk but to the fight as well; he rammed his behemoth into gear, and it roared off.

Jack and a Japanese punk-rock girl, who had just gotten off the Bayshore line, were now the only people watching the driver thrash the German tourist. Jack wondered what had possessed him to stay there observing and not board the just departed bus. The answer was simple – he was hypnotized by the spectacle.

Then it hit him. The bus driver was going to beat this guy *to death.*

A pool of blood appeared beneath the German's curly locks, and he was no longer fighting back. Jack lunged and grabbed hold of the driver's right arm, trying to restrain him. The driver's head sprang up, his teeth bared, his weeping, bloodshot eyes bulging. He quickly stood erect, reaching out to wale on Jack, when something caught his attention, and he glanced down at the tourist. The German's palsied hand had grabbed his pantleg. The driver fell back on him like a stone, roaring.

There was a loud screech, and a patrol car pulled to the curb. Two cops, one Hispanic and one white, disembarked and casually walked over to the driver, calmly pulling him off the now dead man.

"Jeez. Dude really lost it."

They held Jack and the girl there for over an hour, questioning them. Jack was the only one who had witnessed the whole thing from the start on the bus, so his story was the most crucial. If the thing went to trial, he would certainly be called to testify.

He didn't get back to the hotel until two in the morning. He was shocked he wasn't more upset. He really didn't feel much of anything at all, even though he was painfully aware that one man had lost his life and another man had ruined his future. It wasn't just that he didn't know these two men. It was something else deep inside of him, a numbness. He knew his own losses over the years, especially when he sank into the depths of addiction, paled in comparison to the violent destruction of these two men. But it felt as if someone had almost completely burned out his emotion circuits, as if a zap of unrestrained, unregulated wattage had bypassed breakers and had fried everything inside of him that was capable of deep feeling. Sometimes he felt like that, a husk, a man looking in on himself from a ceiling vantage point, just going through the motions of living. Before he had met Linda in 2001, he had only intermittently felt that way. Getting together with her had gradually re-ignited his firing points, and gradually a lot of his emotions had come back. But not all. During that eight-year period, they'd gone through the wasting away-illness of both of his parents and of her mother. And when each of them had died, it had been hard for him to feel much of anything, no matter the guilt, which never seemed to leave him. Sometimes he felt that grief had been his natural state of being for so long, he didn't see how the bar could be set any lower. And then when Linda had left, he had simply wanted to die. He hadn't felt such pain in decades. He had been borderline suicidal, wishing for nothing more than a quick, painless death. It was as if all that they had gone through together in their relationship, every hardship had simultaneously come crashing down on him when she had left. He had felt that way almost every waking moment for months, and he had fought against the feeling because he knew that such grief could, if he gave it the power, literally kill him. He had been a pathetic slave to his emotions for most of his life, and it sickened him.

But how to turn your feelings off *just enough*? Regulate your sensitivity or, better yet, transcend it? Occasionally, he thought he had gotten to that point, the transcendence. But it was something you needed to watch like a hawk, as if you were a tightrope walker, because survival depended on your sense of balance.

He tried to push back a wave of self-loathing, and he wished he could go out drinking. Of course, that would only make it worse. Besides, luckily for him, it was too late, and the bars were closed.

He thought about his new girlfriend, Diana, and wondered if it was too late to call her.

It was.

When he wasn't around, she was usually in bed by midnight.

Maybe, though, she'd left her cell phone on. He hoped so, because he suddenly got a pang, a sucking chest-wound sensation in the well of his being that made it imperative he talk to her.

It would give him a nice feeling to talk to her.

He needed to hear her voice.

RAIL

c. 1948 & 1963, Berneval, France

Joseph was in his mid-eighties when he returned to the town in the still blazing summer of September 1963, exactly fifteen years after the tragic deaths of Mario and Jen. The couple's demise had poured gasoline on the fire ignited by the local version of the still-to-come national 1948 miners' strike, a country-wide stoppage that had been sabotaged by incredibly stupid stratagems and political maneuvers by Stalinist elements in the labor movement.

Joseph had stopped counting birthdays a long time ago. He thought that perhaps he was almost seventy when it had all happened, but he wasn't positive. Just the same, other things stood out graphic-ally in his memory, almost as if they had occurred mere days before. He thanked Providence, or whatever positive energy coursed through his tiny fraction of the universe, for what he believed to be fairly good health for a man of his advanced years. He could still walk a mile or two a day, and he had made this train trip all by himself, despite the protests of his nephew, Etienne. He had come on a whim because something he couldn't even recall had happened two weeks before that had made him remember Mario's vibrant life force and savage sense of humor. And thinking of Mario had naturally made him think of Jen.

He strolled through the dry golden reeds of the parched, rock-hard field and looked across the ten acres that lay before him.

To his left was elevated Berneval, an anemic, yet living village he had once called home for over a decade, and directly to its right was the notorious Mathieu coal mine, looking like the top half of a death's-head skull, carved out of the side of the mountain. It was still in operation, though rumored to be nowhere near as productive as it had been at the close of the last decade. It was startling that there was any coal to be mined at all. He was surprised that the veins had not played themselves out. The mine still roared full-blast all day and all night, although Joseph was surprised when the shift change came. Here it was nearly 4 in the afternoon, and the changes used to be every twelve hours at 6 AM and 6 PM. Maybe after all those years the workers had finally triumphed and won eight-hour shifts.

He'd gotten used to looking at the placid mountain with the skull-like cavities bored into it as if God had been a malicious brain surgeon and decided to practice one day on the otherwise bland terrain. God…that was funny. Why would he think of God? He remembered the way Jen's body had looked when she died.

A high-pitched cross between a whistle and a horn blew. Suddenly what he thought was a stationary line of identical khaki and green bushes began to move into the mountain, and he realized they were people. Beside them, moving faster, streams of men who were done for the day vomited forth from the half parabola that was the mine shaft's deformed mouth.

He ambled over to the battered Citroen in the rutted dirt road and, after pulling a half liter of wine from the boot and closing it again, he propped himself up against it. He uncorked the warm Beaujolais and downed a healthy swig.

Mario, a robust ne'er-do-well looking for hard, simple labor, had come down to the area from northern Italy by roundabout detour through the Loire in early 1946, right after the war. He had been a dockworker in Marseilles for the last two years of the fighting and had fled abruptly back to Milan after the rest of his family had been killed. When he arrived in Berneval in 1948, he was already drinking heavily and had been for quite some time. But he laughed a lot, held his liquor well and didn't seem to care what happened to him. Scars crisscrossed his smooth, muscular torso from his rough-and-tumble life as a longshoreman. His large nose had been broken twice but still retained a patrician elegance that belied his working-class origins. Joseph often imagined he had come from a line of aristocratic Italians who had fallen on hard times, but he knew that was a foolish notion. Mario had never gone into detail about his Italian heritage, and he had barely retained the hint of an accent.

Before the war, Jen had lived further north in some forgotten village – she refused to even tell Joseph the name – with her husband and young son. She was still beautiful in 1948, after years of hardship, debauched living and heavy drinking, so Joseph could only imagine how stunning she must have been in the late 1930s. Her hair had always been a full, short bob, a wavy and lustrous golden color that came down just below the nape of her neck. She had narrow serpentine eyes that made her seem slightly Asiatic, full lips that seemed characteristic of Moorish descent and a snow-white complexion. Her face was broad but not too broad. All in all, she had an unusual, off-kilter aspect to her face, a strangeness of proportion that made her alluring beauty all the more startling. By 1948, her skin had coarsened slightly from tobacco and liquor, but she was still a magnet to men of all ages. She called it her curse. Joseph could hear her as if she was right there in front of him – vibrant, explosive, alive.

"You damn fool men. Why do you think a woman like me would give any of you the time of day? You call me beautiful, but I'm ugly inside and out. My life has a steady stream of vitriol running through it from morning to night. I don't care what happens to any of you, going down like gophers into the bowels of this cursed earth. Die down there, see if I or any of my girls give a damn."

She'd been the madam of a modest brothel in the same building as the village's biggest tavern from the time Joseph had first set foot in the area after fleeing Paris. He had to wipe away a tear as he thought of her, sentimental fool that he was. She'd come to town right near the end of the war, barely alive, full of an angry bitterness at all that had been taken from her, at the humiliation and physical and emotional pain that she had had to endure, at the deaths of her husband and, by default, her daughter at the hands of the Waffen SS.

Joseph took a long swig from the bottle. He squinted at the sun's reflection off the dark green glass.

Mario and Jen. They were like the proverbial oil and water when they first met. They had gotten in an argument straight off after Mario had pinched one of the waitresses going by his table, causing her to spill a tray of drinks. Jen was there in a flash and nearly threw him out. He tried to sweet-talk her but Jen, nearly as drunk as Mario, was having none of it. They started trading insults, with the escalating barrage of sharp-tongued words quickly turning into an acidic deluge. Both had been intent on topping the other until the crush of customers, the bar girls needing Jen's guidance, caused her to cut short her tirade.

Joseph smiled at the rambunctiously raunchy humor of that warm summer night so long ago. He'd been sitting at the table with Mario and a young teenage boy named Herbert, an unfortunate with a clubfoot who had worked right beside them down in the mine. Joseph remembered Mario's indignation at Jen's haughty attitude, but also the magnetic chemistry between the two. Mario's indignation had dissolved when Joseph told him Jen's story.

"After the Germans occupied her village, things went from bad to worse. Her husband, Philippe, forced to work in the German munitions dump just outside the town, was killed in a freak accident. For the first year afterward, Jen held her own under horrible tribulations. The German officers were always after her because of the way she looked, even more beautiful than she looks now. They knew she had a ten-year-old daughter to feed, and food was getting scarce. The good rations went to the Germans, the soldier swine. The officers, a colonel in particular, chipped away at her resistance. The other officers were vulgar pigs, but the colonel played the gentleman, never pushing too hard, always asking after Jen's daughter."

"Scum!" Mario raised his glass, draining it, disgusted at the scenario. He ordered a bottle of Calvados as Joseph continued the story.

"Jen's daughter got sick. The town doctor came and went many times, but she kept getting worse. She needed penicillin, and he had none. He suggested Jen go to the colonel who was always after her. Jen said, 'What! That Nazi beast?' But, as the days crawled by, and her daughter's chances dwindled, she screwed up her courage and her determination to mask her revulsion and went to him. She got the penicillin that night. Within a week, her daughter was well enough to get out of bed. Once she could get around on her own and could stay next door with the neighbors – Jen's and Philippe's relatives were all dead – Jen had to fulfill her end of the bargain.

"It was awful for her. Basically, she became the pig's mistress. The villagers didn't care why she had done it; they stopped talking to her. Her neighbors threatened to stop watching her daughter. Jen lost weight. Then, as if things couldn't have gotten any worse, she found out she was pregnant with the colonel's bastard. It sickened her. She wanted to abort it because she couldn't stand the idea of having the monster's baby. By accident, the colonel found out. He flew into a rage, then took his SS dagger to her himself, slitting her open just above the groin, nearly disemboweling her and leaving her in the street.

Luckily, a young German private risked his life to help her and brought her to the doctor. At first, the doctor was afraid to treat her, but the soldier forced him at gunpoint to clean her wounds, sew her up and treat her with penicillin. He threatened the doctor with death if he didn't keep her there until she was well enough to get about. Needless to say, she lost the colonel's child.

"When she was well enough to leave, the colonel was no longer stationed in the village. Some of the women in town caught Jen one day in front of her daughter and shaved off all her hair, then beat her black-and-blue. The little girl was so ashamed, she ran away. Jen had to look for her on her own because the villagers wouldn't help. It took her days. By the time she found the poor little thing, it had been nearly a week. The girl had been wandering in the forest and had become lost, then perished from the freezing temperatures at night. Jen left the next day, with only a small bundle and the clothes on her back. And do you know where she went?"

"She did what I would have done," Mario, his skin pale, his fiery eyes locked into Joseph's, "She went to find the colonel."

"Yes. And she found him. But she laid low. She joined the Resistance, waiting for the right time. She found her way into the hotel where the swine was staying. It had been over six months, and her hair had grown back. Somehow, some way, she snuck into the colonel's suite while he was sleeping. She made sure he was alone that night and that he had had plenty to drink, courtesy of one of her waitress friends in the downstairs bar – and she crawled into bed with him. The man was so drunk, he responded without alarm, not recognizing her in the shadows. He already had his clothes off, so she brandished her knife, doing the same thing that he had done to her, except worse. She gutted him, slicing across the bottom of his belly. Afterward, she calmly bathed, taking her time, washing off his blood, getting dressed, then sneaking out into the night with no one the wiser."

Mario interrupted, his face anxious. "And what was this colonel's name?"

Joseph finished his drink and wiped his mouth with the back of his burly hand. "Colonel Heinrich Maucheim, Watten-SS."

Joseph was shocked as Mario's face went white. For a moment, Mario was in a cold sweat and seemed as if he was about to faint.

"Are you all right?"

Mario slowly nodded and, with palsied hand, poured himself another Calvados, downing it in one gulp. Mario turned to young Herbert. Purposely not looking him in the eye, he told him he needed to be getting home to his mother, she would be worrying. Herbert started to protest, but Joseph gave him a stern look, shaking his head as if to say, "You better do as he says." Herbert frowned.

"I know why you two are sending me home. And it has nothing to do with my mother. You don't want me to hear what's coming next. Very well." Herbert put on his cap and left.

Mario then proceeded to fill in the details of his own story. How his family had been killed in Marseilles. Unbeknownst to Mario, his wife had been approached by a German colonel stationed there. His wife, being quite materialistic and of not particularly strong character, had acquiesced to the German's proposal and, for several weeks, had carried on a secret affair with the colonel. Mario had been suspicious of her explanation of the great quantity of extra food rations they suddenly had, the gasoline that her father now had no problem buying. When Mario found out the truth, he went crazy. He was told the whereabouts of the couple's rendezvous spot by one of his wife's friends. He found the two in bed and immediately stabbed his wife in the heart, but he only wounded Maucheim. The German put up a terrible fight and raised the alarm. Mario barely escaped, going on the run. Then a week later he heard the news.

His whole family had been slaughtered. Colonel Maucheim had had them rounded up in the street in front of the building where they lived. Mario's father, his aunt (his mother was already dead), his two older brothers, his younger sister and his five-year-old daughter. Maucheim made sure they were all there together when his soldiers called on them. He gave them only one chance to tell where Mario was hiding, not expecting any of them to talk. They didn't.

They weren't shot but were bayoneted instead, in the gutter, pierced through their hearts as Mario had pierced his unfaithful wife, and the colonel had personally overseen the executions, making sure every inhabitant of the neighborhood was present to watch.

It was an overpowering tale that brought a tear to Joseph's eye. He impatiently wiped it with a nonchalant gesture disguised as scratching an itch. He then downed his Calvados.

Tears began to stream copiously from Mario's eyes, and he lunged up and away from the table, stumbling out the front door and then into the street outside.

Jen, watchful of every table lest some bloodshed erupt

provoked by too much alcohol, was immediately at Joseph's side.
"What's with him?"

Joseph motioned her to sit, then told her Mario's story, including the identity of the colonel. It only took a minute or two, and then Jen was out the door. Joseph sat there, overcome with emotion, trying to numb himself with drink but finding the effort futile. The oppressively smoky atmosphere of the raucous, bawdy house, the prospect of another five and a half days of going down into the bowels of that pitiless, suffocating mountain, the black dust in his lungs, his own eternal loneliness, his unacknowledged longing from afar for Jen, knowing her history and then hearing Mario's saga, it was nearly too much, even for a rock like Joseph.

A few minutes passed, and Jen came back in with Mario, one arm snug around his waist and his right arm draped around her shoulders. Joseph could only guess what had transpired between the two outside, but they were obviously now on intimate terms. Jen walked steadily, steering Mario through the maze of tables, her other hand on his chest, caressing him to calm his turmoil. Mario's eyes were clear, but it was obvious to anyone that was sober enough – which meant not many – that he had been weeping. Patrice, one of the more sensitive girls servicing the boisterous crowd, stopped to watch them.

Just when the pair got to the staircase, a hulking presence blocked their path. It was Fallon, the foreman of the main pit, a huge bearded brute. He grabbed Jen's arm, and immediately Mario elbowed the man's ugly, hairy face. Blood spurted, then the two men were a tangle of limbs, tumbling end over end, knocking down drunken miners and smashing at least one table. A couple of the women screamed melodramatically. Jen disappeared behind the bar.

Fallon wasn't as drunk as Mario and abruptly got the upper hand, pinning Joseph's friend to the filthy, sawdust-covered floor. Fallon raised part of a splintered chair to use as a club on Mario's face. Then Jen was there, a cocked American military-issue .45 in her fist with the barrel tucked into Fallon's left ear.

"Get up, you ugly, egg-sucking bastard," she hissed between clenched teeth, "Put that down and get the hell out of here. You are no longer welcome in this establishment."

Fallon's face was livid with rage, but he did as she commanded. He hesitated, then stood upright so the gun barrel came to rest at his stomach. He made a slow turn, surveying the room, memorizing each and every miner's face for future reference. Whether the faces held blank stares, faint smirks or taunting smiles made no difference to Fallon. All of them had witnessed his humiliation at the hands of a whore. He blundered forth, nearly splitting the door in two as he exploded into the street.

Jen grinned and shouted, "A drink for everyone – on the house!" at which the place erupted in claps, whistles and laughter. Then Jen bent down, helping Mario to his feet and up the stairs, undoubtedly to her own room.

Joseph watched them go with mixed emotions, sadness for his lonely self but love for the both of them.

The next two weeks saw the crisis of labor come quickly to a head. There were controversies on shift hours, on short pay for rejected coal, on questionable timbering in the shaft props, you name it; there were countless points of division between the brutally efficient management and the exhausted, impoverished miners. The mine was becoming a living hell, worse than it had been even five years before under ruthless Nazi supervision, and the village was its staging area, a purgatory wracked with near starvation, public drunkenness, chronic illness and a growing climate of malice.

Tension between Mario and Fallon was so thick you could cut it with the proverbial knife. And it was true of not just Mario's relation to the foreman but at least a score of other workers' dealings with him as well. Mario's colleagues, Mansour, Allonsanfan, Goritz, Romita and Faubourg, all had violent verbal altercations with the tyrant, Fallon, who lorded it over them down below.

Much to his displeasure, Mario was switched to a night shift. He knew it was vindictive on Fallon's part. So, when Mario was up sleeping in Jen's bed one hot afternoon, and young Herbert was down below in the mine with Joseph, the tragedy occurred that would serve as the tinderbox for the inferno of tragedies still to come.

Mario had, by default, become reluctant protector of the crippled Herbert, a boy who should never have been permitted to work in the mine; a boy compelled to descend into the depths because of the lack of other employment in the village and the need to support his widowed mother; a boy who was taunted and bullied and abused day in and day out by Fallon.

That afternoon it was bright summer above and a dark brimstone furnace below in the stinking maze of mine shafts. Joseph's team had just pulled out of the vein they had been working. It was too unsafe. The timbering was inadequate and needed shoring up. Some props had fallen, then large slabs of rock. Joseph was left behind with

Herbert, and he cursed the other two men who had crawled, hunched down to half their size, then run the quarter of a kilometer to the main chamber where the elevator promised escape.

Joseph knew that they would be fined heavily if they left behind their pickaxes, and he and Herbert retrieved them, cradling them in their arms with difficulty. Just as Joseph took the lead, bending over to start the long crawl-run out of the vein into the tunnel to the elevator, he heard a crack, then a rumbling boom that made the walls around him tremble. Herbert gasped and, as Joseph whirled around, several sheets of rock and ore pinned Herbert down. Joseph froze, looking into the eyes of the poor boy who was buried to his waist. He was barely visible in the vapor of black dust. They both coughed, gagging, struggling for air. As soon as Joseph made his first decisive step towards Herbert to begin clawing away the rubble, there was another roar of collapsing earth, and they were showered with mud and glistening wet rock. Joseph clutched his lantern to his breast to keep it from being extinguished. He held his breath, or tried to, while the dust settled. But the fine mist of pulverized ore dissipated too slowly. At last, his lungs bursting, he coughed and sucked in the now toxic, firedamp oxygen. He nearly blacked out and raised his dirty handkerchief to cover his mouth and nose.

Through the haze, he saw that only Herbert's head and half of one leg were visible protruding from the slag. Fearful that his movement would cause a further cave-in, he tried to swivel his head around and could just glimpse that the hole behind him was miraculously clear. Deciding to risk it for the fate of the boy, he shuffled slowly to the mound where Herbert was buried. He gently set the lantern down behind him, lest his efforts to pull away rock cause further collapse and plunge them both into blackness.

Herbert was barely conscious, his eyelids fluttering with the ebbing of his life. Joseph reached out to pry away the slab that was propped up against the boy's neck and chest, the main stone pinning him in place. Joseph strained until his fingertips bled. Finally he gave up and decided to try to dig Herbert free from the bottom up, starting at his visible leg. Right off, Joseph was able to dislodge the rock wedged around Herbert's knee. It came away, and Joseph allowed himself a split second of hope before he realized that the whole bottom half of Herbert's leg had tumbled down, too. A ragged fleshy stump, the jagged bone exposed, had been sheared at the small hole in the gritty quicksand of rubble. Another piece of packed, flinty earth rolled off the mutilated appendage, and blood gushed all over Joseph's pants. He could see that the boy was on the verge of succumbing to shock and the trauma of his injuries. He ripped off his shirt without hesitation, twirling it quickly into a coiled cotton rope that he looped as a tourniquet around the torn branch of leg. As he did so, Joseph looked beneath his feet to see that water was trickling from the crushed shale. Seepage. Could he expect any less? That was undoubtedly what had contributed to the cave-in. He automatically grabbed the lantern. He had to get help.

"I'll be back, boy! Keep your courage up!"

Herbert's eyelids fluttered; otherwise he seemed unconscious. Joseph bent down to crawl through the hole, praying that some of the other men were still nearby.

"Don't leave me." Herbert's words were a barely audible croak, but they made Joseph pause. He glanced behind him as he backed his body into the meter-square entrance to the crawlspace.

"I'll be back, Herbert. I promise you. I won't leave you down here."

Then quickly he was scrambling through the cramped tunnels of near darkness. When he reached the elevator chamber and was finally once more able to stand erect, he was greeted with a discouraging sight. All had fled to the surface. All but one man. The man he hated and least wanted to see.

"Herbert's buried up to his neck. Part of his leg's come off. You must help me get him out."

"You sure he's not dead?" laughed Fallon. "Half his leg off, he'll bleed to death in the few minutes it will take us to get back to him. That is, if he's not kaput already!"

"I applied a tourniquet."

"Ah, well, that makes all the difference!" Fallon sarcastically blurted. But he frowned because he knew he had to at least make a slight effort. He pushed Joseph aside, preceding him into the tunnel mouth. They ran in a crouch for several meters until Fallon abruptly stopped stock still, causing Joseph to run into him.

"Imbecile! Turn back!"

"What do you mean?"

"Look, you pathetic fool!" Fallon gestured to the ground, and Joseph saw the water streaming between their feet. It was not rising yet, but already covered the soles of their shoes.

"No. I tell you we can still get him out. The two of us together."

"No, you idiot."

"But we are two big, strong men."

"Imbecile!" Fallon shoved Joseph backwards, sending him splashing and sprawling in the flow of seepage.

Fallon dashed over him down the tunnel toward the elevator. Joseph stumbled erect, bumping his head violently on the low ceiling. He winced but began running after Fallon.

Back in the elevator chamber, Fallon was waiting in ambush, yanking Joseph up by his neck, then planting a bruising kick into his ribs that sent him careening, banging into the elevator cage. Joseph smacked his head on the metal door and saw stars as he slumped horizontal. When he opened his eyes after a precious few seconds, he saw Fallon with a sledgehammer pounding away at the support slats of the timbering props at the tunnel's entrance. Before he could fumble to regain his balance on two very wobbly feet, Fallon had done his damage, and the rock roof of the tunnel mouth cascaded down, sealing off the veins leading to what was now Herbert's death chamber.

Fallon turned on his heel, making for the elevator. Bereft, Joseph slid down the cage mesh exterior, blocking Fallon's way. Fallon flashed by him in a blur of rage and panic, reaching back with his claw-like hands, grabbing and picking up Joseph's head like a melon and heaving him into the elevator, then pressing the 'ascend' button in one brutally fluid motion.

As the gate clanged shut, the cage ricocheted skyward. Joseph lunged at Fallon, head-butting him in the face so blood flowed in spurts from his nose and mouth. But both men's energy was already expended, rapidly dissipating after the adrenaline explosion of onrushing catastrophe. They slumped on either end of the elevator, panting heavily and gazing at each other with stares of hatred.

"You breathe a word and no one will ever believe you."

"Everyone will believe me. Everyone despises you, except for the bosses."

Fallon smirked beneath his blood-soaked beard. "Rightly so. But I prevented the elevator chamber from flooding."

"You hope."

"I know."

"And I know we had a chance to save the boy."

"He was already dead by the time you reached me, and you know it. We would have committed suicide. For nothing!"

Joseph looked away, disgusted, surveying the earth and the dripping wet slime of seepage that always trickled down from above.

Then there was a burst of sunshine that blinded them both.

They had reached the surface.

Mario was beside himself with rage when Joseph related the story of Herbert's death. He told the tale to a full tavern of angry men, rejuvenated from exhaustion by the outrage that was Fallon's existence. And Fallon represented the company. Thus the outrage was at the company as well, a corporation of greedy bloodsuckers who made every man below them expendable.

Jen had begun to get nervous. She could see where it was all headed, and she knew she was completely powerless to stop it. A fuse had been lit. A strike was called for 48 hours hence. The men wished the time elapsed to be no longer. Ideally, they would have struck that very minute. The more time waiting, even to adequately prepare, was dangerous. There were company spies everywhere. Few of the workers guessed just how far they, the strikers, were going to go. Only Mario, Joseph, Mansour and Romita knew that they would blockade the rail line and, if they had to, even blow out the rock on the mountain to cause an avalanche on the village highway.

Jen overheard and had to bite her tongue. She dodged into the back storage room of the brothel's kitchen and wept. Many would be hurt, maimed. And many would die.

The next day was Sunday, fortuitous, as most of the workers did not have to work. Besides, a skeleton crew doing shoring-up repairs in the main pit was Fallon's first priority. There was time for the majority of them to rest up a day for the grueling strike ahead.

Mario was in the mood to celebrate and convinced Jen, Joseph and Patrice to go on a picnic beyond the sun-dappled hills in the first clearing of the nearby forest. It was a bittersweet afternoon. Jen fixed two chickens and a rabbit, brought along bread and cheese and three bottles of wine. After they had feasted and drunk many toasts, the four of them lay drowsily in the warm, late afternoon sun, joking quietly, listening to the buzz of insects and the murmur of an unseen brook.

Joseph dropped off to sleep and had a strange dream. The village was deserted. He was the only one left. But stranger still, the streets were paved with a blanket of rose petals. In the dream, he was barefoot, and the flowers felt soft, almost unbearably sweet beneath his calloused soles. Suddenly the sky darkened, it began raining and his feet felt wet. When he looked down, he saw that the rose petals had changed to blood. A river of blood that was up to his ankles.

Joseph awakened with a start. Patrice gently snored beside him, but Mario and Jen were nowhere to be seen. He lumbered heavily to his feet, nearly toppling over. But he steadied himself, heading for a thicket of trees. Slowly a sound became audible…tender cries of a woman in the throes of convulsive love. The cries grew louder. He slackened his pace lest he abruptly burst upon the missing pair of lovers. Then, through branches swaying in the mild breeze, he saw them stretched out naked in a clearing, framed in a halo of sunlight as they coupled.

Joseph watched for only a second. Finding himself becoming aroused, he grew ashamed and turned away. When he reached the slumbering Patrice, he quietly sat down and rolled a cigarette.

The next morning they were all up before dawn. They met at the great gaping maw of the mine and marched to the railhead. The train was due within the hour to start carting away ore. Not as many miners showed up as they had hoped. Not everyone by any means, but still it was a majority, perhaps two thirds of the mine workforce, including at least a dozen women who had been drafted into service during the war when there was an acute shortage of men.

The various foremen and guards were beside themselves with apprehension. There were too many demonstrating to make a show of force. And Mansour had cut the phone and telegraph lines. The road had not been dynamited, because of disagreement within the ranks about whether it was going too far. Besides the proponents of the tactic had been unable to lay their hands on the explosives. But they still fully intended to block the train with their own bodies.

Fallon was conspicuous by his absence, and his nonappearance seemed to bother only Joseph. When he brought it up, many of the men laughed, Mario the loudest.

The men swarmed the rail line, snaking along it like a herd of insects, giant ants clinging to the hot iron rails that culminated in the loading yard. The crowd stopped, clustering on the tracks a hundred meters out, right where the line pulled way from the gouged plain, shorn, sliced and leveled out of the mountainside.

Joseph looked for Jen but knew the effort was in vain. She had undoubtedly shut herself up in the brothel's tavern, frightened of the barbaric violence of which she knew men were capable.

There had been little resistance from the mining company up until then. When the still faraway train blew its whistle, when the smoke from its locomotive rose in the distance, the men grew excited. The closer the train, the more agitated they became. All of the villagers, including old men, women and children gathered round, spilling down the embankment into the field below to witness the unfolding drama.

Lemond, the manager of the mine, appeared on a horse, strutting back and forth behind the crowd, shouting at them, first in a cajoling way. Then, as they ignored him, his tone escalated from annoyance to anger. Joseph turned to watch him and got the distinct feeling that if the manager had been armed, he would have started firing into the mob.

The train slowed as it always did, then slowed even more as the engineer saw what was ahead, the tracks blocked by human bodies. But he kept on at a snail's pace.

Some of the men in the front became uneasy. It didn't seem that the train would stop. Each miner let his imagination carry him away, images of mangled, bloody limbs strewn on the rails, up the hill on one side and down the steep embankment on the other. Many of the workers jumped off of the tracks and scurried out of the way. Joseph was ashamed that he was one of them. Mansour, Romita and Mario seemed determined to stay the course. Joseph anxiously watched the trio as they lay down across the rails. The train slowed yet again, but it was still coming. Mansour and Romita lost their nerve and crawled off to the side. The locomotive was getting perilously near. Joseph could even make out the expressions on the faces of the engineer and brakeman – they were getting that close. The brakeman reached out to his lever, realizing that Mario was not going to budge.

Unexpectedly, Fallon sprung out of nowhere, leaping up into the locomotive cab, knocking aside the brakeman and barring the engineer from the lever. Fallon wrenched another switchhandle, and the train gathered speed. Mario had not glimpsed Fallon's arrival, and he had been laughing at what he thought to be their victory at stopping the train. Joseph saw Mario's eyes glance sideways in shocked surprise at the last second – right before the locomotive cut him into three pieces, then continued onward through the gates of the loading yard. Screams and shouts of horror rose from the crowd. The mine manager seemed stunned by the gory turn of events, and Joseph himself was dumbstruck. He would never forget the sight of Mario in bloody chunks, the moans of nausea from the men, the weeping of the women and children, making the kinds of sounds that were surely like those audible in the deepest pits of hell.

For whole long moments, minutes that seemed interminable, Joseph watched the train disappear into the loading grounds. Then there was an overwhelming explosion of rage. Joseph, Mansour and Romita led a charge into the yard. The frightened guards fired into their ranks.

But still they kept going.

They found Fallon gloating in the locomotive cab, a demonic caste transforming his already brutish face, making him seem more animal than human. They grabbed him and hoisted him aloft, then flung him into the enraged crowd behind them. Fallon disappeared beneath flailing fists, swinging pickaxes and shovels. Joseph felt all emotion drain out of him as he stepped back down to the ground. Fallon's blood spurted up from the crowd, splattered pell mell this way and that as the foreman disintegrated beneath the angry blows. A few drops landed on Joseph's blank face.

He didn't remember anything more until much later that night, sitting with Jen in the closed-up brothel, they the only ones there, the surrounding darkness of the cavernous tavern kept at bay by the light of a sputtering stub of candle. The power had been cut in much of the village as the strike had taken hold.

Jen had been shut all day in her room. Joseph had had to climb up, then break a rear second-floor window to get inside to see her. The bar girls and whores were cowering in fear somewhere else in the gone-crazy town. Jen had already heard what had happened. In fact, somehow she knew more than Joseph did. Guards had continued firing into the mob, killing sixteen miners and injuring many others. Not only Fallon was dead on the company side. Three guards had been mortally injured, two of them dying hours later, just before the sun set. The third was not expected to live till dawn. And there was a rumor running rampant that, despite the telegraph and phone lines being cut, the military had been alerted and was on their way to quell the disturbance.

Joseph remembered with sadness how white, how drained of blood Jen's face had been. Her beauty had become almost translucent, like some siren mermaid glowing in the blackest depths of the sea. It seemed to radiate outward, casting its own illumination. Perhaps it was because Joseph had had nothing to eat all day and way too much to drink.

"He was the last man, Joseph. The last I shall ever love. The last man I shall ever know. His death is mine as well."

Things Joseph might have said like "Don't be silly, don't be so melodramatic, Jen. You are a survivor. Nothing can kill you," he had not been able to say. He couldn't get the words out. They sounded too trite. Her pain was too all encompassing, and the anguish from her eyes made him catch his breath in his throat. He reached out and placed his hands over hers. They were ice cold, like smooth marble.

A day later, the military arrived. They were too late to stem the violence, but the company breathed a sigh of relief. About half the demonstrating workers had come to the conclusion that the strike was futile, and they went back down into the earth. Joseph and many others, perhaps one hundred, had refused.

Two days later, Joseph had walked through the very field where he sat now, basking in the sun with his wine. It had been a little greener then, but otherwise not much different. He had been wandering back and forth aimlessly, straying closer and closer to the gravel-strewn embankment that supported the railroad tracks. He had tried to guess how high it was – perhaps 20 meters? He recalled squinting up at the blinding sun and the warmth that had spread across his flushed face. He had shielded his eyes and moved his gaze to the tracks down the line, closer to the village and the mine's loading yard. He had strayed out into the middle of the field by then, and he thought he noticed someone, a woman, kneeling beside the rails.

The rumble of the approaching train shook the ground, and its whistle gave off shrill calls as it came around the bend. Joseph thought it was perhaps a kilometer away. When his gaze returned to the woman, he suddenly had a terrifying revelation. The woman was Jen, and he knew intuitively what she planned to do.

Joseph relived those agonizing few moments in his aged memory, and the vision stood out in crystal clarity. Him running, stumbling on stones, shouting Jen's name, his voice increasingly drowned out by the approaching train. Jen had not moved. She wasn't on the tracks but was very close, perhaps two or three feet away. She held her back rigidly straight as she knelt there. At last, Joseph reached the foot of the embankment. She was up there to his left, and he could plainly make out her stoic profile. He knew he would never get to her in time. He prayed that she wouldn't go through with it, that she would change her mind or lose her nerve. But as soon as those thoughts entered his head, he knew with an awful certainty that she would most surely do what she had set out to do. The very qualities in her that he loved so much, those were the qualities that would spur her to unflinchingly meet her fate.

Just as he reached the top, he could see that he was still almost fifteen feet away. The train was starting to pass him. The locomotive whistle shrieked as the engineer saw Jen bend over. As she laid her head sideways on the rail, her eyes met Joseph's, and she gave a faint smile. Joseph collapsed as the braking locomotive passed over, crushing Jen's head. He tumbled down the embankment in a swoon, his eyes scrunched closed, his mind inside Jen's mind, seeing what she must have seen as the heavy iron locomotive wheels squealed mere inches from her beautiful face.

Joseph had come fully back to consciousness as he hit bottom, and he had whirled to his feet, edging backward, staring up in a vain hope that Jen had rolled aside before the train could reach her. But, no – her body was spreadeagled on its stomach with outstretched arms, a blooming flower of thick blood spreading in a mandala from where her head had been.

Jen's death galvanized the village. Men who had given up went back on strike. The truckers who had previously come and gone on the highway with little interaction with the villagers – except for maybe a quick drink or lay at Jen's tavern – ended up blocking the road for several miles for over a week. Mansour and Romita, miraculously still free, dismantled the tracks around the bend of the mountain one moonless night, causing the next afternoon's train to derail. More troops were sent, twenty more people died and unknown numbers were injured.

Joseph sighed and finished off his wine. He tossed the empty bottle onto the hard, packed soil at his feet, then stared up at the railroad embankment again, seeing plainly the spot where Jen had died. For a few seconds, he saw the giant rose of her crushed, bloodstained skull there and then the bouquets of wildflowers that had been strewn across the tracks in the following days. Just as quickly, the images were gone.

Joseph blinked. The sun would be setting within the hour. He shuffled over to his car, pried open the creaking front door and fell wearily into the seat behind the steering wheel. He glanced up at the embankment one last time as he slammed the door shut. He started the ignition and steered the car onto the rutted dirt road that led back to the highway.

Thank yous...

need to go out to Donna Lethal, Eve Golden, Byron Coley, Lili Dwight, Thurston Moore, Eddie Muller, Kat Milne, Peter Maravelis, John Doe, Lydia Lunch, Grace Krilanovich, Mary Woronov, Jerry Stahl, Alan K. Rode, Alex Maslansky, Liz Garo, Billy Shire, Shepherd Stevenson, Benjamin Rew, Brendan Mullen, Eleanor Whitledge, Erika Wear, Jane Reardon, Mike Minky, Richard Modiano, Claudia Colodro, Tosh Berman, Patrick Paeper at Alias Books East, Mark Rainey and Julia Smut at TKO Records

Chris D. is the author of the novel *NO EVIL STAR* and the collection *DRAGON WHEEL SPLENDOR and Other Love Stories of Violence and Dread*. His anthology *A MINUTE TO PRAY, A SECOND TO DIE,* a 500-page collection of selected short stories, excerpts from unpublished novels and scores of dream journal entries, as well as all of his poetry and song lyrics, was published in December 2009.

His non-fiction *OUTLAW MASTERS OF JAPANESE FILM* was published by IB Tauris (distributed by Palgrave Macmillan in the USA) in 2005.

He saw release of his first feature film as director *I PASS FOR HUMAN*, in 2004 (and its DVD release in 2006), and worked as a programmer at The American Cinematheque in Hollywood, California from 1999-2009.

Chris D. is also known as the singer/songwriter of the bands, The Flesh Eaters, Divine Horsemen and Stone by Stone. He also was an A&R rep and in-house producer at Slash Records/Ruby Records from 1980-1984.

Other recent books include the novels *MOTHER'S WORRY* and *SHALLOW WATER*, and the long-in-the-works non-fiction *GUN AND SWORD: An Encyclopedia of Japanese Gangster Films 1955-1980*.

Upcoming books include the novels *TIGHTROPE ON FIRE, VOLCANO GIRLS* and *TATTOOED BLOOD*.

The life of recovering addict and Nam vet Milo unravels when ex-CIA friend Dave goes off the deep end. Not only is Dave the heist man whacking NYC drug dealers, he's also hatching a scheme to plunder mob boss Nunzio's art treasures pilfered in WWII. Complicating matters, Yuen, an ex-Viet Cong with a grudge against Milo and Dave, arrives in New York.

"A healthy authorial sense of curiosity and generosity lends weight to NO EVIL STAR's intersecting lives, where Chris D. ably traces out the contours of human torment in a manner recalling American films of the 1970s."
– Grace Krilanovich, author of THE ORANGE EATS CREEPS

AVAILABLE NOW

FROM POISON FANG BOOKS

The long-awaited complete collection of poetry and song lyrics by Chris D., singer/songwriter for the bands The Flesh Eaters, Divine Horsemen and Stone by Stone; plus numerous dream journal entries, short stories and excerpts from his novels. 500 pages.

"Chris D. presents...an immense encapsulation of his life's work...a literary autopsy of a man not yet dead but of one who has died a thousand times and somehow miraculously between crucifixions used pen as shovel to prevent himself from being buried alive...It speaks in revelations... of the limbo that we live in drawn and quartered at the alley's mouth by the Pain Gods of our own creation..."
– Lydia Lunch, author of PARADOXIA and WILL WORK FOR DRUGS

A MINUTE TO PRAY
A SECOND TO DIE

A Collection of Writing by
Chris D.

Preface by Byron Coley
Foreword by John Doe
Afterword by Lydia Lunch

The year is 1987, and outlaw Ray Diamond's mother is the queenpin of crime in Mystic, GA. After his Navy discharge, Ray knocks over a mob-connected El Paso liquor store, not counting on Eli, the owner's psycho son, dogging his trail. Back home in Mystic, Ray's girl, Connie Eustace, resorts to stripping at Mama Lorna's club to make ends meet. Witness to a murder by the local sheriff, she goes on a drug-and-drink bender, jumping from the frying pain into the fire.

"...a crazy dive into a universe populated largely by monsters...a classic update of the Gold Medal/Lion Library loser noir tradition. Great work..."
– Byron Coley, writer for WIRE magazine, author of C'EST LA GUERRE: EARLY WRITINGS 1978-1983

MOTHER'S WORRY

a novel
by
CHRIS D.

AVAILABLE NOW

FROM POISON FANG BOOKS

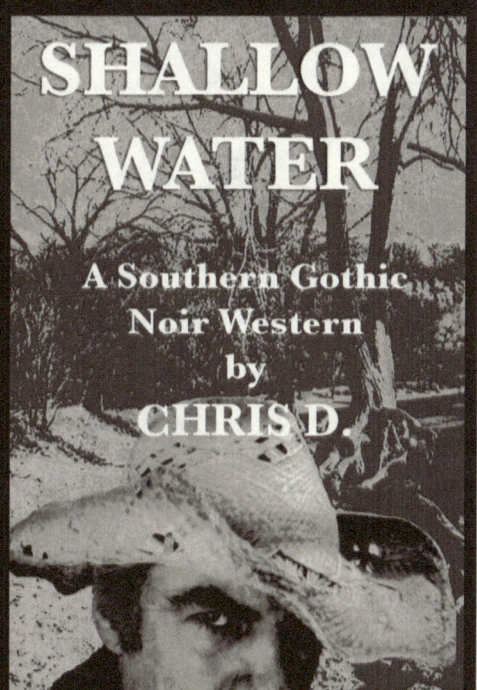

SHALLOW WATER

A Southern Gothic Noir Western
by
CHRIS D.

Post-Civil War, bitter rebel veteran and bounty hunter, Santo Brady, drifts through the Deep South. When he rescues halfbreed Indian prostitute, Lucy Damien, from one backwater town, he has the whole world fall in on his head. They embark on a freight-train-hopping odyssey to New Orleans, unaware that Lucy's rich white father and homicidal brother are tracking them. A tragic tall tale plunging head-first into a wild heart of darkness.

"One sinsister serpent of a story, an old Republic Pictures western serial scripted by James M. Cain and reimagined by Sam Peckinpah. I loved it."
– Eddie Muller, author of THE DISTANCE and SHADOW BOXER

Two New Novels from Chris D. Available October 2013

Half-sisters, schoolteacher Mona and junkie punk rocker Terri, are uneasy roommates while taking care of their sick mother. When their boyfriends, cop Johnny Cullen and killer Merle Chambers, clash due to labor struggles in their small town of Devil's River, the two women are pulled into the fray. To make matters worse, jealous female sheriff, Billie Travers, decides Mona is intruding on her faltering love affair, and quiet small town life amps up into an apocalyptic nightmare of uncontrollable violence and destruction.

Corrupt female police detective, Frankie Powers, is treading water in her small desert hometown of Sweet Home, California. Burned-out and emotionally numb after losing her husband and child in a mysterious fire ten years before, her conscience is reawakened when her affair with a Bakersfield narc brings new facts to light. Frankie's mob boss uncle, Jack Richman, has been kidnapping under-age girls for his Vegas prostitution syndicate; he's also been victimizing his own teen daughters, Frankie's twin bad girl cousins, Valerie and Vanessa. Soon Frankie finds herself singlehandedly fighting tooth-and-nail against not only wicked uncle Jack but also his dominatrix wife, Marilyn and their degenerate hitman, Cal Nero. Can a lone shewolf survive against the bloodthirsty pack?

from **Poison Fang Books**

www.ingramcontent.com/pod-product-compliance
Lightning Source LLC
Chambersburg PA
CBHW030503260626
47157CB00005B/1622